COMES THE WINTER
By Samantha St. Claire

For Those Who Wait

CHAPTER 1

THE wagon lurched sideways as the sour-faced, bewhiskered driver hit yet another deep rut along the narrow mountain road. Lena Sommer tightened her grip on the bench seat to keep herself from toppling into the lap of the driver or out of the wagon entirely. The metallic taste of blood on her tongue made her question what the road had been *before* its reputed improvement.

Lena grimaced as her fellow passenger dug fingernails into her arm. Face pale, the young woman beside her gave Lena a weak apologetic smile before releasing her grip. Lena wondered if she looked as vulnerable. Although she questioned her sanity at times for this venture, she felt more resolute than fearful of the outcome. Over the course of days traveling by train and stage, the faint glimmer of hope burned brighter, giving her the courage she needed to pursue a new direction for her life.

A smile teased the corner of Lena's mouth watching the young woman once again fold the worn piece of paper and return it to her cloth handbag. Lena bent near her traveling companion, lowering her voice. "That must be from someone you care about very much."

The young woman's cheeks flushed, her hand closing protectively over the bag in her lap. "My betrothed." Her smile broadened until it touched her eyes.

Lena nodded, finding a sudden affection for the girl's frank manner. The young woman's response did not surprise her. What else brought an obviously respectable young woman of marriageable age traveling alone into Idaho Territory? She shifted her gaze. Indeed, why would she, Miss Alena Sommer, be traveling to such a remote outpost of the civilized world?

Her companion's expression brightened, eyes fluttering to the bag in her lap, then back to Lena. "His name's Bartholomew Long. He's working at a mine in Sawtooth City, where we're heading, you know." Her cheeks colored. "Well, of course you know. You're going there, too, aren't you?"

Lena nodded, encouraging, preferring to hear the other woman's story. Stories were very personal things, delivered with gift wrap and ribbons while others lay tucked away inside drawers of yellowed newspaper clippings or closed attic rooms. Lena believed this one must be wrapped in flowered paper and tied with pink satin ribbon. She smiled to herself. How fanciful her thoughts and how unlike her!

How might her story appear to others, neatly wrapped, secured by a lavender ribbon? A reader would find no great number of pages, little worthy of print. Perhaps, that was about to change here, where new and even exciting chapters of her life remained to be written. A sudden shiver of anticipation, and when she was honest with herself, a modicum of uncertainty, prompted her to draw the wool wrap tighter about her shoulders.

The young bride-to-be launched into her story, obviously unaffected by the presence of their driver. "We've been writing these past eleven months now. He's a wonderful writer." Her voice took on a dreamy quality, her gaze drifting past Lena. "He's going to earn enough to buy a farm in Oregon. He said his brother's staked a claim and that the soil is richer and better than any they ever worked back in Illinois. He said that one more year in Sawtooth should give him enough to buy the land, build a cabin and start a family. She giggled and cast her gaze to her bag as if Bartholomew himself might have been inside and overhearing her. "Of course, he needs a wife for that, doesn't he?"

"Yes, I imagine so." Lena found the young woman's candor refreshing, lacking the common restraints of conversations with strangers. "You must be very happy."

"Oh yes!" Her blond locks bounced, her face aglow with hope. She reached into her bag again, this time pulling out a small photograph, as worn as the letter. She handed the image to Lena as though it were a living entity, fragile. "He's very nice looking, don't you think?"

Lena peered into the boyish face, incongruous with his dour expression. She searched the image for any indication of personality, of temperament or character. The photographer had captured little of that. They seldom did. The photograph she kept layered between the folds of her linen handkerchief depicted an image of a child of eight.

Nothing in the likeness revealed the effervescence that once animated those blue eyes.

She returned the photograph to the young woman. "He has a kind face, I think."

After tucking it carefully back in her bag, the woman thrust out her hand to Lena. "My name's Jessica Leach." She scrunched her face for a moment. "Isn't that a perfectly dreadful name? Of course, it won't be for too much longer." She tossed back her head and gave out a laugh, startling in its unselfconscious expression. "Please call me Jessie. Everyone does."

"Well, Jessie, soon to be Mrs. Long, I'm Alena Sommer. You may call me Lena. I am pleased to meet you." She accepted Jessie's hand. Jessie shook it with the same enthusiasm that punctuated her speech.

"I'm sorry. My family always tells me I talk too much." Jessie lifted her hand with finger wagging at Lena, her eyes squinting as she adapted a high-pitched voice. "'Girl, I don't know how you come up with enough words to say with so few brains in that head of yours. You haven't had a sensible thought in your life!' Well, that's what my mama always says."

She laughed again, giving Lena the impression that humor colored this woman's view of life as much as tragedy might shade the view of another. She felt a pang of envy.

Jessie's voice returned to normal as she said, "But I had one sensible thought after all. I found a fine young man who thinks I'm special, special enough in a good way. May I ask what brings you here, Mrs. Sommer?"

"You may ask. But you must not ask Mrs. Sommer, for my mother is not here." She watched as Jessie processed that remark, saw the slow smile of revelation. "I'm not married. At least not yet."

Jessie leaned back, her eyes wide. "So, you're a mail-order bride as well? How wonderful!"

The wagon driver threw Lena a curious glance. Lena recognized the look, one she'd seen before. No, she was not a young woman, not like Jessica, as most mail-order brides. She'd always been called handsome or comely, but never stunning or even attractive. *Big-boned like her father*, her grandmother had frequently pronounced her appearance. But her grandmother had little good to say of anyone, be they kith or kin.

In her eight years of service as a governess, Lena had learned how to dress and style her hair to best highlight her positive features, few though she thought they might be. At least, she was confident she appeared stylish, but conservative as her station in life required. Her brown eyes flecked with amber, shadowed by thick lashes were similar to those of her father but her attractive auburn curls were the inheritance bequeathed by her mother. However, those thick locks of hair were far less resplendent, tightly constrained as they were into a twist at the nape of her neck. They were, much as Lena's life had been, restrained by circumstances and necessity.

At thirty-two, Lena knew odds did not favor love to be found in any conventional manner. A mail-order bride was in essence what she'd become. By answering the advertisement for a wife and accepting Mr. Nash's business proposition to manage his boarding house, she had secured a two-for-one contract that suited her needs as well as his, a home and the respectability of marriage.

Beyond the hills, sharp peaks pierced the sky, some snow still sheltered in crevasses. The sight filled her with an inexplicable sense of peace. That was one expectation she dared hope for—permanence. She longed for a hearth to call her own. Whatever else this wild land held for her, she determined to find a way to be settled and put behind her the events shadowing her for the past few months. She fingered the brooch pinned at her throat. The gift, chosen by Miranda, had become a talisman of sorts. But unlike the letter that symbolized Jessie's hopes, the silver brooch represented those precious people and the life Lena left behind, relationships locked away in a hidden chamber of her heart, like the ruby set in silver.

Another teeth-jarring jolt sent Lena's hands searching for something solid to hold. With one hand grabbing the back of the wagon seat, the other clutched the beefy arm of the driver. Muttering words not quite appropriate for the company beside him, he took a new purchase on the reins. He looked at the gloved hand gripping his arm, then up at Lena's face. "T'ain't nothin' to worry about, Ma'am. These here mules been walkin' this path all summer deliverin' freight, from Ketchum to Sawtooth City and beyond. They know what's waitin' on the other side of the pass so they'll get us there, by gum."

Lena pulled her hand back into her lap. "I am very grateful, sir, for your assurances. The mules do seem most sturdy."

"Oh, that they are. They'll get us into Sawtooth City before sunset." He kissed to the mules.

After weeks of traveling by train and stage wagons, weary and covered in dust as she was, what were a few more hours?

Evan Hartmann pulled the sweat-soaked hat from his head and wiped an arm across his brow. Beneath his dark bush of a beard was hidden the face of a much younger man than he first appeared. It was a face marked by a strong, square jaw and riveting green eyes shadowed by thick black lashes. Those eyes had been the inheritance from an Irish grandmother on his mother's side, a woman in her youth to have been considered the fairest flower of County Cork. Although both brothers had been blessed with that striking color, Evan always knew the ladies were first attracted to Jimmy.

With a groan, he lowered himself onto the slag heap of yellow rock, sending a shower of small stones tumbling into the stream twenty feet below. Squinting up at the sun's position, he allowed himself the privilege of a break for some victuals he had stuffed in his pack. Stale bread and a hunk of dubious looking cheese were poor nourishment for the energy he'd just expended. He dug in.

The sound of his teeth crunching against the hardened bread crust pushed back at the silence pressing in that quietness that had settled into his head, so different from the constant chatter of his brother's cheerful optimism had departed.

He caught the movement beneath the sage brush before seeing two hungry gold eyes studying him from an oval, black furry face. A pink tongue flickered out of the cat's mouth as though in anticipation of a morsel from Evan's meal. Here was at least one new habit. He tossed a tidbit of cheese beneath the bush. Only a moment of wary watchfulness passed before the creature pounced upon it.

"If you'd just let me help you, I could find you a nice hearth to keep you warm through the winter. You just need to learn who to trust, little girl."

The cat appraised Evan, waiting. Picking up a second piece of cheese, she moved deeper into the shadowy undergrowth.

Evan slouched against a rock, tearing off another chunk of bread, watching as the sun slipped behind the peaks. Soon that familiar, suffocating silence would overtake him. He jumped to his feet and began packing his tools. The soft mew of the cat stopped him. Turning, he saw the cat sitting primly a few feet out from the bush, her thin body revealing that her efforts to find nourishment for herself were less than adequate.

"Well, there's a switch. Feeling brave, are ya?"

The cat lifted a paw to her mouth. Her tongue extended, grooming herself.

Evan dropped to one knee, pulling the last of the cheese from his coat pocket. He stretched out his hand, palm open.

The cat paused in her cleaning to consider the proffered gift. Her gaze flickered from Evan's hand to his face.

"Come on," Evan coaxed. "I'm your best option for getting through this winter."

She took a tentative step before the sudden raucous squawk of a crow sent her scurrying beneath the bush and out of sight.

Evan tossed the cheese in the direction the cat scurried. "We might still come to an understanding."

He shrugged on his back pack and headed down the hill toward town, whistling to drown out the silence waiting to overtake him.

Chapter 2

THE little traveling party of three rode in silence for a good measure of miles before the wagon driver spoke. "That there pass we just come over won't be open to travel much longer. Snows come early here and stay. I'm a hopin' you two ladies know what yer gettin' into. Sounds like ya' might have men folk waitin' for ya' in Sawtooth or Vienna. That right?"

Jessica's pale cheeks colored again, her eyes once again drawn to the handbag in her lap. "Yes, sir, Sawtooth City."

He winked at the girl, causing her to blush a deeper shade of pink. "That's a good thing then. Vienna's got mine trouble. But that's the way it is up here, boom town today, ghost town tomorrow. And it be good you've got men folk, cause there ain't much in the way of womanly companionship up that way unless you're in the business..." He stopped himself in time and shot a glance at Lena whose eyes remained fixed on the mountain range. "Sorry—I just mean that a woman needs a man up there to take care of her, is all."

Lena understood the man's thinly veiled reference. Women would find little opportunity to earn a living in a place as remote as this unless they chose to sell their charms. So, without the support of a man, well, it always came down to needing a man in some capacity. She straightened her shoulders, looking forward to stretching her legs and working out the damage done to her spine after the torturous wagon ride.

Before them stretched a wide basin where a narrow river snaked against low foothills on the north side. Scattered along the river was an odd assortment of structures, a surprising number rising a lofty two stories. This *city* could scarcely be compared to the older settlement of Hailey to the south where both electricity and telephones brought eastern civilization to the frontier. She recalled the lovely bookstore she'd visited there and doubted such luxuries of culture appeared here.

Jessie leaned in close to Lena's ear whispering, "Oh! It's smaller than Bartholomew described."

"I actually thought it a bit more substantial than I'd imagined." One of these must surely be the boarding house owned by Mr. Nash, a place soon to be her new home. *Their* home. That was a thought that made her throat constrict and stomach clench. She'd be expected to make a home with a stranger, because Mr. Nash was little more in spite of their letters.

Lena glanced over at Jessie and saw her bite her lip while she brushed a nervous hand at a wayward lock of hair. This anxiety they shared filled Lena with a rush of empathy for the younger woman.

"Where are you staying until you're married?" Lena asked, hoping to distract the girl from her obvious nervousness.

She glanced at Lena, her eyes wide. "I...I don't know. We didn't talk about that."

Lena realized her question had only increased the poor girl's anxiety. "I'm sure your young man has thought those details through. I know for a fact that there is a boarding house here."

Jessie brightened at that. "Oh yes! My Bartholomew lives in one at the edge of town."

One last hill and the trail widened, becoming the main street of Sawtooth City.

"Here we are, ladies." With that announcement, the driver jumped from the seat, landing with a heavy thud, his feet stirring a cloud of dust.

"Jessie?" Both women turned. A red-headed youth sprinted up to the wagon, hat in hand, breathless.

Standing so quickly that she startled the mules, Jessie lost her balance. Lena reached out a hand to steady her, but the girl's momentum spilled her out of the wagon directly into the arms of her Bartholomew. It was an accident that the young man obviously did not find objectionable as he stood there holding his young bride-to-be.

Jessie gasped, "Bartholomew!"

"Yes, Ma'am! At your service." He lowered her to her feet then took a slow step backwards, his hands still holding her arms as if he were afraid she might shatter. Neither one of them said a word for a long moment as if by staring into each other's eyes they might see the answers to the questions each could never ask in months of written correspondence.

Clearing her throat in a ladylike manner, Lena broke into their silent communion.

Bartholomew stepped around Jessie. "Oh, here, let me help you." He reached a helping hand to Lena.

"Thank you." After brushing at her hopelessly rumpled skirts, Lena surveyed the dusty street and clapboard buildings lining it. She'd expected Mr. Nash to meet her. Did her last letter announcing her arrival date not in time?

"Oh, Bartholomew..." Jessie started.

Bart held up a hand. "You gotta call me Bart. No one knows me by my full name here. Too long to shout." Bart grinned at Jessie and Lena had the distinct impression he was on the brink of falling into her eyes again.

"All right, Bart. I wanted to introduce my friend, Miss Sommer." All smiles and happiness again, she gestured to Lena.

Lena shook Bart's hand. "A pleasure to meet you. Could you possibly direct me to the boarding house run by Mr. Nash?"

Bart's face drained of color, leaving only his freckles behind clustered across his cheeks in constellations. The grin slipped into a grim line. "You're Miss Sommer?"

Lena tilted her head, confused by his sudden change of expression. "Are you all right?" For a moment, she wondered if he might be ill, overcome by his emotions at seeing his bride-to-be for the first time.

He licked his lips, his smooth brow wrinkling. "You're the Miss Sommer that Mr. Nash was expecting?"

Lena felt a rush of relief. "Why, yes!"

She saw his countenance fall, his eyes shifting between Jessie and herself. He sucked in a breath, then said, "I'm sorry."

As suddenly as the moment of relief had come, it departed, leaving behind the awful dread that his next words were about to alter her world yet again.

"There was an accident two weeks back." He stuttered out the rest in a rush. "Mr. Nash got hurt real bad, dragged by his horse."

Lena stiffened. She'd faced injuries, disease, fire. Whatever it was, she could handle this. "Please, take me to him, then." She blinked, reading in the next moment the truth in Bart's young face. Mr. Nash would not be greeting her—ever. The man with whom she'd hoped to build a future was gone.

Gripping her elbow more firmly, Bart shook his head. "I'm so sorry."

CHAPTER 3

A LITTLE cry sprang from Jessie's lips as she pressed her hand to her open mouth. "Was that your intended?"

A familiar specter cast a shadow across her path once more. Not a friend but neither a stranger, death had come again to reshape her world.

Bart, recovering himself, stepped closer to Lena, as if he thought she might be inclined to faint at the news of Mr. Nash's death. "Miss Sommer, would you like to go someplace where you can sit? I could move your bags over to the boarding house if you wish."

Lena met Bart's concerned expression, a momentary pause as she considered his offer, then a faint smile. "How kind. Yes, that sounds just the thing." She squared her shoulders, taking in a deep calming breath. Details could be attended to in time. Not now.

Bart's buckboard solved the issue of transporting the two women and their luggage. Although Jessie took the middle seat closest to Bart, she remained solicitous to Lena. Few words were spoken, but at one-point Jessie stretched her arm around Lena, giving her a hug. "We'll make a pot of hot tea as soon as we arrive. That will help put things to right."

Lena nodded once and said, "Yes, that would be fine." Then she pulled back inside her quiet center where she'd learned to file news and occurrences requiring thoughtful meditations. Years had taught her that hasty decisions often led to regrets.

With less enthusiasm than was probably his nature, Bart pointed out a few of the sights in town, the livery, the mercantile, the small church standing alone at the end of the street, looking lost and unwanted. Of course, there were four saloons with second stories devoted to business Bart prudently managed not to mention.

The dirt street climbed to a higher bench providing a view of the town below and the mountains rising to the east. A two-story structure, sedate and sturdy nestled into a copse of aspen commanded a view of the town. The aroma of fresh cut cedar suggested the house was little more than months completed. The newly painted sign planted at the side of the road declared the establishment to be the Nash Boarding House. A wide porch wrapped comforting arms the length of the south and west facing sides. Someone had made good progress in stacking wood under the southern eaves in preparation for winter. All in all, the house made a striking first impression as she climbed the three white-washed steps.

"Pretty, ain't she?" Bart asked. "Mr. Nash sunk everything he had into this place. Think he hoped to turn it into a proper inn for those touring folks they say will be traveling the new roads soon. Folks around here who know more than me say those peaks and the lakes will draw them. There's a real pretty one, a lake, not far from here. An old miner staked a claim on the north shore. He's building cabins for folks to come just for enjoying the view and the fishing. Imagine that?" He'd turned to face the mountains, his arm flung wide to the valley rolling off to meet the foothills. 'Some say it's them Sawtooths that will bring them here, as grand as the Colorado Rockies."

Jessie stood beside Bart, her arm boldly linked in his. "They look so forbidding. Does anyone go there?"

"Oh yeah. There's some mighty pretty lakes up there with water so clear that if you hung from a tree by your knees, it'd be hard to tell the difference between the sky and the water. Good fishin' too." He grinned at her. "You'll see soon enough. I'll take you there."

"There must be plenty of wildlife living there."

Bart seemed to puff up at her interest, adding color to his description. "They aren't just up there in them high mountains. The big cats and bears find pickings good here too."

Lena could see that Bart's descriptions were doing his young lady no good deed. She had enough to adjust to without fueling her imagination with the makings for nightmares. "And I'm sure that you and the other men of the town are quite good at defending yourselves. Isn't that correct, Mr. Long?" Despite her shock at learning of Mr. Nash's death, Lena already felt a motherly protection for the younger woman.

"Oh yeah! We can sure do that!" With a grunt, he hefted two satchels and led them through the wide front door.

The entry led them into a room that spanned the width of the house, providing views to the mountains from the eastern windows. Along the far wall stretched a massive stone fireplace with an opening as tall as a man. A hearth of smooth river rock spilled out into the broad plank floor, giving Lena the impression of a riverbed flowing into the house. Close to the hearth and scattered under the windows were oversized chairs constructed of pine logs stripped of bark, wood gleaming in sunlight filtering through large panes of glass.

Lena scanned the room, stunned by the craftsmanship. It was more complete than she'd imagined from descriptions in Mr. Nash's letters. This was to be her new home earned in partnership with a man she'd come to admire through their correspondence these past six months.

Unlike Jessie's arrangement with Bart, Lena and Mr. Nash had worked out a very amiable business proposition. Along with a modest investment from her savings, she brought her experience in managing a household. It had all been reasonable and well-planned. For Lena, it provided both an escape and the one thing she desired most in the world, a permanent home and a hearth of her own.

And now? Now, the dream had vanished like morning mist, burned away by the harsh light of reality. She brought her fingers to touch the brooch at her throat, tracing the design.

Another small exclamation slipped out of Jessie's open mouth. "Everything is so big!" Her gaze rested on a straight-backed chair in the corner with arms the size of a man's thigh.

"Well, it's too bad you never met Mr. Nash. He was a big man with even bigger plans." Bart threw a worried look at Lena. "You sure you're all right, Miss?" Bart exchanged a look with Jessie. "Why don't you two make yourselves comfortable while I unload."

Jessie nodded and said, "Here, let's make you a cup of tea. Would that be all right, Bart? Where's the kitchen?"

"Oh! Through that door on the west end." Bart waved vaguely to a wide door opening at the far side of the room. "Stove is hot. I made some stew. If you're hungry, help yourselves."

Although a frontier kitchen, this one lacked nothing in functionality. As much as the kitchen offered in its modern wood stove and ample counter space, the windows held Lena's attention. Framed like a masterpiece painting, the Sawtooth mountain range gloried in golden afternoon light. Who would be able to concentrate on recipes and mundane chores while distracted by such grandeur?

Behind her, Jessie had shifted for herself, locating a tin of tea and tea cups. In short order, she'd stoked the fire in the stove. The tea kettle sang happily atop the wood stove.

"Lena, you should sit down."

Jessie's voice drifted through the cloud insulating Lena from the realization that all this was lost to her.

Stretching not less than eight feet down the middle of the kitchen sat a massive table with wide benches on either side and two chairs at each end. Jessie tugged at the heavy chair for Lena. "Now, sit yourself down. And see? I found some tinned biscuits."

Smiling at the girl's kind, motherly attentions, Lena obeyed and took the seat.

Jessie laughed a nervous little trill. "I feel a bit like Goldilocks here, like I've stumbled upon the home of the three bears, you know?"

Lena brought the teacup to her lips. She stopped, contemplating the cup in her fingers. "This is real china, isn't it? How very odd."

Jessie stared into her own. "It is! Who'd have thought a man would collect such finery."

Taking a cautious sip, Lena felt her muscles relax. She stared into the steaming cup, a look of bemusement lifting her lips. In a deeper voice, hinting at a British accent, she quoted, "So I says, 'My dear if you could give me a cup of tea to clear my muddle of a head I should better understand your affairs.' And we had the tea and the affairs too..."

Seeing Jessie's perplexed expression, Lena shook her head, chuckling. An explanation might be in order. "Don't look at me like that. It's just a silly phrase from a book I once read by Charles Dickens. I can't seem to recall the name of the book just now."

"I'm sorry. I've not heard of it."

Lena could feel Jessie's eyes observing her. No doubt, she was puzzled by Lena's unnatural calm at receiving such news as might have sent another into fits of fainting or wailing. Perhaps she should feel faint. But she did not, just numb.

"Bartholomew says that I should stay here tonight. There was a couple closer into town who offered me a place to stay with them, but considering all, well I can stay with you until you sort out what you're going to do. Bart says it's not proper for you to stay here alone with this house full of men and all." Jessie took a breath, waiting for a reaction.

"I'd appreciate that, Jessie. Your company might be just what I need. And you could see more of your young man." She was touched by Bart's thoughtfulness.

Jessie studied her teacup with more attention than it deserved. "He's even more handsome in person than in his picture, don't you think? He was worried about your reputation staying here. How many men would have thought of that?"

"You are a very fortunate woman to have made such a match."

Again, that thin line formed between her eyebrows as Jessie must have realized the disparity of their situations.

"Is that stew I smell?" Lena rose from the table and strode to the stove where she found an enormous pot of stew simmering, filling the air with an irresistible fragrance. Long days of light fare were beginning to catch up to her. The savory aroma of the stew set her stomach to rumbling.

Bart stepped into the room, brow beaded with sweat. "Think I've moved everything inside. What's in the crate, Miss Sommer? Felt like bricks."

"Oh dear, I should have warned you about that one. I brought a few of my most treasured books, those I just couldn't leave behind. They're friends, you see, and one must never abandon friends."

Bart passed her a blank expression, then said, "Well, it felt like there might have been at least one body in there, for certain!" His ears flushed red. "Sorry." He nodded to the stove. "Hungry? I made a pot of stew for dinner."

"Famished, Mr. Long, simply famished!" Lena said.

Neither Lena nor Jessie could fight the demanding call for sleep. Not even Jessie's desire to linger with Bart could enable her to keep her eyelids open any longer. Bart showed them to Mr. Nash's upstairs bedroom, explaining that it was the largest room and most comfortable. He lingered in the hall, his eyes adoring on Jessie, then said good night.

They closed the door, grateful to at last rid themselves of their dusty traveling attire. Bart's provision of two basins and a pitcher of warm water for bathing further proved his sterling character to Jessie. Lena shared her glowing observations, agreeing he was a remarkably thoughtful man.

Clad only in her cotton chemise and petticoat, Jessie perched on the edge of the bed, her feet dangling above the floor. "See, even the bed is Papa Bear size."

The dresser rose to a lofty height, with the mirror mounted above it far too high for Jessie. Lena, however, could just see her face. Surprised by the dark circles beneath her eyes, she was grateful for the thin layer of dust obscuring her reflection. She gave that dim reflection a wry smile as she removed the pins holding her hair. The ritual of brushing it slowed her breathing. She turned to the basin when she'd finished, scrubbing her face until it stung.

When she looked back to the bed, a towel pressed against her neck, she smiled, seeing Jessie curled like a cat, still in her petticoat and chemise, fast asleep. Lena pulled the covers from her side of the bed over the girl, careful not to disturb her. It was such a familiar act of caring, one she'd performed so many times for little Miranda.

Little Miranda. How she missed her precious charge! Nearly every night for eight years, she'd tucked her into bed.

Even the girl's mother had not shared that nightly routine with her as much as Lena had. She closed her eyes for just a moment as she tucked the memory back into its secret place.

A desk sat nestled under the window looking out over the distant river, a sliver of silver. Dusk altered the color of the landscape to a monochrome of blue. With little thought to what she was doing, her hand roamed the top of the desk, touching a silver writing pen, a horse shoe weighting a stack of important looking papers, a smoking pipe. She lifted the pipe to her nose, and sniffed, pleasant hints of apple and tobacco. Her father had smoked a pipe, a habit that helped deepen her memory of their little bookstore; the scent of tobacco smoke mixed with the musty scent of aging books.

She recalled the small photo Mr. Nash had sent her, so little to explain the man who'd penned the letters. How strange, apprehending the essence of the man without ever having really known him. She wouldn't even be haunted by his ghost because nothing bound them in this world aside from an agreement to marry. This was a grief of sorts, she supposed, not for herself, but for a future that might have been. Perhaps their relationship might have become more than one of business. The unlikely event that love might grow from such a relationship had not even tempted her. She was a realist, honestly born to it by two very pragmatic parents.

A sudden rise in men's voices from the room below was followed by a whispered hush, as though someone had remembered the women were asleep in the room above them. That act of consideration she found endearing.

Strangers can be kind. Somehow the kindness of these strangers touched her as the news of Mr. Nash's passing had not. A single tear rolled from her eye to drop upon the pile of papers atop the desk. She brought her hand to her cheek and wiped it away. No more need fall. One was enough.

For a long while she sat in the oversized chair, *his* chair, with her feet tucked up beneath her. From here she had a view of the shadowy form of the mountains. The voice of her father whispered in her memory. *Beware the dangers of making decisions after the sun sets. Best to tuck your worries under your pillow and sleep on them till morning. Sometimes in the night the worries will be ironed out by your sleeping head.* So, she resolved not to decide what to do tonight. That decision would wait until the clear light of day.

But sleep refused to come. When all sounds in the room below had ceased, she wrapped a quilt around her shoulders, slid her feet into her slippers and tiptoed down the stairs. Opening the front door, a cacophony of night music met her. Gently closing the door behind her, she padded to the west end of the porch, settling herself in a generous chair with a view of the western sky where the ragged edge of the mountains made a darker shade of night. Stars danced above the distant peaks, and the moon cast a pale light upon the mountain's craggy face.

A calm that should not have been her companion after a day of upheaval took a seat beside her. She had no idea when her weary body succumbed to its need for rest and her eyes closed in sleep.

Dead tired, Evan stumbled up the steps to the porch. His body yearned for sleep even more than food. A full day of back-breaking work followed by a one-hour ride in a stiff saddle made the prospect of a soft bed all the more enticing.

A sound and small movement to his left brought him fully alert. An animal, a bear perhaps? One had taken to roaming the river bank this summer looking through garbage. He pulled his gun from its holster, taking slow quiet steps across the porch. The shadow moved. Now he could discern the pattern not of fur but a quilt. Maybe one of the men had come home drunk and decided to sleep it off out here.

Then a slender, bare ankle, attached to a pale white foot, emerged from the corner of the quilt. A woman? Here?

He slid the gun back into its holster. Standing in front of her now, he saw the face framed by dark curls, softly falling across her cheek. Standing there with the moonlight caressing each curve of her face, he wondered if *he* were asleep. Maybe he'd come off the mountain, walked inside the house and was already dreaming of this angel.

She shifted, sending Evan scuttling back into the shadowed edge of the porch. He held his breath lest she see him and think him up to some mischief. Drawing her foot back within the folds of the blanket, she settled back into sleep. In a moment, her breathing changed to that of a very human being, not at all angelic. He considered that for a moment. Who was he to say angels didn't snore?

He remembered then, Nash's expected lady. This must be her. Most conjectured her to be an older woman, certainly not a woman possessing such an ankle as this one, or a cheek as comely.

Evan frowned. Bad business, this. The poor woman. He scratched at his beard, newly sprouted for the coming winter months. Turning back to the door, he left the sleeping angel to her dreams. He had little doubt she'd be on the first wagon out of the basin, off the mountain before winter locked the doors to the outside world. Or she would if she knew what was good for her.

CHAPTER 4

LENA awoke with a start. Disoriented, she sat up, blinking back sleep. So cold. She pulled at the heavy quilt, drawing herself into a small ball to conserve body heat. And with the chill on her face came the return of memory: the trip up the mountain, the shock of discovering Samuel Nash's death, the breathtaking beauty of the mountains surrounding this isolated community. She shivered and knew she'd be warmer inside, but something held her there.

Something moved just beyond the porch. Straining through the gray light of predawn, she watched the bulky creature lumbering along with obvious lack of concern for her presence. It rose on its back legs, standing quite still, its beady black eyes observing her. She was certain his eyes were more adapted to the dark than hers, likely both seeing and smelling her quite distinctly.

She'd seen one once in captivity when she'd visited the Lincoln Park Zoo with Miranda. It was a bear cub much like this one. If she'd known more, she might have flown back into the house and under her covers. But the moment held so much magic that all she could do was gaze in wonder at the creature. Apparently, finding little amusement in his study of her, the young bear fell back onto all four paws and lumbered along the length of the house before turning to the creek.

Letting out a long-held breath, she settled back into the chair, the quilt tucked beneath her chin. High on the tallest peaks, a faint pink glow heralded a new day. As she held her breath, waiting, the sun spread its light down the face of the mountains, flowing like golden water into the high valleys. Lena listened to the songs of birds unfamiliar to her city trained ears, their songs announcing the morning as surely as the milkman on his daily rounds. But this was so different, quiet, and yet not. The longer she sat there absorbing the growing presence of day, the more she heard.

How unlike the gray skies of Chicago! How lovely! In the east, rays of gold fanned out along the horizon, chasing back the last shadows of night to foreign lands, far beyond the mountains in the west. Her breath caught as the sun emerged from behind the hills, drawing with it a canopy of pale blue. If anyone had witnessed this greeting between them, they would have seen Lena's face aglow in sunlight. And had Evan seen her, his thoughts of her as an angelic being would have seemed confirmed.

Sounds of waking life drifted from inside the house. Someone had stoked the fire in the wood stove; a kettle, metal on metal. Men's voices drifted from the rooms, reaching to her ears here in her warm cocoon. Reluctant to leave this peace, she pushed her feet from beneath the quilt. Holding it tight to her body she padded across the cold wood floor and slipped inside unobserved.

Moments later, dressed in a wool skirt and high-neck blouse, her hair pulled up into a bun and shoes back on her feet, she looked less the angel and more the matron. Bart looked up, startled by her sudden appearance in the kitchen. "Good morning, Miss Sommer."

"Good morning, Bartholomew. Looks like you've taken on the feeding of this house of men. Smells delicious."

"When my ma passed away, it was eat my pa's attempts at cooking or teach myself. I do like food, so I did the cookin'." Bart waved the spatula, pointing to the stove. "There's a pan of biscuits in there. If you wouldn't mind, you could take them out before they burn."

Happy for a task to do, Lena found a towel and pulled the pan from the oven.

"Did you sleep well? Know this place must be strange for you, bein' from Chicago and all. Never been there myself, but I heard it's a big city, like New York."

The sweet earthy aroma of brewed coffee sent Lena searching for a mug. It took several tries before finding the correct cupboard in the unfamiliar kitchen. "It is. Since the fire destroyed so much of the city in '71, the buildings are new and quite grand, even if less charming in character."

Bart carried the plate piled with biscuits to the center of the table. "They must have electric lights and even telephones like Hailey. Have you ever used one of those contraptions?"

"Indeed, I have. My employer, Mr. Simpson, was quick to convert his house from gas to electricity. He was fascinated with anything and everything he considered a modern innovation."

"Well, I don't think we'll be seeing any of those things here in Sawtooth anytime soon. Hel—Heck! We only just got a decent road put in a year ago."

Lena clasped the mug close to her face, breathing in the warm steam. "So, what date have you and Jessica set for your wedding? She's a lovely young lady. You are a very lucky man."

A furrowed brow on the young man halted the progress of her cup to her lips. This was not the face of a happy groom-to-be. She set her cup on the table and waited.

"It's a long trip here from back east, time when people can't talk to each other for weeks. Things happen." Bart stopped and looked up at her, a crease between his eyebrows forming a deep canyon. "Sorry. Guess you know that."

Lena nodded, her hand gripping the cup a little tighter.

"Well, the Campbells had this nice little house just outside town, with a cabin where Mr. Campbell lived when he first started prospecting. I asked if I could rent it from them for me and Jessie. They were all for it. Mrs. Campbell said she'd appreciate the company. So, I used my free time fixin' it up. Put in a nice hearth and a couple of new windows with a view to the mountains." He sat down heavily on the bench across from her.

"After the mine started layin' off workers, he and his missus decided they wouldn't take a chance of being stuck here through the winter. So, they sold it. They offered it to me first, but, well I ain't makin' much."

"Have you told Jessie yet?" Lena took a sip of her coffee. Seeing Bart's tortured expression, she guessed the answer before he responded.

Bart seemed suddenly engrossed in the coffee dredges cooling rapidly at the bottom of his mug. "Haven't had much chance yet."

"Well, she seems to think the world of you. I believe she'll understand and the two of you can come up with a solution."

"I do hope so, cause I surely think the world of her, and half again! She's so full of spunk and hope. I hate to be the one to disappoint her."

Lena hesitated to offer any advice without being asked, being unqualified as she was in matters of the heart. However, despite feeling she should keep her own counsel, she said, "I think if it were me, I'd want to know straight out. If I guessed you were keeping the truth from me, I'd be more hurt."

Before they could continue the conversation, two young men burst through the kitchen door.

"Well, you'll get to meet the rest of us now, ready or not." Sidling up to the taller of the two, he slapped him on the shoulder. "This is Carrick Ferguson and that ugly one's his baby brother, Donal."

Lena took in the handsome good looks of the black-haired younger brother, smiling to herself at Bart's facetious description—*ugly indeed.*

Behind the two brothers, a trim older man with gray flecked temples and close-trimmed beard padded into the room. He nodded graciously to Lena as Bart introduced him. "This is Ely. Don't let him scare you. He doesn't smile much, but he doesn't bite too hard."

Ely bowed. "Ely Beckert, miss."

"Very nice to meet you, Mr. Beckert."

"There's one more fella, that we don't see as often these days. When he's not workin' here for the company, he's off at his claim." Bart set a steaming bowl of sausage gravy onto the table. "Dig in while it's hot."

"Do you all work at the company mine then?" Lena asked as she joined them at the table. Bart served her a plate heaping with enough sausage gravy for two.

Donal answered for everyone while Carrick busied himself squeezing three biscuits onto his plate beneath a river of gravy. "About that...The mine bosses seem considerable confused about how to proceed. They've brought in supplies, enough they say for us to continue through the winter. But they've let a few men go. They say they might bring them back on, but nobody knows. Carrick and I don't want to be stuck here through the winter if there's no work. We'll wait for a few more weeks, and if them bosses haven't made up their minds by then more'n us will be heading down the mountain."

A cool breeze announced the entrance of one more member of the house. The man shuffled into the room, closing the door behind him.

"Evan! You look awful!" Donal greeted him cheerfully.

"Why thanks, Donal. Thanks for noticing." Evan pushed a hand through his tousled hair and shuffled over to the open seat beside Ely. He greeted Ely with a nod.

"Even though you haven't had your cup of coffee, pull yourself together and be civil."

Evan's half-lidded eyes widened as he appeared to focus on Lena for the first time. He sat a bit straighter, brushing a hand for the second time through his unruly shock of black hair. "Sorry, ma'am. Nice to meet you."

It is generally good that not all first impressions are lasting, though sadly, many are. Lena's first impression of the gawking, disheveled Evan Hartmann was far less than favorable. Evan had not managed to improve that impression as he still looked more like a fish out of water, with his mouth agape.

Lena met Evan's steady gaze. "Mr. Hartmann, nice to meet you."

"So that's it then. Evan's the last of us," Bart said. "We have room for one or two more, but no one's filled them rooms yet."

Jessie joined them as Bart concluded his introductions. Bart met her at the door, taking her elbow in his hand, guiding her to the table. "Your turn to meet the rest of this bunch."

Polite conversation, restrained by the women's presence, resumed. Evan had little to offer aside from requests for a bowl of this or a platter of that, finishing his meal before anyone else. Excusing himself, he left the room. Lena puzzled at his hurried, gruff manner. Shortly thereafter, Carrick, Donal and Ely left, leaving only Bart, Jessie and Lena.

With her cup refilled, Lena leaned forward, her arms resting on the table. "So, Bart, if you would, please tell me everything you know about Sawtooth City. How many hotels are here, how many residents, the condition of mining? I need to make an informed decision regarding management of this boarding house. To be frank, I need to understand what my risks are in staying through the winter."

A surprised expression opened Bart's blue eyes wide. He rubbed the back of his neck while his lips pursed and a little puff of air escaped. his face going through a series of awkward gymnastics, looking anywhere but at her. "You're thinkin' of stayin' here?"

"I am studying my options, Bart. I know that the first would be to place my bags on the next wagon back to Hailey. But this boarding house needs a manager. There are men enough to nearly fill the rooms. It seems reasonable to contemplate taking on the role I traveled here to assume." She saw their expressions and added, "I'm quite experienced in managing a household. This one has only a few more residents."

Bart shot Jessie a perplexed glance. Jessie shrugged. Bart scratched at his stubble of a beard, then tapped his tooth with a fingernail before saying, "Well, I'm pretty sure Nash had a will. His lawyer was Mr. Baxter, here in town. Think Nash had a sister back east." He paused, his brows knit together. "And I suppose you'd like to see Mr. Nash's ledgers."

Jessie clapped her hands, eyes sparkling in pure delight. Her cheeks glowed pink as she picked up her fork and dug into her breakfast. "This just might be fun!"

CHAPTER 5

LENA left Jessie and Bart at the sink where they worked to clean the breakfast dishes, chatting happily. Watching them, she confirmed her earlier opinion that they would work out their difficulties. Lena left them to become more acquainted. Allowing Bart time to explain his disappointment seemed the prudent thing to do.

Sunlight bathed the valley in a warm glow, enhanced by aspen leaves just changing from their summer attire to the gilded colors of fall. Gold speckled the distant hills where frost transformed the leaves from green to yellow.

Lena ran her fingers along the log post framing the railing, cool and smooth to the touch. She found it hard to believe the buildings here had been constructed so recently, appearing so permanent, almost as though sprouting from the ground itself. Perhaps the illusion came from the raw materials employed, logs that looked as though only recently removed from their forest home where they'd provided shelter to birds, not people.

Again, the contrast struck her, the difference between her recent cited past and this wild landscape. Instead of inhaling the sweet scent of pine, she'd be wincing at factory smoke and the stench of littered streets. There her skyline was marked by multi-story buildings not granite cathedrals.

But she had to consider those options she'd so boldly declared she possessed. Would any reasonable person believe such options existed? She was a single woman. Tucked away in her valise was the money given to her by her employer when he saw her off at the station, tears pooling in the corners of his eyes.

It had been hard for him to say goodbye. With her leaving, the reality that the purpose of her presence in the house was gone, must have struck him hard. With both wife and child dead, what need was there for a governess? His tears were not for her, but for what she represented—life, laughter, the hope for the future. All changed when Miranda and her mother were killed in the carriage accident. All Lena had left of the child in whom she'd invested so much of her youth and love, were fading memories and a silver brooch.

But all of that was behind her, chapters from her past. Was this her future? She believed it to be despite Mr. Simpson's doubts and concerns for her. So, her tidy mind began to count the costs of a new future. With his final gift and her modest savings from the sale of her parents' bookshop, perhaps she could create an option apart from returning to the city. But was she the woman for such a challenge? Was she prepared for this life?

There was the third option that she hadn't shared with Jessie or Bart. When she'd been delayed in Hailey, she'd strolled about the town to entertain herself. She found it surprisingly modern with electricity and even telephone service, a city in its infancy.

On a side street next to a small hotel with a cafe, a quaint bookshop caught her attention. Surprised to find it there, she spoke with the man who owned it. A writer himself, he seemed interested to learn of her parents' shop and her experience working there as a young woman. He mentioned his thoughts to hire someone to manage the shop so that he could devote more of his time to writing. At the time, she dismissed the idea, thanking him politely. But now, might this be the better option, one that her experience prepared her to take?

A distant melody, familiar and sad, pulled her from these thoughts. This was not some memory stirred but the very real sound of instrumental music drifting from the trees bordering the stream north of the house. Like the Pied Piper of legend, the music drew her.

She hesitated on the porch step, recalling the bear cub of the morning. For a moment, she contemplated the sensible knowledge that she was a stranger here, unfamiliar with the dangers of this wilderness. But the melodious vibrations of bow upon string floated upon the breeze, an irresistible beckoning. Casting her sensible nature aside, she followed the melody to the edge of the stream.

A game trail followed the stream's rocky bed north into a grove of alders. Light danced upon the slow-moving waters as though in appreciation of the music. The music swelled, as the violinist lifted the melody to a crescendo, a slight pause as the notes rose as though they were birds released from the trees by a sudden breeze. Then came the answer to the refrain, softer in tone, played with passion.

Afraid to go farther, for fear she might frighten this fairy creature away, she stood quietly listening as the violinist finished his concerto to the woods. And surely, this must be some magical creature to be playing here with only the trees and forest animals to listen. But curiosity drew her along the path until at last the artist was revealed as not a fairy but a man of flesh and blood. She recognized the worn woolen coat as that of the solemn German, Ely. The violin still tucked beneath his chin, he seemed locked in a trance, his eyes fixed at some distant point above the trees.

Lena cleared her throat softly. Ely stiffened, turning. Upon seeing her, his shoulders relaxed, and he gave her a polite nod. "Miss Sommer."

"I'm sorry to disturb your playing. But the melody was so lovely and unexpected. I wanted to find out who played such music." Lena smiled, hoping that her intrusion had not offended him. His unreadable expression made her uncomfortable, and she found herself fumbling for words when silence might have been best. "I have attended a good number of concerts, but the concerto you just played is unfamiliar to me. What is it called?"

Ely studied her for a moment before answering. "It is the violin concerto No.1, in G minor. Have you heard of Max Bruch, Miss Sommer?"

Lena shook her head. "I'm afraid his name is unfamiliar to my amateur study of music. The tune reminds me a little of Johannes Brahms. Is it in the same style?"

The man's countenance brightened. "You are familiar with the German Romanticism style then?"

"My former employer was most generous and would allow me to accompany the family to concerts. He felt that as his daughter's governess I should be culturally as educated as she. But I confess that my knowledge is quite limited.

Although, I do enjoy listening so very much even if I am unable to place a name to every piece."

"Every melody deserves an appreciative ear." He knelt on the moss and lay his instrument in its case.

She noticed his long fingers, his hands not like the others who made their living in the mines, clawing at rock. The observation made her wonder what work he performed there. "And do you find the ears of the creatures here appreciative, Mr. Beckert?" She lifted a hand to the trees about them. "Are there any others here who might equally appreciate your music?"

Ely rose stiffly to his feet, his case in his hand. Lena noticed that, unlike so many of the men here, Ely was clean-shaven. His over-all appearance made him more identifiable as a venerable professor than a miner. He cast his eyes about him, taking into consideration the forested glade and the stream before answering. "It seems a very good place to share such music, yes?" His eyes held a hint of a smile.

Lena followed his gaze with a smile. "Indeed, Mr. Beckert, it does."

They strolled together back along the path. There was little need for conversation, where the world about them carried on its own dialog. As the house came into view once more, she saw Bart sitting close to Jessie on the front porch. Their voices low, Lena assumed Bart had shared his disappointment about the promised cabin.

Ely and Lena pulled up, both reluctant to interrupt what appeared to be a serious conversation. Lena turned to Ely and asked softly, "May I make a cup of tea for you, Mr. Beckert? That's one task in the kitchen I can perform."

Ely ran a hand down his face. "That does sound pleasant. *Ja.*"

Lena led the way to the side door which opened off the kitchen. Ely lay his violin case on the table and walked to the cupboard to pull two mugs from the shelf while Lena sprinkled tea leaves into the kettle.

"You must be most disappointed, *ja*? You will leave us, then?" Ely asked his questions in that same somber tone that seemed his normal manner of speech.

Lena confessed her uncertainty. "I suppose it would be prudent to return at the end of the week with the freight wagon to Hailey."

"*Ja.* Prudent is an interesting word, is it not? It seems a word that comes before many more." Lena thought she saw a quick wink, but discounted that as something such a gentleman would not have done.

She saw in his eyes that same softness that had shimmered there as he spoke of music to the forest. Surprising herself, she spoke her thoughts aloud. "It is this. I have little to return to in Chicago. The four people I loved most in the world are gone."

"*Aha.*" This time she was certain of the sympathy in his grey eyes, a compassion perhaps born of similar loss.

"But, I suppose I should leave before the snows come. What if the mines fail? What if no one remains to need a boarding room? Perhaps I should leave now and take the job I was offered in Hailey. There's a lovely little bookshop there."

"*Aha!* You seem well-suited to such a position. May I ask what makes you hesitate then? It would be in a place offering so much more than Sawtooth City. You might even enjoy a concert from time to time. There must be more musicians in a town of its size. And there would be young ladies and perhaps young gentlemen to fill your days with happy conversations."

She didn't reply at first, but sipped from her cup instead and then used her finger to trace the rim in slow circles. "I'm not sure. But I think I would regret leaving if I were to ride away without trying to stay a little longer. I would be haunted by what might have been."

"To keep from being haunted perhaps you must stay."

"Perhaps." There were enough ghosts in her past. She'd rather not invite more into her life. Besides, most opportunities were accompanied by risks. This opportunity, most fraught with risk, also offered her the greatest chance to redefine her life, the very chance that had drawn her west.

Lena folded her gloved hands in her lap, meeting Thomas Baxter's eyes with a steady gaze. "I think my offer is reasonable, and I honestly can't see what you have to lose by giving me an opportunity."

The solicitor sat back in his chair as Lena explained her plans to run the boarding house in Mr. Nash's place. For long disquieting moments, Lena feared he would simply burst into laughter and politely escort her from his office. But he remained with his fingers forming a little steeple, his blue eyes studying her. She forced herself to remain placid, resisting the urge to squirm under that steely eyed gaze.

He leaned forward in his chair, taking a heavy breath before speaking. "And you do understand that I will still have to notify Mr. Nash's next of kin." He shuffled through the file before him, pulling out one piece of paper. "Virginia. Yes, his sister lives in Richmond. I should find out from her how she wishes to proceed. Because you and Mr. Nash did not marry, any spoken contract between you has no bearing on this. I admit, that is an unfortunate situation for you."

Lena detected a note of sympathy in his voice, finding in it encouragement.

"I will explain all of this to her in a letter, including your offer to purchase."

"Thank you, Mr. Baxter."

"Well, that does not exactly settle the matter for the immediate future, does it?" He stroked his close-trimmed beard, a frown deepening the lines on his face. "I want to help. I really do. You seem an intelligent and sensible woman."

Lena responded to his compliment with a soft smile.

"You propose to run the boarding house through the winter or until we receive news from Mr. Baxter's sister."

"Yes."

"Even with the mining company laying off men, and the future of the town itself unknown, you'd rather invest more of your own money into what might be a dying town?"

"Yes, Mr. Baxter. I would like to believe that Mr. Nash correctly foresaw the opportunities here, that one day this area would be a place for people to visit to appreciate the beauty of the country, not just for its direct economic interest."

"I see." He stood and took a step to the window with a view of the mountains where men worked deep beneath the earth to coax riches from its bowels. "I wish I could share in your optimism, Miss Sommer. But I do admire your pluck to try. And as you have so well said, it is your choice to make."

Lena did not especially like the sound of the word *pluck*. She doubted it would have been a word most would chose to describe a man's determination. But he obviously meant it as a compliment, so she accepted it with grace.

"I can see no harm in your remaining at the lodging house and even running it through the winter. God knows, I've seen enough merchants pull out this fall, leaving fine buildings standing empty."

"Thank you, Mr. Baxter. I appreciate the opportunity."

He turned back to face her, hands folded behind him, a stern expression darkening his face. "But the winter here is not kind. It is harsh and at times brutal, even deadly. The passes close, leaving us isolated. You should prepare for that. If you find this becomes too difficult, I would strongly suggest you reconsider your plans and leave before November snows."

Her shoulders lifted as resolve filled her once again. "I appreciate your concern, sir. I will consider your kindly given advice. But I wish to try."

Baxter extended a hand as Lena stood. "I suspect the ladies of our new city will be glad to welcome a lady of culture such as yourself. Heaven knows how few of you there are here."

Lena found the comment unsettling, managing to keep her expression placid, hiding her thoughts behind a practiced reserve. "I do look forward to making my acquaintance with Sawtooth society."

The man held her hand for a moment, giving her a wry smile. "Well then, welcome to Sawtooth City, Miss Sommer. I wish you all good fortune."

Lena stepped into the kitchen where Jessica stood beside Bart peeling potatoes. Not hearing her light footsteps, they both looked up surprised. Jessie dropped her knife on the table and rushed to Lena's side, grabbing her gloved hands in hers. "Tell us how it went! Quick, or I'll just die of curiosity! Don't leave anything out!" She pulled Lena to the chair and flopped on the bench next to her.

"I hope he was civil. He's used to dealing with men, you know." Bart said while he poured a cup of tea and passed it to Lena.

"Oh, he was very civil. He's not the dreadful solicitor you had at first led me to believe him to be." She took the proffered cup and sipped cautiously, relaxing as she took comfort from the familiar. "He was very respectful and listened to my plans to attempt to purchase the property over time."

"So? What did he say?" Jessie bounced on the bench beside her.

"He said that he would have to contact Mr. Nash's sister and ask her how she wished to dispose of his assets here. But he promised to present my offer to her."

Jessie looked up at Bart then again at Lena. "That's good, yes?"

"Yes, for the time being. But I might need help."

"Anything," Bart answered, his honest face lighting up. "What can I do?"

"If I'm running a boarding house, I need to offer not just a room but board." Lena's expression took on a wry twist.

"Well, yeah. That's the usual way." Bart said as he shared a puzzled look with Jessie.

"There's one problem," Lena said. "The only thing I can cook is toast."

With his shift in the mine cut short, Evan saddled his horse and headed back to his mine upstream. The sun offered thin warmth even at the middle of the day. This used to be his favorite time of day—that is, until last winter. At midday, if he and Jimmy were working their claim, they'd stop for lunch and swap daydreams, how they'd spend their wealth, how many girls they'd attract because of it. Those daydreams grew more outlandish with each passing month since staking their claim along the north end of Beaver Creek. Of course, Jimmy could out dream him by a mile and a half. He could imagine what it might be like to own a fleet of fishing boats off the deep waters of the Pacific. It didn't matter that they knew nothing about boats, let alone the sea. Neither did it matter that not long ago, Evan had his own plans.

Jimmy, the baby of the family, always a dreamer. More than once, big brother bailed him out of another grand scheme gone sour. This one, this search for gold, took them farther from home than Evan ever thought he'd go. Certainly, Evan never planned to wander so far from the green hill country of southern Indiana. But when their mother learned what Jimmy planned, she pleaded with Evan to go with him, just for a year, and look out for him as he'd always done.

What Evan planned for his life didn't matter; his mother's words made his purpose clear. "Bring him home, Evan. When the gold doesn't pan out, bring him home. Give him a year, then bring him back home."

It hadn't panned out. There were signs, an ounce here or there, good signs, but the strike bringing them riches just hadn't happened. And even if Evan found the elusive vein, Jimmy wouldn't be going home. Not ever.

With Jimmy gone, just the dreams remained—Jimmy's dreams. In a sense, the dreams replaced his brother. As pointless as they might be without the dreamer, what else did he have?

He spent a few hours picking along the stream, finding little. His hunger turned him to the trail back to Sawtooth. Unlike his fellow workers, he'd never been one to drink away his earnings, choosing instead to save every hard-earned dollar. Neither was he one to indulge his yearnings for female companionship. That was not to say he did not have them, but that too would only postpone his dreams. His brother was quite the opposite, and while he lived, their savings never seemed to grow. Evan would return to the house and deal with his feelings concerning Nash's lady.

With any luck, she'd be gone by the end of the week, and the disturbing way she made him feel would not be an issue. What a fool he was, to give her more than a passing thought! And it was darn certain she gave him not even a passing one. The last thing he needed was another woman in his life.

After bedding down his horse, he walked back to the boarding house with a sour expression and a shuffling gait.

"Why the dark look, Evan?" The soft purr of a woman's voice stopped him. He turned.

Naomi greeted him from across the street, her emerald silk dress standing out as a sharp contrast to the drab clapboard siding of the building behind her. Naomi, like her dress, provided a contrast that softened the hard edges of the men's lives who worked in the mines. She saw her disparity as a purpose as well as a business.

"Just tired I guess." Evan recognized the truth in that. Reluctant as he was to return to the boarding house, he took the opportunity to delay. He crossed the street, falling into step with the woman.

"Don't see much of you since your brother..." Hesitating, she looked up at him before finishing. "How you doin', Evan? Sorry none of the girls made it to the funeral." Her ruby-painted lips curled into a sarcastic smile. "Didn't think the respectable folks would find our presence desirable." Her smile dissolved into a hard line, "That's just the way it is."

Evan cast his gaze down at his feet. "I do. But Jimmy wouldn't have minded. Neither would I."

She smiled, a genuine expression that transformed her entire countenance for just a moment.

His focus drifted back to his feet, voice soft. "How's Vicki?"

"Ah, you know. Good days. Bad days. She's not like the rest of us. This business came to her hard. Man ups and dies on her in the middle of winter. What's a young woman to do to survive? We were the only family to take her in."

Evan remembered stories of the man, Vicki's husband, the miner who'd died a year before he and Jimmy arrived in Sawtooth. Pulling up his pace, he turned to her. "You'll tell me if there's anything I can do, won't you, Naomi? You promised."

Naomi placed her hand lightly on Evan's sleeve and looked up with old eyes. "I told you I would. She's written a letter to her ma like you asked her to. She doesn't have much hope, but..." She shrugged. "Who knows? I'm not one who's much for believing in miracles, but I think that's about what it'd take. Forgiveness comes hard for those that put too much stock in their own cracked mirrors."

Evan shoved his hands into his pockets and looked up above the rooftops to the raw edge of the mountain. "Jimmy did love her. I'm sure he did. Had he known she was in a family way, he'd have married her for sure." His jaw tightened. "It wouldn't be any other way for a Hartmann."

Sympathy softened Naomi's eyes. She patted Evan's shoulder. "You've been a good friend to Vicki, and you were a good brother, Evan Hartmann. He might have had the looks to melt a woman's heart, but you were blessed with a heart bigger than all outdoors. It's a fine thing you helping Vicki." She cocked her head, studying him with narrowed eyes. "But I'm thinking this isn't helping you."

"What do you mean? It makes sense I should be looking after her." Something familiar stirred his blood. He prepared himself to defend his right to take care of her.

"Maybe. Like I said. It's a fine thing, more than most in this town full of do-gooders." Naomi's lips formed a straight scarlet line. "But what are you doing out there, scratchin' at the dirt like the rest of these poor souls? You've got more goin' for you, Evan. You've got more head sense than most anyone I ever knew, and that's sayin' a lot." She threw him a wry laugh before her face turned serious again. "I could understand it when Jimmy was alive, but what's holding you here now?"

Hadn't he asked himself that question a dozen times? He didn't have the answer any more now than he did then. Except, at times, he felt he was waiting for something. Like a hovering, half-formed thought, yet to resolve itself into any solid form he could latch on to. "Don't know, Naomi. God's truth. I don't know." He felt her dark eyes on him and met them. "Sometimes a man's just got to put one foot in front of another until he finds his way. Can't see where he's going until he looks back to see where he's been."

She scowled. "Evan, that makes about as much sense as a moth flying into a flame and burnin' itself plumb to ashes."

Evan threw out his arms in a gesture of surrender. "What do you want me to do?"

"That's your problem, Evan, right there! You're waiting for someone else to give you a roadmap for your life. You been following after your brother's dreams so long you don't know how to make your own!"

Evan pursed his lips in an effort to hold his tongue. Her words touched a nerve he'd been protecting for months.

"Ah, Evan, I'm sorry. But dang it all. I hate to see a man like you turn into a drifter." She wrapped her arms close to her body. "You shouldn't have asked if 'ya didn't want me to bust out with an answer."

After a long awkward moment, Naomi shook her head. "Life deals you a hand and you gotta play it. Jimmy's was a mixed hand with no aces and no kings. Vicki's, well, we'll see how she plays it. There still might be some surprises." A short mirthless laugh followed with a sigh tacked on the end, like an afterthought.

Evan shrugged. "I suspect you may pick up more news on that front than I do. You see a lot more of those in charge here than I would." He regretted having said it. Naomi's expression didn't change, but he quickly added, "Sorry."

"Don't be sorry. It's the truth. But no one seems to be talkin'. Seems odd. I'd sure like to get a handle on which way the wind is blowin' before winter sets in hard. I got my girls to consider, too."

A sudden burst of loud laughter came from the doorway across the street. Two very satisfied customers sang a tune to carry them home.

"You get along, Evan. I got business to tend to." She took a step toward the stairs at the side of the building. "I'll tell Vicki, you said hello." When he didn't walk away, she frowned at him, then turned back, giving his shoulder a shove. "Get on with you. A sad face like that's bad for business."

Passing her a smile, he turned back in the direction of the boarding house.

CHAPTER 6

"THIS is good!" Carrick elbowed his brother and took another bite of soda bread. He talked around a mouth full of heavily buttered bread. "You gotta' try this, Donal. Almost tastes like Mom's."

Donal sniffed the slice in his hand, a grin spreading across his face. "Ah, heaven" In three bites, the slice was consumed.

Lena said, "Well, I'll be."

Jessie threw her arm around Lena and hugged her. "You see? You can cook!"

Lena lifted an eyebrow. "I see that it's a very good thing that Bart showed me how to use the bread starter. Our results might not have been so favorable. She stepped to the counter where a book lay open with flour dusting the pages. After carefully folding a corner of the page, she tapped the recipe printed there. "And in place of a mother to teach me, *Mrs. Parloa's New Cookbook* will do quite nicely."

Jessie thumbed through the pages and read, "Curry of Roasted Rabbit. That sounds interesting. But what's this? *Vol a vint*. What language is that?"

Lena peered over her shoulder. "French! Vol-au-vent." She sighed. "My former employer hired a French pastry chef for a dinner party one Christmas." She closed her eyes as scented memories rushed past her tongue and into her mind visions of golden, flaky pastries. "They were so light and filled with the richest lobster sauce imaginable. Oh, they were heavenly. I forgot how wonderful they were."

"French chef? You worked for a very rich man, then." Jessie tilted her head, a quizzical expression inviting an answer.

"He did well for himself in shipping." She offered no more, turning her attention back to the book. "Look at this one! Chicken Croquettes. We should try that one tomorrow."

Jessie leaned in close. "Yum!"

"I also brought this one." Lena pulled another book from the shelf beneath the counter, laying it before Jessie.

"*Breakfast, Dessert, and Supper* by Mrs. H.L. Knight, Two Hundred and Seventy-Five Practical Recipes, The Result of Long Experience and Thoroughly Tested.'" Jessie read aloud. "My mama never used a cookbook in her life. She surely thoroughly tested everything on us, over and over and over again. But it never made anything she cooked taste any different from just plain awful!" She poked an elbow in Lena's arm and laughed.

Turning to the last half of the book, Lena placed a finger on one page. Jessie read the title aloud, "Apple Dumplings."

Evan avoided the kitchen when he heard voices, heading for the stairs instead. As hungry as he was, he wouldn't face the woman looking as he did, like a tramp. After a day in the mine, he was filthy, and he didn't want those dark eyes appraising him in that same way they had this morning. Taking the stairs two at a time, he quietly closed the door to his room. A basin of somewhat clean water rested on a side table. By the time he'd finished dousing his face and beard, the water looked a bit more like weak coffee.

A small mirror propped onto the window ledge provided a poor reflection of a man who still looked more grizzled than his years. He frowned while sorting through his kit. With razor in hand, he strode back to the basin. Again, he squinted into the mirror as he pulled the straight blade across his cheek. Grimacing, he continued his efforts until a younger face peered back at him. He scowled and leaned closer. A few drops of blood appeared at the cleft point of his chin. He stepped back, looked down at his sweat-soaked shirt and scavenged about for the second one he kept at the foot of his bed. He sniffed it and made a face.

Clean of whiskers, Evan's pondered his reflection. What he saw was a square jaw that looked as though it could stand up to many a blow. A thin scar at the corner of his lip remained as a reminder of the life he might have lived had he followed in the footsteps of his two pugilist uncles. He'd been encouraged in that direction even before he'd grown into his feet. Their expectations took his thoughts about the matter into little account. His uncles, dismayed that he was squandering his God-given talents, accused their sister of spoiling the boy with unnecessary book learning. But she understood that Evan's strength, though considerable, lay not in the power of his fists but in the power of his heart and his good mind.

"You're lookin' all Saturday night, Evan," Bart said, his voice teasing, but friendly.

"Yeah, I was feelin' a bit itchy." Running a hand along his now exposed cheek, Evan stepped into the kitchen and slipped into a seat next to Bart.

Lena turned from the stove with more biscuits, stopping in mid-stride. For a moment, perhaps even two, she thought this must be a boarder she'd not yet met. With a start, she recognized the eyes of the man. How much younger he looked without the beard! He wasn't just younger than she'd first assumed, he bore the chiseled good looks of the plaster statues exhibited of late in the Chicago Museum of Art. Her breath caught as it had this morning watching the surprising sunrise over the mountains.

What had become of the dirty, bear-of-a-man who'd sat here this morning? Surely, a simple shave would not account for the transformation.

"Lena, are you all right?" Jessie whispered to her. She followed Lena's gaze. Jessie's eyes widened at the sight of Evan's appearance.

Recovering from her shock, Lena looked at Jessie with a carefully recovered mask of nonchalance. "Oh quite." She quietly slipped the plate onto the table, spinning back to the stove where she found the urgent need to stir the stew.

Jessie was at her elbow. "He's certainly the handsome devil, isn't he? Those eyes! I've never seen green eyes of that shade before. Emeralds, right? That's what they call those jewels."

"Oh, are they green?" Lena kept her head down, stirring methodically from one side to the other.

"Liar." Jessie whispered. "Don't pretend you didn't notice."

"I suppose he is rather above average in his person."

"Phfft! What nonsense are you talking?"

"What are you two whispering about?" Bart leaned in close to Jessie.

"I suppose if we'd wanted you to know, we'd have spoken to you." Jessie said before tossing her head and turning away. Jessie scooped out a portion of stew into the bowl and placed it in front of Evan. The force with which she set it on the table produced raised eyebrows on both Ely's and Evan's faces. "Sorry," she said as she stormed out the door of the kitchen.

Lena turned at the sound of the bowl hitting the table. The men looked to her for explanation but all she could do was shrug. She headed for the door.

"Jessie!" Lena found the girl in tears standing on the banks of the creek. "What's wrong, dear?"

"I'm sorry. It's that..." Sobs shook her small shoulders, her words coming in short spurts. "Well, you plan for months for something wonderful. You have to answer all the questions from friends and family about the man you've never met. You have to put up with their advice about rushing into things." She paused for breath, wiping her eyes with the back of her hand. "You just convince yourself after a while that it's all going to be all right, despite their thoughts differently. You know?"

Not at all sure that she did know, Lena put her arm around the girl and patted her shoulder.

"And then it's suddenly not." She stopped as another spasm of sobs shook her shoulders.

"You mean he's not what you imagined him to be?"

"Yes! I mean, no! It's not Bartholomew. Not entirely anyway. I mean I think he meant the things he wrote to me. But now what are we to do? We can't live here." She pulled up a corner of her apron to dab at her eyes and runny nose.

"Well, as far as I'm concerned you can. The room upstairs on the end isn't being used right now."

"But then I think maybe it is Bartholomew, you know? Maybe he's just not right for me." She pulled away from Lena, lips quivering, face flushed, as if she'd seen a revelation. "Maybe it's me!" A wail escaped her lips as she covered her face with the apron.

Lena rested both her hands on Jessie's shoulders. "This is a lot to take in, Jessie. You have every right to be confused and even disappointed. Even though you've written each other for months, there's been no time to become truly acquainted with one another."

Jessie plopped down on the bank, drawing her legs up under her skirt, her chin on her knees. "Bart told me that he explained to you about the cabin. But it isn't just the cabin. I think we need some time." She looked up at Lena reaching for her hand. "You know? Like you said. Writing is one thing. A pen is a whole lot less talkative than a tongue. And you can scratch out the words you know you shouldn't say."

Lena sat beside her. "Sounds sensible. Have you told Bart what you're feeling?"

"Not yet." She plucked at a blade of grass. "I'm afraid he'll take it that I don't care about him. But I do care. I care very much. He's kind, and he makes me laugh." She pulled up a handful of grass and tossed it away, heedless of dirt showering her white apron. "I just need some time. Do you think that's very silly of me? People back home always called me silly. I mean I came here ready to marry him. Oh, I don't know what's wrong with me."

Lena reached across the space between them and cupped Jessie's chin in her hand. "It's anything but silly. It's extremely logical. And if he loves you in return, he'll understand. And if he doesn't, then he really isn't the man for you, right?"

At that, Jessie threw herself into Lena's arms. "Oh, thank you." She sat up again, wiping her eyes furiously with the back of her hand. "May I stay here with you a little longer? I mean at the boarding house. I can help you in the kitchen or washing the linens, whatever you need."

"Of course, you can. I'd welcome your help."

A smile replaced the grim line that had defined her mouth moments before. "I've never had a sister. If I had, I'd have wanted her to be just like you!"

"I'm flattered you should think so," Lena said. Neither had she experienced the confidences of a sister, the late-night confessions. She supposed that Miranda's mother was the closest to becoming a sister as anyone.

"I do! And as your sister, I would tell you that you are blind if you don't see how attractive Evan Hartmann is. If it weren't for Bart, I'd sure set my cap for him! And I know you saw him the way I did too." She pointed at Lena's chest, her eyes narrowing to slits. "I saw that glimmer in your eyes."

Lena granted her the mild smile. "His eyes are very attractive. But this isn't the subject, now is it? You need to dry your eyes, wash your face, and sit down with Bart. Tell him what you told me." She grinned. "Well, perhaps you can leave out the part about setting your cap for Mr. Hartmann."

Jessie giggled.

By the time the dishes were cleaned and put away, one of the men had kindled a fire in the great room. Carrick and Donal sat in the corner by the window, a game of checkers on the table between them. Ely rested in a chair near the hearth with his pipe clenched in his teeth, his eyes locked on the growing fire.

Evan stood by the mantel, a poker in his hand, occasionally adjusting the logs. Lena walked in, leaving Jessie and Bart in the kitchen to discuss their uncertain future. Ely rose and motioned for her to take the seat near the fire. She smiled and accepted.

Lifting her voice a bit louder than was her habit, she addressed them all. "Gentlemen, I wanted to speak with you about my decision that affects all of you."

Carrick slapped his brother on the arm and inclined his head in Lena's direction. Donal scrambled to a chair while Carrick perched on the arm of it.

Surprised to find her voice dry, she cleared her throat. "I spoke with Mr. Baxter today about the disposition of Mr. Nash's property, including this house."

Carrick nudged Donal, giving him a wink. Ely stood nearby, listening as he puffed rhythmically on his pipe.

"I've asked him to allow me to continue to operate the boarding house until Mr. Nash's sister makes her wishes known to Mr. Baxter. I know there are some who would view this as a poor decision and hastily made, but it is my decision and I believe I have carefully weighed all possible factors. I do hope you all will stay and not seek rooms elsewhere. I will do my best to provide you with the same quality of services as Mr. Nash."

"Well, if you can just keep makin' bread as good as we had tonight, there's no other place I'd rather be sitting down to table in all of Sawtooth. How about you, little brother?" Carrick punched his brother again.

"Yup. Seems fine to me to just stay put. At least as long as the mine is payin' us a fair wage."

That last brought the room to a very quiet place where the only sound was the crackling of the fire.

A span of moments elapsed until Lena cleared her throat again and rose to her feet. "Well then, gentlemen, I'll excuse myself for the evening. I'm still in need of catching up on my sleep."

Evan's deep voice stopped her. Almost too soft to assume he'd addressed her, she hesitated.

"Mr. Hartmann?" Lena waited.

"Have you considered the winter that's coming, Miss Sommer?"

She met his gaze steadily, chin up. "I believe that I have, Mr. Hartmann."

He continued in a level tone. "The snows that come here aren't like those you're used to. They come with fierce storms that blow through any crack or loose chink. They'll be no returning to the low valleys once they hit. Have you considered that?" The blankness of his expression and his flat tone acted like a knife cut through her resolve.

"I have been warned of what to expect, yes."

"Have they also spoken to you of the avalanches that thunder down from the mountains without warning?"

She stood motionless, feeling indignation kindling like a coal caged in her ribs.

He turned back to the fire. "As long as you know, Miss Sommer."

Who was he to think he knew what might be best for a person? He had no idea of her strength of character, her tenacity, her ability to care for herself. She suddenly became aware of the silence about her and the tension that had balled her hands into fists at her side. "Thank you, Mr. Hartmann, for your concern." She turned to the stairs wanting to say more, but not trusting herself to maintain her composure.

With the door closed behind her, she stepped to the bed and sat staring out the window at the mountains in silhouette. Holding her arms tight about her, she tried to control the shaking that seized her. Even her teeth chattered. Not knowing whether fear or rage gripped her, she tried to sort logically through the events of the day. She'd sought out counsel from both Bart and Ely, looked at Mr. Nash's ledgers, considered her reserve of cash against the expenses of running the house. Why shouldn't she be able to do this? What did this man know that she did not?

She paced to the window, gripping the frame with white knuckles. Who was Evan Hartmann to fill her with such doubt? He knew nothing about her. Did he know that after her parents had died of influenza when she was a girl of eighteen, she'd been making her way? Of course, not! Did he know that alone she'd found good employment as a governess and become an excellent teacher? No!

Then, as though a veil lifted from her eyes, her logical mind dampened her anger. The questions changed. Had she considered the winter snows? Why wouldn't she have factored that into her calculated risks? Had she? Or had she missed something? What made Evan Hartmann so sure of himself and so ready to frighten her with stories of avalanches? Of course, she'd heard of such things, but until now, thought they only occurred in such faraway places as the European Alps. Was he simply trying to scare her into leaving or was his concern genuine? She frowned and gripped the window ledge until her nails dug into the soft pine.

She'd been on her own for these past years, but not entirely. That was the truth. The child had been her focus, her immediate concern. She'd been a part of that family, their fortune determining hers. She'd not been concerned with the details of her existence apart from her duty to the child. Decisions like the one she faced now would determine her future. She might lose everything.

Did she really have a choice? Yes! Of course, she did! But had she made the right one?

CHAPTER 7

BEFORE sunup, Lena, with her sleeves rolled above her elbows and apron cinched around her waist, tackled one of Mrs. Knight's two-hundred and seventy-five *practical* recipes. The book assured her that each recipe had been "The result of long experience and thoroughly tested" by Mrs. Knight herself. Although she lacked the *gems pan*, called for in the book, she chose the recipe for popovers since she recalled happy memories eating those with Miranda in a cheery little tea shop one fall day last October. The recipe used few ingredients and seemed straight-forward enough. The fifteen minutes of beating the eggs, flour, and milk was a bit tiring, and she doubted the necessity of such effort after about seven of those minutes passed. It occurred to her that had she possessed the *Propeller Egg Beater,* called for in the recipe, she might have had an easier time of it. After a quick search, she located a muffin tin and poured in the hard-earned golden batter, imagining the lofty crusts to come in just ten minutes.

She stepped back, admiring her filled tins, and felt quite satisfied with herself. Let Evan Hartmann say what he would, she could make a success of this.

Carrick's and Donal's arrival in the kitchen was preceded by their Irish brogues engaged in some good-natured teasing. She greeted them with a broad smile as they took their accustomed places at the table. They sniffed at the air as they waited, grins spread wide. Ely followed them, greeting Lena with a "Good morning" and what might have been a hint of smile. Jessica and Bart arrived together.

Jessie rushed to Lena's side. "Sorry, Lena. I should have been here to help you."

"It wasn't a problem. See?" She hefted the open cookbook from the counter, grinning. "Mrs. Knight's been teaching me. At that, she turned to the oven, towels in each hand and opened the door. A little "Oh!" followed by "Fiddlesticks!" could have been as foul a word as any sailor could utter in the way she spat it out. Whatever manner of magic she'd hoped for had failed to develop within those ten minutes, leaving the popovers, most definitively, un-popped.

Mr. Hartmann walked into the kitchen at that unfortunate moment. Embarrassment and frustration stirred together as a deadly concoction boiling within her. For Evan, the man who seemed to know what was best for her, there to witness her failure, only made matters worse. If the human body could generate a deadly degree of energy to match that of lightning, and the eyes could conduct such a charge, Evan would have turned to ash in an instant.

Before the men left for their shifts at the mine, Bart gave Jessica and Lena some simple instructions for preparing stew. As tempted as Lena was to try yet again another recipe, she allowed her common sense to over-rule her new adventurous spirit. *Mrs. Parloa's New Cookbook: A Guide to Marketing and Cooking* could wait for another day.

Dinner that evening was a success, as everything served was quite edible. Though not up to Bart's level of culinary expertise, no one complained and seconds were accepted.

Lena dished out a second helping to Evan, though unsolicited, a smug smile tugging at the corners of her mouth.

Later in the evening, even though Lena thought she could not stay awake much longer, she remained downstairs for the sake of propriety so that Jessica and Bart could talk. In the far corner of the room the two sat chatting. From where Lena sat it seemed Bart had as much to say as Jessie.

Sitting close to the fire in the large oversized chair, her feet warming on the hearth, Lena opened a book she'd purchased from the small book shop in Hailey. It was a rather recent publication she'd heard much about before heading west. But until moving away from the city of Chicago, she'd had little interest in such provincial writings. She much preferred the works of Jane Austen, Victor Hugo or Alexandre Dumas. Had she chosen to read an American author, she would have picked a book by Nathaniel Hawthorne, but not one by such a writer as Mark Twain. But such was the book she held in her hands now, *The Adventures of Tom Sawyer.*

Although she struggled to keep her eyes open through the first chapter, by the second Mr. Twain had reeled her into the story. Her quiet smiles at Tom's foolery changed to soft chuckles when the lovesick boy lay under Becky Thatcher's window, sorrowful to death for his unrequited love.

Jessie scooped up her skirts and knelt beside Lena's chair, "What is it? I want to hear what makes you laugh." Bart placed another log on the fire, then perched on the arm of the chair to the right of the fireplace. "Surely, Lena, we'd love a good story."

Putting her finger in the book to mark the page, she looked from one eager face to the other. "Well, the dialect is a bit troublesome for me, but I suppose I could try. It's this boy, Tom, that makes the story so appealing. He's fallen under the charms of a little girl named Becky." She picked up the book, found her place and began where she'd stopped earlier. '...he was showing off with all his might— cuffing boys, pulling hair, making faces—in a word, using every art that seemed likely to fascinate a girl...' It's perfect!"

Jessie giggled. "It is! Every boy I've known was just like that!"

"What do you mean?" Bart frowned at them, first at Lena, then Jessie.

Jessie answered, "Oh, come now, Bart, it's exactly the way little boys behave. I had the experience with my brothers to prove it."

"Well, maybe little boys, I suppose." Bart conceded.

"You think such "showing off" stops in childhood?" Lena challenged. "I can recall many instances of men using their strength to show off to ladies. It's the same thing." She couldn't repress the laugh when she saw the wounded look on Bart's face. "Surely, you know what I mean."

"Seems you could have asked for help with those trunks the other day." Jessie shot him a teasing look.

Bart's good nature sparked again, his eyes softened as his face broke into a self-effacing grin. "I suppose. Maybe. Sometimes." He squinted at them both as he added, "And I suppose it isn't common for the ladies to preen and prance before the men, with fancy clothes and colored cheeks?

Seems it works two ways." He made a little pantomime, arms flourished, head tilted coyly.

A moment of silence followed before all three dissolved in laughter.

"Well, make yourself comfortable then, Jessie. Sit yourself in that chair next to Bart. I'll read one more chapter and then we all should take ourselves off to bed." Lena resettled herself and picked up the book again, reading aloud, "*Monday morning found Tom Sawyer miserable...*"

Half-way through the chapter, Evan entered through the front door sending a rush of cold night air across the room. Lena met his gaze, the heat in her eyes from earlier in the day now gone. He nodded to them as he unbuttoned his coat. "Cold night." For an awkward few moments he remained there as if uncertain what he should do. Without a word, he continued down the hall to his room, closing the door behind him.

"Is he always so unpleasant?" Lena asked.

Bart tipped his head. "Unpleasant? Never would have called him that. Serious maybe."

"Oh, I see." Lena turned back to the open book.

"Read another chapter, Lena. Please?" Jessie asked.

"Two more pages and then I must retire. And so, should you." She picked up the book and started in where they'd left off. "*'Thomas Sawyer!' Tom knew that when his name was pronounced in full, it meant trouble.*"

CHAPTER 8

Taking the early shift in the company mine allowed Evan time to work his claim for a few hours in the late afternoon. If he skipped dinner, he bought himself even more time, but with meals improving lately he had more reason to pull up to the long kitchen table. Besides, he was a big man that needed more than a bit of jerked beef and hunk of bread to satisfy him. Miss Sommer, though improving her cooking skills, was still troubling his mind and sometimes that tension he felt in her presence caused him to rush through his meal. That just wasn't something a Hartmann had ever wanted to do.

With a swing of his pick, he broke a large chunk of quartz from the rock wall and carried it outside into the sunlight where he could study it better. His teeth showed white against the grime coating his face. There was promise in this hole, this proved it. Maybe he wouldn't hit it this fall, but come spring he might, with a bit of luck and persistence. Persistence was something he had in spades—luck, not so much. But maybe luck could change like the seasons.

Tucking the quartz sample into his saddle bag, he secured his tools and headed out, back down the smaller stream that fed into Beaver Creek. Maybe he'd grab his dinner from the saloon and head over to Naomi's and see how Vicki and the baby were getting on. Along with a bit of that luck he was wishing for himself, he wished even more for it to shine on Vicki and her little girl. They certainly needed it more than he did. That luck might soften the heart of a mother back east and a letter would arrive welcoming Vicki and the baby home. But even as he thought it, he knew it would take more than luck. Naomi had it right. It'd take a miracle.

Evan tied his horse to the post in the alley behind Naomi's place. Dousing his grubby bandana in the watering trough, he scrubbed hard at his face, managing to lighten his skin tone a shade and bringing a tint of color to his newly shorn cheeks. The bandana was worse for the use, but Evan felt more human because of the quick wash. His bare cheeks felt the chill of the wind coming off the mountain, and he cursed his vanity.

It was a bit early for customers to come knocking at Naomi's front door, so Evan hoped to find her and maybe Vicki in the kitchen. But he was greeted by the buxom redhead, Katie, already dressed for the evening, or as it might be said, undressed for the evening.

"Evan! Aren't you lookin' fine! I like your boyish new look. Makes me want to take you in and be your mama." She laughed. "I do love a man that still blushes." Stepping to the side to allow him to enter, she managed to make the opening between the doorframe and her person as narrow as possible. Evan squeezed by and found Naomi sitting at the table holding the baby, Rebecca.

"Come on in, Evan! What brings you callin' at this hour? Doubt you're here on business." She patted the chair next to her with her free hand. "Sit yourself down. Katie, bring Evan a cup of coffee. Should still be hot."

"I was hoping to see Vicki and find out if the little one needs anything. We got a paycheck yesterday."

"She'll be done in a bit. Business." Naomi lifted an eyebrow in the direction of the stairs.

Evan frowned. "I thought she was done with that until she heard from her mother. Thought the extra cash might help keep her from having to..."

"We gotta pay the bills and this ain't a charity house nor some home for wayward girls and orphans." She gave a rueful laugh. "Well, maybe it might be a bit of that. Besides, this one's a nice chap, polite and clean. We try to keep her from workin' as much as we can." Naomi pulled her finger from the child's grasp. "Here!" She held the child out to Evan. "Want to hold her?"

He shook his head. "No! Thanks, but no. I'm no good with kids."

Naomi pushed the child onto Evan's lap and stood, smoothing her taffeta dress. "I've gotta' change. You'll be fine. Just talk to her like she was your horse."

He held the child on his lap at arm's length, balancing her awkwardly on his knee. She was just old enough to begin giggling at those small things which amused her. Apparently, she found amusement in Evan. Her laughter brought a grin to Evan's lips, and he made a face at her, provoking more giggles. "You are a pretty little thing. You got the clear look of a Hartmann about your eyes, but the softness of your mama everywhere else."

"She does, doesn't she? Makes me feel like Jimmy's still here with us." Vicki stood in the doorway at the bottom of the stairs. Evan could see that she'd taken the time to change out of her working clothes and into a simple, sky blue cotton dress, a color that matched her eyes perfectly.

Evan stood as she entered. The habits of childhood still dictated his actions where a woman was concerned. He held the child out to Vicki's open arms. "You're looking well, Vicki. And the little one is growing so fast. I'd heard she wasn't feeling well, but she looks plenty healthy now."

"She is. Thank you for your help, Evan." She kept her eyes on the baby, nestling into the crook of her arm. "I'm sorry about..." She tipped her head slightly toward the stairs. "I wouldn't be still..."

Evan shifted his feet, uncomfortable at the change in topic. He moved to the stove and poured more coffee into his already full cup, an excuse to avoid her apologies. He remained there for a while, fiddling with the hot pad, his back to her. "You don't owe me any explanation. It's your life. I just want to help if I can."

He could hear the soft sounds of the child, more like a lamb than a human, he thought.

"I'm just sorry a woman has so few choices. And those you got, well..." He forced himself to turn back to her.

Vicki said, "When my husband died in that mining accident three years ago, I thought things couldn't get much worse." She moved to the table and sat in Naomi's empty chair. "I was wrong." The child grabbed a strand of Vicki's long hair. "But when I met your brother—I had hope again. I thought things might be looking up."

Vicki's face wore the look of one who'd cried all the tears within her, the reservoir dry. A faint smile on her face, she looked up at him. "I will choose to believe that, Evan. And take comfort in it."

Putting down his cup in the sink, he shuffled the few feet to the door. "I'm praying for a miracle for that little girl. Think she deserves one." He slipped his hat on his head as he headed for the door. Hesitating at the door, he turned, saying, "Let me know when the letter comes. Somehow we'll get you off this mountain before winter comes."

Evan arrived at the house after everyone else had finished eating dinner. A single plate lay on the table. Drying the last dish, Lena stood peering out the window when he stepped into the kitchen. She turned at the sound of his footsteps. "Good evening, Evan. There's chicken and dumplings on the stove. Please help yourself."

He simply nodded his head, mumbling a thank you. From the corner of her eye, she watched him scoop creamed chicken onto his plate. Surprised that it could be possible, she thought that he looked even more somber tonight than last night. In that moment, she felt more than curiosity about his sullenness. A stirring compassion made her want to ask what troubled him. But nothing about his body posture or countenance invited such inquiries. Instead of hastening out of the room as she'd done on previous evenings, she lingered.

"Ely told me the company has started payroll again. That's certainly good news." She tried a topic that might break through his reserve, hoping to engage him in casual conversation.

"Yes, they paid out last week." He mumbled, working a mouthful of biscuit past his teeth.

"Must be quite hard for you men."

Evan glanced up, his green eyes shadowed with dark circles, making him look older and more worn down than ever. "It's harder on the men with families. This isn't a good place for women and young ones." The words came out hard. A muscle in his jaw worked, but not at chewing his meal.

The utensils rattled as the drawer shut with the force of Lena's bristling temper. "And why is that, Mr. Hartmann? It seems this is a city after all. Cities usually attract both men and women, and where there are the two genders, there are inevitably children. Do you have something against cities?"

"This is a boom town, Miss Sommer. 'City' is hardly what I'd call it. Boom towns have that name for a reason. They explode with activity; businesses come to take advantage of the gold and silver... and anything else, and then they move on. They live for a short time, fed by greed, and then they die. And heaven help the man or woman stuck in them through a winter."

Turning her back to him she stopped herself in time before throwing the towel into the sink. With supreme control, she folded the towel into a neat rectangle, placing it on the counter. Gathering her remaining composure, she walked from the room. "Good night, Mr. Hartmann."

CHAPTER 9

USING the complaint of a headache, Lena excused herself from the promised reading to Bart and Jessie and retired to the upstairs bedroom. Carrick and Donal sat in the corner playing poker, an agreement they'd made with the young couple for propriety's sake. Lena's head, in fact, pounded from the effort to restrain her anger.

Lena kicked off her shoes and sat at the foot of the bed for a while. Feeling her frustration bubbling up again like a bad case of heartburn, she flung herself back on the bed staring up at the ceiling, intentionally counting the knotholes in the beams stretching from one end of the room to the other. After forty-two, she stopped, sitting up again. Still, the anger churned a tempest in her stomach.

In that temper-simmering state, she picked up the faint lilt of violin music. She slipped on her shoes and a wrap, following the violin's singing to the end of the upstairs hallway. A narrow doorway crouched at the end of the hall, unexplored and unnoticed by Lena until this moment. Hand pressed to the smooth wood, she listened with her ear close to the door. As the melody spiraled toward completion, she quietly turned the handle and found that it opened onto a small balcony, tucked beneath the eaves.

Ely looked around at her, violin still nestled under his chin. "Evening, Lena." He said in his soft, quaint accent.

"I hope you don't mind the intrusion. I seem to be doing that to you frequently." She hesitated at the threshold. He'd obviously come here to play without an audience or he'd be downstairs in the great room. But she hoped he'd allow her to stay. She had felt her heartbeat slowing, the pressure in her chest subside in the presence of his music.

"Oh, no, it is fine. Come, there is room on the bench for two." He scooted to the side, propping the violin on his knee. "It's a fine night, don't you think?"

Lena sat beside him, pulling the woolen wrap close about her shoulders. A bright canopy of stars spread out to the gray shadow of the mountains marking the horizon. She agreed. "Lovely." The crisp air rushed into her lungs with every breath, clearing her mind of the confusion and frustration she'd experienced just moments before. She closed her eyes, fully appreciating the sensation of breathing in the fragrance of the night. *Delicious.* Somehow, the air here seemed richer, almost intoxicating. It was as if her lungs had never been satiated before. As though she'd been living with less oxygen for most of her life. This made her feel more alive.

After a time, sitting together listening to the quiet of a fall evening, she turned to him. "Will you play some more, please? I do enjoy your music."

"*Ja*, of course. What would you like for me to play? Do you have any favorites?"

"I like the concertos by Johann Bach. But I'd be happy with anything you decided to play." Feeling her teeth chatter a little, she drew her knees up beneath her skirts, hugging her arms about herself. But whether from the cool air or the thrill of sitting here beneath the wide-open skies with the anticipation of listening to her own private concert, she was unsure.

"I will play for you. One, perhaps, you may know. It is older." With the grace of a dancer, Ely lifted the instrument and placed it firmly beneath his chin. He held that pose, his eyes closed, as if playing the melody first in his head before applying his fingers to the strings. Lifting his bow, he held it hovering above the strings for a moment more before the first note cast its voice into the night sky. The bow flew across the strings; his fingers calling forth the melody rapidly at first then slowing to the gentle rhythm of a lullaby. The beauty of it, at times melancholy and at others joyful, enveloped her completely.

When the last note vibrated to silence, Ely lifted his bow from the string and lowered his hand to his lap. Neither of them spoke for a long while. At last, Ely sighed softly and lay the violin within its case. "It is too bad he did not write more of those, *ja*? Many say that he did not write this one, but I disagree. It has his voice, I think."

"At first it reminded me of the fast-moving streams, tripping notes like water over stones. How lovely!" She touched his sleeve. "You play so beautifully. Thank you, Ely."

Ely dipped his head. "You are welcome. I am glad it pleased you."

She shivered, definitely from the cold this time. "Would you ever consider playing for all of us one night? It might be a bit warmer downstairs."

He laughed with her, shrugging his shoulders. "I do not wish to bother anyone."

"Oh, Ely, how could you bother anyone with such beauty? Please do join us tomorrow night. I will read for a little while and you will play."

His expression conveyed his skepticism.

She grinned at him. "You will play for us, *ja*?"

Head wobbling from side to side, between a nod and a shake, he said, "My old fingers feel the cold more keenly these days."

Again, she pressed him for an answer. "Then you will join us, *ja*?"

He smiled then. "*Ja*."

Plumping the pillow for the third time, Evan ceased his fidgeting, turning his head to the open window where the music drifted down from the balcony. The tune swirled through the room like smoke. He liked that Ely had chosen the place above his room to play his violin. For a few moments, he felt a bit of peace, the anxiety he felt for Vicki and the child fitting into the larger picture of life. The injustice of the life she and the child faced enraged him, but there were so many injustices and hers was just one more. His brother should not have died so young, nor Vicki's husband.

Why did he stay? If the mining company should close for the winter, he could work his claim. Maybe with another cycle of seasons he could fill his pockets with enough silver to buy that cattle and horse ranch he and his brother had dreamed of owning. But the thought of living in the shadow of the mountains that had promised so much and then swept all those dreams aside like so little chaff...

Unjust—that was how he'd behaved to Lena tonight. He'd taken out his fears and frustration on the poor woman. *What a fool I am.* She was just trying to make the most of her disappointments in life. Learning the news of Nash's death had to have been hard on her. But this notion she had that she could make her living here was foolishness. She'd be flat broke by spring, or worse, forced to join Vicki working for Naomi.

The swelling of the musical refrain distracted him from his dark thoughts. Forcibly shifting his focus, he listened to the insistent voice of the violin, feeling his tense muscles relaxing at last. After the final note faded, just as he'd closed his eyes, he heard the woman's voice. Soft and indistinct, her words drifted down from the balcony followed by a light musical laugh.

She didn't deserve to be martyred by his demons.

CHAPTER 10

J ESSIE, her feet fairly skipping as she walked along the boardwalk with Lena, pointed ahead to the livery stable. "Let's go see Evan's stallion. Bart says he's a beauty." She wrapped her arm through Lena's, tugging her away from the boardwalk into the dirt street. "Come on! We have plenty of time to do our shopping."

With an indulgent smile, Lena allowed herself to be towed to the open doorway of the livery. The scent of newly milled lumber intertwined with the fresh fragrance of hay and earthy horse manure greeted them even before crossing the threshold. Lena breathed deep, enjoying the wholesome warmth of it. The snuffling and stomping of the horses sounded muted in their well-bedded stalls.

Releasing her hold on Lena's arm, Jessie peered into the first stall where a sweet-faced chestnut bay lifted its head to stare out at the two women. "Oh, aren't you a dear!" Jessie ran her hand down the mare's soft neck. "You remind me of my little Sugar, only she had a blaze right there." She touched the horse's forehead, prompting the animal to toss its head to the side.

"She's a small one, isn't she?" Lena cautiously reached out her hand to stroke the mare's nose. Having lived in cities for most of her life, her knowledge of horses could have been contained within a few paragraphs. Most of those facts would have centered around the type of horse most suited for carriages or those used for deliveries. She liked to look at them and could appreciate their beauty, but had never had the opportunity to interact with any for any long period.

"My Sugar was the gentlest thing! I'd had her since she was a foal. Daddy detested the way I spoiled her, dressing her in my bonnet and feeding her carrots from Mama's garden." Jessie rested her head against the mare's neck and in return received a soft huff. "I do miss her so."

Lena marveled at the velvety softness of the mare's nose, the perfect curve of her nostrils, surprised by their size. "It must have been hard for you when she died."

"Oh, she didn't die. Daddy sold her to a man in town in exchange for a couple of pigs." Jessie stepped back, folding her arms across her waist. "I hope you've got yourself a good mistress." She spied a bucket of grain and looking about her scooped up a handful, offered it to the horse in her open hand.

"What makes you think it's a mistress. Why not a man?"

"From the size of her I'd guess she'd be best suited to a lady. Too small for most men."

Lena tilted her head to observe the animal with this new information. She turned to Jessie with a flash of a smile. "Do you suppose I could try? To feed her?"

Jessie demonstrated how to open her hand, fingers extended. She placed a handful of grain into it. The horse sniffed once before using her lips to gather the grains into her mouth.

"Oh my, but she has large teeth!" Lena enjoyed the sensation of the mare's whiskers brushing her palm. "Did that taste good?" She stroked the mare's neck, marveling at its silky, smooth texture.

Within moments of feeding the mare, a chorus of whinnies rose from the other stalls deeper inside the stable. The scent of freshly ground grain would not go undetected by any horse's sensitive nose.

"We're in for it now." Jessie scooped another small handful to offer the next horse.

Lena followed her example and did the same for the next one, a blue roan. "Ouch!"

Jessie laughed at her. "Forgot to keep your palm open?"

Sucking her injured finger, Lena nodded.

Nine horses watched them with their heads poking out of their stalls, munching like curious old men chewing tobacco.

"Wonder where this horse has gone?" Lena peered into the empty stall.

"That'd be Gambit's bunk." The familiar voice brought her head around much like the mares had at the sound of their voices. Evan stood silhouetted in the doorway, leading a horse whose head barely cleared the open door. He tipped his hat. "Morning, Jessie, Miss Sommer."

Jessie brought her hands together in a soundless clap. "Evan! That must be the horse Bart told me about. He's just as fine as Bart said! May I pet him? Is he comfortable with other people?"

Evan glanced at the giant beside him, giving Lena the impression the man and horse exchanged some understanding. *Something* had passed between man and horse. Fascinating.

"He's not so friendly with other men, but I've noticed he favors the ladies. You could pick up a handful of that grain over there and offer it to him. He'd be certain to take a liking to you, then."

Jessie scooped up another handful. Taking slow steps and speaking softly as she approached, she crooned, "Handsome boy, I've got something you'll like."

The horse jerked his head up just as Jessie was within reach of his muzzle. "Whoa, boy, steady." Evan stroked the stallion's neck. "You know you like what she's offering."

Lowering his head, the bay sniffed at Jessie's hand, threw his head up, then blew once. A moment of caution passed before he mouthed the grain with his lips. A good portion fell to the ground. Neck extended, he chewed the rest, appearing decidedly content.

Jessie slowly lifted her other hand to his nose. "Nice boy. Bart says you have plans to buy a ranch and use Gambit to start your own herd."

Still stroking the stallion's neck, Evan nodded. "Been ruminating on it." Redirecting his attention to Lena, he asked, "Would you like to give the boy a pat? I'm sure he'll be quiet for you, too."

Pulling her hands behind her back, she straightened her shoulders. "I'm quite sure he would, Mr. Hartmann. But we have errands to run. Perhaps another time."

Jessie looked back over her shoulder. "Lena, you must touch him. He's like silk."

With Evan, the horse, and Jessie standing between herself and the livery door, she had little excuse to refuse.

"Very well."

Jessie stepped aside as Lena moved closer. "Just take your time. Don't come up to him straight on, 'cause he can't see you as well. Come over this way and let him take a good long look at you before you touch him."

Moving to where she could see the stallion's dark eye appraising her, she waited until Evan nodded for her to move closer.

Evan said, "That's the way. Just slowly move your hand to right behind his ears. That's his sweet spot."

Gambit stomped a foot, tossing his black mane as he did, prompting Lena to jump back.

"Whoa, boy. It's just fine," Evan soothed.

The stallion quieted, blew once, and lowered his head as if inviting her approach. She tried again, brushing the soft hair behind his ears with two fingers. In spite of her intended reserve, she smiled at the pleasant sensation. "Nice, Gambit. Good boy." She glanced at Evan, asking, "Do you ride him?"

"I've always thought any horse not worth riding wasn't worth owning. Yes, I ride him from time to time. Mostly I ride my horse, the gelding over there. I know him and he's gotten used to me after all these years." He patted the stallion's neck. "But Gambit and I are getting on."

"I see." Clasping her hands in front of her, Lena had to ask. "Interesting name, Gambit. Do you play chess, Mr. Hartmann?"

Evan chuckled. "Not me. That was the name he was given by the Scotsman I bought him from. I know it's a chess term, though, having something to do with giving up something small to gain something bigger."

"Yes." Lena studied Evan as he indulged the horse in more scratches. The man seemed different this morning. Even at breakfast she thought she detected a change in his manner. He made eye contact with her when he brought his plate to the sink for her to wash, thanking her with the barest hint of a smile. Curious. She took a step back, looking at Jessie, said, "Jessie, we really must be going. We've not made bread yet."

Lena edged carefully to the side between the door and Evan, then side-stepped her way out the opening. "Good day, Mr. Hartmann."

Catching up to her on the other side of the street, Jessie said, "Wait up! What's the hurry?"

Lifting her skirt an inch above the toe of her boots, Lena strode with purpose down the boardwalk. "I told you. We've work to do."

Jessie tripped along beside her, a smile drawing the dimples to her freckled cheeks. "Evan seemed quite nice, friendly even, don't you think?"

"Did he?" Lena considered the politeness of his greeting, the barest suggestion of a smile tugging at his lips, a difference that made his handsome features even more appealing. Yes, he did seem different.

"I wonder if he's having lady friend troubles."

Lena glanced at Jessie. "Oh? Why would you think that?".

"It's just that men can get as moody about women as we do about them. You never knew with my brothers what face you'd see staring back at you come breakfast on Sunday morning. If some girl had danced or at the least made eyes at them on Saturday night, they'd be all smiles and howdy-do. If not, oh my! And they say women are broody about such things!"

"Does he have a lady friend then?" Lena asked, keeping her voice casual.

"I'm not knowing that for a fact. Maybe I could ask Bart."

"Oh, I should think not!" Lena's forward momentum hitched as she threw a frown at Jessie.

"Why forever not? Seems a handsome man like Evan would make a nice catch." It took three more steps for Jessie to realize that Lena had stopped.

"You can't be suggesting…"

The mortification must have shown on Lena's face, drawing a laugh from Jessie. "Why forever not? This is a hard country for a woman to be alone in. Seems Evan might be just the man to keep a lady safe. Like I said, if Bart hadn't stolen my heart already, I'd be making designs on him myself."

Lena's frown deepened. Starting forward again, she stopped to turn a flinty eye on Jessie. "I've been taking care of myself since well before I was twenty. I've not needed a man in all this time. And I would certainly not make *designs* to catch one. If a man can't love me for myself without my luring him with traps, then he's not the type of man with whom I'd care to attach myself."

Jessie's countenance wilted. "Sorry, Lena. I just thought…"

"Well, you thought incorrectly." Aware of Jessie's crestfallen state, Lena reproved herself. Remorseful, she reached out a hand, laying it on Jessie's arm. "I appreciate your concern, Jessie, but marrying the first eligible man I find is not a solution." Linking her arm through Jessie's, she started off again, pulling the younger girl along. "Let's see if we can find a respectable establishment where we can have a cup of tea, shall we?"

Finding a small table by the window with a view to the street, both women settled themselves. The only other patrons were two older women, who nodded cordially as Lena and Jessie entered. "This is nice," Jessie whispered. "Cloth tablecloths and china teacups make it real special."

Lena, discretely used her nail to pick off a dried crust of food from her saucer, considered her friend's opinion in light of the somewhat dingy surroundings. She tried to imagine the place from Jessie's perspective instead of her own. Perhaps she might one day better appreciate the simple touches of cotton tablecloths and gingham curtains. Much about this wild country would require her to adapt, to adjust her thinking to a wider world.

If the surroundings were less refined than Lena had come to expect, the pie satisfied her palette quite beyond expectations. "This crust is exceptional!" Lena murmured as she touched the napkin to her lips.

"It surely is! Maybe the cook would share her secret with us." Jessie looked to the door leading to the kitchen. With a mischievous wink, Jessie stood and tripped across the room, peeking through the door.

Before Lena could stop her, she was through the door. Although she could feel the eyes of the women across the room watching her, she chose to ignore them, studiously finishing her pie.

She watched the parade of industry outside. It had such a different flavor than the Chicago daily bustle. Instead of carriages, rough freight wagons and men riding by in heavy leathers and furs, their horses and pack animals laden with all manner of what she assumed to be mining gear and supplies. The few women that passed within her sight wore dark-colored homespun skirts and wraps, no silk gowns or parasols here. The horses weren't the only ones sensibly shod. Everything had a functional purpose, from head to toe. There was a harsh practicality about this place, and in that, a kind of elegance that only one of Lena's pragmatism would appreciate.

"Excuse me. We thought we'd introduce ourselves." A round-faced, ruddy-cheeked woman, stocky and looking to be in her middle years hovered before her. Her friend, tall and vaguely skeletal, was her opposite in every way except for exhibiting the same curious expression.

Lena gave them an open smile, standing to greet them. "I'm Lena Sommer."

"I'm Edna Jordan and this is my sister *and* sister-in-law, Thelma Jordan. Aren't you the woman who Mr. Nash was engaged to marry?"

At first, Lena was a bit taken aback. How would such personal information become common knowledge? In the next moment, she laughed to herself as she considered the population of Sawtooth City. Yes, it was quite possible for personal details to become the bread and butter of news hungry citizens.

"Yes." She felt no need to be defensive or evasive. It was a fact just as his untimely death was a fact.

The shorter woman clutched at her cloth bag. "I'm so sorry, my dear. It must have been a terrible shock."

Thelma leaned over and patted Lena's arm with a bony hand. "What a tragedy for you. You have our deepest sympathies."

A tragedy it might have been had she truly known the man, but she was hardly the grieving widow. Still, she should show some measure of sympathy at the man's passing if only for the sake of the story these ladies might be able to embellish to their friends. "Yes, it was a surprise. His letters led me to believe he was a very kind man."

"Oh, he was! Why, if my husband's brother hadn't finally gotten the hint that my sister, Thelma, was just right for him, I would have picked Mr. Nash myself for her to marry. He was one of our most respectable bachelors, not like most of these miners around here, drinking away every penny they make."

Mrs. Thelma Jordan made a clucking noise with her tongue. "Edna's husband and his brother, my husband, own and operate the sawmill. It's been quite a good business for them these past three years."

Mrs. Edna Jordan beamed. "Indeed, it has. I don't mind telling you we've made a tidy little profit moving from one boom town to the next for these past twenty years. But I hardly get to know anyone and we're off to the next one. There's always a need for lumber to build even the smallest shacks, you know."

Lena nodded. "Must be a little hard on you to have to pack and move every few years."

"Not so bad as all that. Now that my sister has moved out here, I always have someone to talk to. But it does look like we might be moving on soon. What with the mines having trouble with investors and such and most of the businesses already built, seems we'll be moving on to the next mountain with a promise of quartz."

"I see." The significance of her observation was not lost on Lena. How little she understood of boom towns and Western life in general. This was a land where the rules that governed the East simply didn't hold. Adaptability seemed a much needed attribute, not only to thrive but to even survive.

Jessie returned at that moment and Lena quickly introduced her friend.

"So, you're a mail-order bride! How charming you are!" Mrs. Edna Jordan's eyes sparkled with this new bit of gossip. "Does that mean we'll be having a wedding soon?"

Jessie glanced at Lena, then rejoined confidently, "Well, Bart and I are giving ourselves a little time to get to know each other better. Miss Sommer has asked me to work for her in the meantime."

In unison, both women swung heads back to Lena. Edna's hand flew to her breast, as if she forcibly had to keep her heart in place. "You mean to say that you're staying, Miss Sommer? Surely not."

"Why, surely, I am, Mrs. Jordan. I will continue to run the boarding house until an arrangement can be worked out with Mr. Nash's next of kin."

"But a woman alone?" Mrs. Edna Jordan threw her sister a significant look. They looked like two remonstrative owls.

With a quick smile, Jessie answered before Lena could form an appropriate response to the obvious innuendo. "Oh, we're quite safe, Mrs. Jordan. We have five men to look out for us, you know. There's my Bart for one, and Mr. Hartmann surely won't let anything happen to us."

"But... is it respectable? I mean..." Mrs. Edna Jordan began.

"Oh, I see what you mean. Why it surely is that! Miss Sommer and I look out for each other." Jessie suddenly clapped her hands together as though she remembered something. "Oh, before I forget what I learned from the cook just now... it's gin! Mr. Seewald said he uses half gin and half water in his pie crust. Imagine that!"

The Mrs. Jordans' eyes grew even wider. Mrs. Edna Jordan took her sister's arm in hers, starting for the door as she threw back a hurried goodbye to the two younger women.

"Now, I wonder where they're off to in such a hurry," Jessie said.

CHAPTER 11

L ENA sat close to the fire, reading from *Tom Sawyer* to a captive audience. Only she appeared to note Evan's arrival. She stopped her reading, greeting him. "Mr. Hartmann, you look as though you've had a long day. Your dinner is under a dishtowel on the table."

Evan nodded to her as he took off his hat, hair springing out haphazardly. "Thank you, ma'am."

Lena resumed her reading.

"'Please Becky—I'll whisper it, ever so easy.'

Becky hesitating, Tom took silence for consent, and passed his arm about her waist and whispered the tale ever so softly, with his mouth close to her ear. And added, 'Now you whisper it to me—just the same.'

She resisted, for a while, and then said, 'You turn your face away so you can't see, and then I will.'

He turned his face away. She bent timidly around till her breath stirred his curls and whispered, 'I—love—you!'"

"Oh, Bart, would you have talked to me that way had you known me as a little girl?"

"Well, it's for sure the right thing to say to any gal you'd be courtin'."

Jessie turned a skeptical eye on Bart. "But that boy's a bold-faced liar, muddle-headed too. That Becky should see right through him if she had a brain in her head. Fiddlesticks! I wouldn't trust the scamp to mean it."

Lena exchanged an amused expression with Ely, before noticing Evan at the back of the room, a vaguely grey dusty ghost. "Mr. Hartmann, why don't you join us? Come warm yourself."

Evan shifted uneasily, alternating between pushing at his unkempt hair and fiddling with a tear in his right sleeve. "I'm a mite too dirty for the company. Maybe another time. Thank you."

Lena watched him disappear down the hall, a frown pinching her brow.

Lena marked her place and turned to Ely. "Won't you play for us now, Ely? My voice is worn out to a whisper."

Jessie clapped her hands, and jumping to her feet, grabbed Ely by the arm. "Oh, yes! Please, play for us."

A twinkle of pleasure gleamed in Ely's eye. "I have a tune in mind that you might enjoy." With that he picked up his case and pulled out his violin. Plucking at the strings for just a moment, he threw a quick glance at Lena before bringing the instrument to his chin. She nodded reassuringly.

For a full twenty minutes, the room was silent except for the rich melody vibrating from the strings of Ely's violin. At times playful, while at others serene and plaintive, the music transported his audience beyond the confines of the warm room to the mountains and streams beyond the walls. When he had finished, the violin still tucked beneath his chin, no one moved. It was as if they each had held their breath until at last Jessie leaped from her chair and threw her arms around Ely, encompassing him, violin and all. With the silence broken, Bart began to applaud, joined no less enthusiastically by Carrick and Donal.

Lena stretched out her hand to touch Ely's sleeve. "Thank you, Ely. That was lovely."

With one arm tucked behind his neck, Evan lay on his bed listening to the concert through his half-open door. When Ely finished, Evan's face grew serene, a faint smile softening the hard lines of his face. If a soul could sing, surely, it would sing such music. There were times when he was riding in the wild lands, where the high ranges shed their icy waters into the clear blue lakes, that he felt such swellings of gladness in his chest. At times the beauty of those sacred places bruised him with their loveliness. It was the aching yearning of a mortal body trying to comprehend something too vast to be bound by the shackles of human understanding.

As the soothing strains faded, Evan felt in their absence all the confusion of recent events grow darker by contrast. He'd been his brother's north star for most of their lives and just when it seemed Jimmy had, at last, corrected his course, he'd lost his life. That loss had altered not only his life but that of Vicki and her child. Where was the sense in it?

Together, they'd finally made a sensible, not a pie-in-the-sky dream, but a practical plan for their future. With a claim that showed promise, a wide-open country waiting to be tamed, and their combined experience with raising livestock, they stood a good chance of making their mark. But without

Jimmy's optimism and exuberant spirit, clouds obscured the path ahead. The question swirled about him like a veiling mist. What did he, Evan, want from life?

Naomi's remarks cut deep and true. If he'd pry his fingers loose from his brother's dreams, might he dare to imagine his own? The ranch seemed something he'd wanted as much as his brother, wasn't it? He closed his eyes remembering the music again, letting it carry him beyond the room in which he lay. Perhaps he would dream something new.

As the last embers glowed within the stone fireplace, Lena remained where she'd been all evening, her feet propped before the grate. Everyone had long since retired, but Lena's mind still spun through the events of the day. Recalling the conversation of the two women at the café, their aghast response to her continued residence, their disturbing comments about the future of the town, all conspired to keep sleep from visiting her any time soon.

She knew the danger of such a double-minded state. She had committed to stay through the winter, and so she must put her mind to that end and not waver. Tomorrow, with Bart's help, she would make an extensive list of chores that needed doing to prepare for the cold months ahead. She would consult her ledgers once again and balance her accounts against her savings. She would make this work. She must.

Footsteps in the hall startled her. She looked over her shoulder. Evan, face now scrubbed but hair still disheveled, stopped upon seeing her. From his stunned expression, she felt certain he was not expecting anyone. She saw him button up the top button on his undershirt, a charming modesty. It made her feel that same strange empathy for the man that had caused her to drop her guard once before. How did he appear so vulnerable one moment, and then in the next breath, snap at her with words of stinging recrimination?

"Sorry, ma'am. Didn't know anyone was up at this hour."

Now it was Lena's turn to feel self-conscious. "I… I was having trouble sleeping."

They simply stared at each other, both unsure what the etiquette called for in this awkward moment. Evan gestured vaguely toward the kitchen. "Thought I'd see what might be in the kitchen to help me stop my stomach from grumbling."

"Oh! I think there's some biscuits left over from breakfast." She tucked her feet back in her shoes and rose to her feet.

He lifted a hand. "Don't bother, ma'am. I can fend for myself."

"Oh, it's no trouble, Mr. Hartmann. I rather think my stomach might be saying a few things to me as well. A warm glass of milk might be just the thing." She avoided his gaze, slipping past him into the kitchen.

Evan seated himself at the table, watching Lena gather a jar of honey and dish of butter from the larder. After setting them in front of him, she stepped back, hands on her hips. "I really don't think that's sufficient. Would you like a few eggs to go with those biscuits? I'm sure I'd enjoy some." Without waiting for a reply, she pulled four eggs from the basket, and stirred the stove back to life. Before cracking the shells, she put two back, mindful of Bart's admonition to use them judiciously.

"That's a lot of trouble, Miss Sommer. I could have made do with most anything. I feel bad having you go to all this fuss."

"Nonsense! I'm fully awake and it'll help keep my mind off my…" She'd started to say troubles, but thought better of it. "day," she finished.

She poured a glass of milk for herself and another for Evan, setting them both on the table before turning back to mind the eggs. "How about you, Mr. Hartmann? What's keeping you from sleeping?" Was that too bold? With her back to him, she winced, wishing she could be more prudent. Jessie's impulsive nature seemed to be rubbing off on her.

"Guess, the day keeps playing back in my head, too," Evan offered quietly.

It seemed to her that working in the mines day-after-day would bring little to trouble his sleep. Shouldn't he simply be exhausted from the manual labor? But she kept her questions to herself, laying the plate of eggs before him.

"Looks good." Evan dug in, slavering honey on three biscuits.

For a time, he ate in silence. Lena stole a glance at him before asking, "When did you come to Sawtooth, Mr. Hartmann? Were you one of the first to arrive?"

Evan threw back the last of his milk. Lena hadn't supposed that one could swig milk. "Suppose I was, Miss

Sommer. He tipped his head to one side, then shook it. "Seems a long time, doesn't it?"

"Depends on how the time was spent, I would suppose. It can seem a very short time when you're doing what you enjoy." She thought of the years she'd had with her darling charge and how brief those years seemed now in retrospect.

"There's some truth in that." He suddenly rose to his feet, stood there for a moment as though more needed saying, then picked up his plate and took it to the sink. "Thank you for the snack, Miss Sommer."

He hesitated at the door, but if there were words he'd wished to say he kept them to himself.

Lena watched him go, feeling she knew even less about him than before. There was this cloud of mystery about the man, whether made of trouble or sorrow, she hadn't the faintest hint of a clue. But she sensed that there was some burden, that stayed close to his heart, like an old friend.

Chapter 12

M ARCHING into the kitchen with the egg basket in her hand, Jessie announced, "Those girls aren't all doing their job this week. I only gathered six eggs. Two of those hens seem to have lost interest."

Bart put down his cup of coffee, laughing. "It's cold, Jessie. Didn't your folks have chickens?"

"Sure, we did. But it's not even November yet."

Lena looked over her shoulder, curious. "What are you two talking about? Are the hens sick?"

"Oh, nothing like that." Jessie deposited the eggs on the counter and sidled up to Bart. "Hens just slow down their laying in the winter, is all. Some just give up on the whole matter."

Bart added, "You forget our winter days are shorter than they are back where you come from. Those hens need daylight and warmth."

"You mean there won't be any more eggs?" Lena turned, startled.

"'Fraid not as many, anyway. You might get a few if you're mindful of keeping the coop dry and warm. Mr. Nash set a lot of store by those hens. He built a sturdy coop and laid in a lot of straw for bedding." Bart offered his coffee cup to Jessie.

Lena sat across from them, her stirring spoon forgotten in her hand as it dripped onto her apron. "I hadn't thought of any of that. I suppose their water will freeze as well. Oh my, the poor things." Here were more preparations to add to her growing list.

Bart suggested, "Some folks butcher their hens before winter sets in."

Lena shuddered. "Oh, I wouldn't wish to do that. There must be a way to care for them through the winter." She handed the spoon to Jessie and hurried from the room.

Mr. Nash's downstairs' desk sat near a westward facing window. Two stacks of papers flanked the work surface. Lena scribbled notes on a pad of clean paper. Little details that slipped her attention disturbed her. She should have asked about the chickens. What else did she need to consider? Perhaps she should consider stocking in more cooking supplies. Did the freighters continue to bring in necessary items throughout the winter months? She hadn't thought of that either. Laying her pen down, she cast her gaze to the mountains.

What was that quote, the one she'd heard years ago from a seminary student who'd boarded with her parents? It had struck her as poetic, something she didn't associate with the Bible. "I will lift up mine eyes unto the hills, from whence cometh my strength." Resting her chin upon her hand, she recalled Evan's words to her last night. It seemed a tendency here to ascribe human characteristics to nature. A mountain or a season could become a killer, as if they were capable of intentional enmity toward men. It was nonsense of course.

She had to admit that the city she'd grown accustomed to insulated her to some extent from the realities of nature's fury. Even that seemed like rather anthropomorphic language for an indifferent, unfeeling force. Was she coming to understand this perspective of man in a battle against nature? An uncomfortable prickle rippled up her spine.

Heavy footsteps from the porch distracted her. The footsteps were followed by a thump, and then another. She rose to her feet and peered out the window. Evan stood a little distance away, lifting a chunk of wood onto the chopping block. Hefting the axe, he drove it down into the wood, splitting it neatly in one blow. Tossing it aside, he pulled another chunk onto the block, repeating the action.

Curious. She assumed she'd hire someone to do the work. And judging from the pile of split wood already stretching around the porch four feet high, she thought she'd have plenty stockpiled. But here he was, stripped to his undershirt, sleeves pushed up, adding to the stacks.

Smoothing her hair back from her face, she opened the front door and stepped out onto the porch. "Mr. Hartmann, I'm surprised you're still here. Aren't you usually at the mine at this hour?"

"They've cut our shifts again. Had the day free, so thought I'd help out here." He swung the axe, the satisfying crack of wood echoing off the lodge walls.

"At the rate you're going, we'll have wood enough for two seasons." She slipped her hand around the giant porch post.

Evan glanced up, wiping sweat from his brow with a rag pulled from his pants' pocket. "Not by half, ma'am. Pardon me saying, but you don't know the winters here."

She felt herself bristling again, but checked her retort. "As you've said." Despite her sudden rush of anger, she noticed a change in his expression at her reaction. There was no real heat in his eyes this time.

"I'm sorry, ma'am. I've no intent to offend you." He dropped the axe head to the ground as if he had more to say.

Concern? Was this what she saw reflected in his green eyes, genuine concern?

"Thank you, Mr. Hartmann. I'm sure it will be used." She turned then, taking a step back to the door. Before she reached it, the axe rang again. Hesitating at the door, she looked back at the man. Muscles straining the cloth of his shirt, the axe buried a good three inches in the cutting block this time. It struck her that he was a man built for such an environment. What attributes would a woman require to survive here? Were wits and determination sufficient?

Evan made sure he was back from the claim before dinner. The conversation at the table turned to the mine's troubles with Eastern investors. Much of what they knew was derived from hearsay with little to substantiate. Ely remained quiet, confirming only that the investors were holding up funding.

Glancing up from his plate, Evan noticed how Lena's body had stiffened as the conversation drifted from one piece of bad news to another.

Jessie scowled at the men. "What's the good of talking about what you don't know anything about, I say."

"Well, Jessie, if the mine's gonna' close, we'd like to know and move on. It's that simple." Bart picked up his plate, taking it to the sink. Then he took Jessie's hand in his. "But Swenson, my shift foreman, says there's plenty of gold left in that quartz down the tunnel we've been working this month. I'm thinkin' they'll convince that group back East and work will pick up in the spring."

Carrick snorted, "But can we wait till then?" He shot a glance at his brother. "We heard that there's some color showing farther up the Salmon near Stanley Basin. Might be a good time to head up that way."

Lena pushed herself away from the counter, her face calm considering the disturbing talk. "Gentlemen, Jessie, I think we need a little distraction. There's nothing anyone can do about this tonight. Let's take these cookies in by the fire and see what shenanigans Tom's up to in Hannibal."

The tension broke in the room; the gloom dispelled for a time.

Lena took the chair by the hearth, Bart and Jessie to her right, before the fire. The others settled into the oversized chairs as though this new routine was something they'd been doing for years. Evan found a place by the window where he could stretch his long legs. The position also offered him a good view of Lena, a view that was easy on his eyes.

Flames brought out highlights in her auburn hair and cast a warm glow along the gentle curve of her cheek. Her hair fell against her long neck, sweeping low to touch her breast, the curl resting there rising and falling with her every breath.

What could he offer a woman of such refinement as Lena? Even as the unbidden thought skittered across his mind, he felt like a cad. He already had a woman and child in his life, even if they were his brother's. A dream, if he should settle on one, would have to be attainable. But then a small traitorous voice whispered in his ear, *"Will everything in your life, even your dreams, belong to the ghost of your brother?"* Shutting out the doubts, he settled himself back into the timbre of her voice, letting it weave its way into his imagination. He was Tom, romancing young Becky. He was Huck, fearful of his father. He was a man spinning a dream, a hopeless piece of fiction.

"'Injun Joe sprang to his feet, his eyes flaming, snatched up Potter's knife and went creeping catlike and stooping, round the combatants, seeking an opportunity. All at once the doctor flung himself free, seized the heavy headboard of Williams' grave and felled Potter with it—and in the same instant the half-breed saw his chance and drove the knife to the hilt in the young man's breast. He reeled and fell partly upon Potter, flooding him with his blood, and in the same moment the clouds blotted out the dreadful spectacle and the two frightened boys went speeding away in the dark.'"

Jessie let out a little cry that caused Lena to stop, looking up sharply. "Oh my! That Huck was sure to get our Tom in trouble!"

Carrick nudged his brother in the ribs and said, "Sounds just like our cousin, Michael, back in the old country. He was one to get himself in the worst scrapes what with his hot-headed ways. Trouble seemed attracted to him like fleas on a dog."

"That's for certain," Donal agreed. "It was always a good thing to be as far away from him as possible when he got himself worked up about some injustice, real or imagined. But this Tom, well, he seems too smart to get himself in any real trouble. I'm thinking he'll come out of this smelling like a rose. Come on, Miss Lena, tell us how he escapes."

Lena cleared her throat, reaching for her tea, now cooled in her cup. "I'm afraid my voice is giving out. Perhaps we'll have to wait until tomorrow to finish."

"Oh no!" Jessie wailed. "It's just getting exciting."

"I'm sorry, Jessie." Lena's voice, raspy and soft, convinced everyone else of the truth of it.

"I can read for you."

Lena looked up. Evan stood before her, his hand outstretched. "Thank you, Mr. Hartmann. I think you'll see where I left off." She gave the book into his hands.

Evan took a seat on an upturned log at the opposite side of the hearth. He cleared his throat and in a sonorous tone began the story where Lena had left it. Stumbling at first over Twain's diction, he pushed on until a few pages farther he captured the dialect. He gave himself to the story, his voice suspenseful where needed. He read the final chapters to an alert audience.

"So, endeth this chronicle. It being strictly a history of a boy, it must stop here; the story could not go much further without becoming the history of a man. When one writes a novel about grown people, he knows exactly where to stop—that is, with a marriage; but when he writes of juveniles, he must stop where he best can."

Evan closed the book, handing it back to Lena as his audience applauded his performance.

Lena who had watched him with rapt attention, seemed too stunned to comment.

"But we'll never know if he married Becky, now," Jessie pouted.

"It was over way too quick," Bart frowned. He looked first at Evan and then Lena. "What will you read next?"

"Well, I'm not sure. I'll look through my small library and find something if you like." Lena clutched the book to her breast, a glow of contentment on her face. She looked over at Evan. "Thank you for that. You read wonderfully."

"My mother was a school teacher with a love of good books. Our family took turns reading at night, just like you're doing here, Miss Sommer."

"Really? My family had the same habit."

Good nights all around, interrupted the flow of their exchange. Lena waved to Jessie, promising not to stay up too long.

Evan turned to go, but Lena stopped him with a touch of her hand on his arm as he passed. "Mr. Hartmann, I wanted to say that I'm grateful for your concern for my well-being. I think I'm beginning to understand why you were so insistent that I not stay."

He took in her slender, white fingers resting on his sleeve, then closed his eyes for one moment. When he opened them again, he was looking down into her dark eyes, so lovely and hopeful. What did she want from him? Did she hope to receive his blessing for her ill-advised decision? He couldn't do that. But as much as he believed she'd be wiser to leave, a hope stirred that she would stay. It was a selfish thought with the danger of turning into a prayer that she would never leave.

"I'm glad that you do." It was all he could say, not trusting himself to say more.

"Good night, Mr. Hartmann."

"Good night, Miss Sommer."

CHAPTER 13

WITH Bart's bandana over her nose and mouth, ends knotted behind her head, Lena blinked back tears as she carried more of the soiled, stinking straw from the chicken coop. Bart had instructed her in the need to provide clean, dry bedding for the hens. Since Mr. Nash's accident, no one had taken care of the job, so Lena attacked the coop with the naïve zeal of one uninitiated in poultry farming. She had quickly found out exactly *why* no one had 'remembered' to clean out the henhouse. Amidst the fussing hens and thoroughly saturated by the odor of ammonia-infused droppings, Evan found her.

"Miss Sommer?" Evan's head briefly appeared in the small enclosure, then sharply withdrew with a fit of coughing.

Lena looked up through a film of tears, blinking until she could make out the details of his face beyond the doorway. "Yes?" The word came out muffled, so she pulled down the handkerchief. "Yes, Mr. Hartmann?" Lena saw the bemused expression and the smile lurking at the corners of the man's mouth. He could think of her as he wished.

"I found something I thought you might enjoy." He held out a small parcel wrapped in cloth.

Stepping around a particularly vociferous hen viciously pecking at her boot laces, she emerged into the sunlight. She took a deep, grateful breath, waving her hand before her face. "Oh my! That's not a job that should be put off for so long."

"No, ma'am." Evan seemed determined to keep the smirk from his face.

"What was it you said?" She removed her gloves, a second pair of fine kid ones she'd sacrificed for the job, tucking them into her apron pocket.

"It's this." He handed the parcel to her, smiling now with genuine pleasure. "My mother's favorite. She gave it to me before she passed. I've carried it with me all these years because I enjoyed it so much as a boy. I thought you might like to read it aloud to folks."

Lena carefully unwrapped the stack of books from its silk cloth cover. The three leather volumes were lovely and well preserved but obviously old. She traced the title with a finger, trying to recall why the title sounded vaguely familiar. Turning to the title page, she gave an involuntary gasp. Sir Walter Scott! "This is a first edition!"

Evan's smile broadened. "I think it was a gift to my mother. She tutored students at the university who were frequently bestowing her with gifts, some no more than an apple and then others like this one. I know she treasured it."

What a delightful surprise! Here so far from the world she'd left, to find something like this, a reminder of her parents' world, was nothing less than amazing. "Mr. Hartmann, this is *Ivanhoe*, a first edition copy no less!"

Nodding, Evan confirmed her observation. He knew.

"This would be a lovely story to read." Her hand still laying reverently on the cover of the first volume, she saw his face lighten with the particular joy of giving a gift well received. "Thank you, Mr. Hartmann. Thank you, we will start it this evening."

He turned to go, but she called after him. "Will you be joining us for dinner tonight?"

"Yes, ma'am. I'm on my way to work at the claim today, but I'll be back in time." He tipped his hat and strode off. A few seconds later, Lena heard him whistling as he turned the corner of the house.

Lena addressed the bothersome hen pecking at her shoe. "That man is full of surprises."

The hen squawked. Lena interpreted it as an agreement.

That evening, Ely let the violin fall from his chin and dipped his head, sitting quietly for a few moments while the music hung ethereal in the air about them. "I like that refrain, but it always reminds me of home and therefore it also makes me a bit nostalgic."

"There is a quality of melancholy about it, even if it does not remind one of home," Lena conceded.

"Maybe the man who wrote it was homesick as well. Didn't you tell us many of the men who wrote these were not living in countries of their birth?" Jessie picked up Ely's case and lay it on his lap almost reverently.

"*Ja*, it is true. But for many, home was not the same as they remembered. Like for me, *ja*. The home of my memory is not the home I would find today."

A heavy silence blanketed the room as though each were recalling the homes they too had left behind, and likely would never see again.

Lena reached her hand to her side. "We have a treat," she began "Thanks to Mr. Hartmann, we have a new story to read. This book changed the way people thought of books for entertainment alone. Mr. Scott's writing would influence many authors to come, including Mr. Charles Dickens. Would you mind, Mr. Hartmann? Could you start the story for us?" She offered the first volume to him with an encouraging smile.

"Here, Evan, take my seat." Ely moved to the side of the room, his violin tucked within its case at his side.

Nodding his head to Ely, Evan settled himself into the chair across the hearth from Lena and took the book, their fingertips touching for half a breath. For a full minute, he thumbed through the first pages, as though reacquainting himself with the characters before introducing them to those gathered expectantly about him. He looked up once, an audience of eager expressions before him.

"Maybe I should tell you a little about the story before I begin. When my mother first read this to me as a very young boy, I was caught up in the whole story of knights and swords, fighting for honor, and the exciting medieval times of England. But as I grew older, reading it the second and then the third time, I knew it was about more than what they called chivalry."

How could he explain the themes of this little book that had so defined his perspectives of life? This was not the tale of Tom Sawyer. He knew that there were one or two similarities in the author's loathing of prejudice, but Ivanhoe... This was a man of uncompromising principles, a man who lived for justice. Seeing Bart's face, mouth slightly agape, anticipating the tale, he reconsidered that the simpler story, daring and dangerous as it was, might be enough. It certain had been for him. And as much as he'd like to share the deeper lessons to be taken from the story, he decided that this might not be the place or the time.

Evan lifted the book from his lap. Sinking deeper into the cushions, he began, taking his time with each phrase to capture the beauty of the author's prose. *"In that pleasant district of merry England which is watered by the river Don, there extended in ancient times a large forest, covering the greater part of the beautiful hills and valleys which lie between Sheffield and the pleasant town of Doncaster."*

Lena quickly changed into her sleeping gown and wrapped a blanket around her shoulders to ward off the chill of the upstairs bedroom. She stood by the window looking out on the moonlit peaks while Jessie jumped into bed.

The younger girl pulled the quilt tight beneath her chin, sitting up with her back propped against her pillow. "Sure is cold tonight. Bart says there'll be frost on the ground tomorrow morning."

"Yes, I suppose so," Lena replied absently.

"Lena, Bart wants to take me out to the lake tomorrow. He says it's real pretty and that we should see it now before it freezes over. Won't you come along as a chaperone? Evan said he'd come too. Since he's providing the horses and all."

Lena turned from the window to look at the girl's face alight with enthusiasm. "You want me to ride a horse? But I don't ride well at all, Jessie. You'd be spending your time trying to keep me from being thrown off."

"Evan said he has a real gentle mare he can pony for you. It isn't that hard. Just hang on to the saddle horn and he can lead you. Oh, do say you'll come. It would be so fun for the four of us to go. We can take a picnic, and Evan and Bart can fish."

Too chilled to stay out from under the covers any longer, Lena crawled in beside Jessie. "You're sure that Mr. Hartman agreed to go, knowing I'm just a... What do they call me? A greenhorn?"

"Bart said he didn't have to do much convincing. Evan was *more* than willing to go." Jessie snuggled up to Lena's arm for warmth, waggling her eyebrows. She whispered conspiratorially, "I think he might be sweet on you."

"Jessie, you are such a romantic. I fear reading *Ivanhoe* will only encourage such fanciful imaginings."

"Why shouldn't he be sweet on you? You're a fine-looking woman, kind and generous, not a bad hand with a rolling pin..."

"Jessie, I'm not a young woman anymore. Not like you." The direction of this conversation was not one Lena wished to follow.

"Age hasn't anything to do with it! Besides, you aren't that old. I had an aunt who lost her husband in..."

"Jessie, I'll go with you, but please don't try to play matchmaker with me." Lena hoped that would stop the girl from pursuing her notion.

"Oh, you will? Thank you!" Jessie threw her arm over Lena and hugged her. "It'll be fun, you'll see."

Lena replied tersely, "If I don't break my neck."

As Jessie's breathing deepened into the slow, gentle rhythm of sleep, Lena lay with eyes wide open. In her head, the sound of Evan's voice reading, soothing and expressive, continued to waylay her sleep. The puzzle of the man became more complex each day. He looked every bit the part of an uncouth cowhand in his dress and physical appearance, but when he read aloud, there was no mistaking the education and training he'd received somewhere in his past. Surely the tutoring of his mother alone could not account for it.

She couldn't deny that he was an interesting man. No one else she'd met since leaving Chicago seemed to possess quite so many complicated, beautiful layers. Surely that was all this was, not a romantic attraction. Most of their exchanges had ended in a bristling reaction from one or both. Besides, how foolish of her to even entertain such notions.

Still, she lay with eyes wide open thinking of the man. Curiosity, that's what it was. However, that curiosity stirred some peculiar feelings.

CHAPTER 14

EVAN helped Lena mount up, doing his utmost to avoid more than a glimpse of white leg as she swung up into the saddle. With her skirts tucked modestly about her legs, Lena fidgeted with the reins. Evan waited before tapping her booted foot, drawing her attention to her position in the stirrup.

"Keep your toe in the stirrup," Evan explained. "If you need to dismount in a hurry, it'll make it easier."

Lena nodded.

Evan reached up and patted her gloved hand gripping the saddle horn. "You can keep a light touch on the reins because I'll be ponying Rosie for the first part of the ride until you feel comfortable."

Lena nodded again. He could see her mouth twitch upward as though she were mustering the courage to smile.

He kept his hand on hers for a moment longer than necessary, watching her fear battle with her reason. "It's going to be all right, really." He patted her hand. "You couldn't ask for a gentler mare. I'll be right by your side. Relax."

"Thank you," Lena whispered.

Evan mounted his horse, looping the lead of Lena's horse loosely around his saddle horn.

Bart and Jessie led the way from the livery stable out of town through the sparkling fall morning. Evan followed with Lena tottering in her seat at his side.

At first the road continued along the river track, one heavily beaten down by the feet of men and beasts. Winding along the creek, the trail kept to the lower elevations, but less than an hour out of town the trail diverted from the lowlands, beginning to snake lazily up and around a gentle cluster of hills. As they passed beyond the last vestiges of civilization, the vistas opened to the wilder upper meadows. The granite cliffs stood out in stark contrast to the meadows, colored with autumn gold.

To their left, a half-mile distant, a large herd of elk were making their way along a distant creek. He reached across the space between them and touched Lena's hand, motioning with his free one to the two dozen head of elk.

Evan twisted in his saddle. "Elk."

"Are they dangerous?" Her smile faltered a fraction.

"Only if you cross them."

"How might we do that?" Lena asked, her brows knit together in obvious alarm.

"Well, you don't ever want to get between a cow and her calf, that's for certain. And you wouldn't want to cross the path of a bull in fall." He watched the peaceful passage of the herd, meandering through the valley on their way to warmer elevations.

His practiced eye caught sight of one more beast ambling behind the herd. He pointed it out to Lena. "Now that's a critter you don't ever want to stumble across no matter the season."

"Oh! I know what that is. A bear!"

"That's a brown one, though, so not as much to worry about. It's the grizzlies that grow huge up here. They're a bit more irrational than the brown ones."

He watched her knuckles whiten as she gripped her saddle horn more firmly. "I saw a cub the first day I arrived. I suppose that means his mother wasn't far away."

"Most of the bears who come into Sawtooth are brown ones." Evan urged his horse forward, tugging Lena's sedate mare along behind.

The wildlife was astir on this fall day, making use of these last warm days to gather food and prepare for the coming cold. Looking down on the stream a hundred feet below the trail, Evan pointed out a family of beavers. He pulled up so she could watch the younger two scamper along the rocky shore while the older pair labored at their dam. The youths were tumbling in typical sibling play, falling into the water and scrambling out again to engage in mock combat.

Lena covered her mouth to suppress a laugh, but Evan barked out his laugh, drawing the attention of the older pair. They appeared less frightened and more curious at the sound and the intrusion. Such behavior could only be explained by the remoteness of the area where humans had not yet brought their dominance fully to bear.

Evan glanced over at Lena. She was grinning like a girl, delight shining in her eyes. She might be a city girl, but she was certainly game for experiencing the new and unknown. He kneed his horse gently into a trot, causing Lena to grab the pommel to balance herself against the sudden forward momentum.

He kept the pace steady, catching up to Bart and Jessie. As they rounded a low hill, the trail began a gentle downward angle back to the stream now bordered by cedars. The trail turned downhill again, bringing into view a long narrow lake of crystalline water.

Jessie stood in her stirrups and swiveled to look back at Lena, a broad smile spread across her youthful face. She waved. "That's the prettiest sight I think I've ever seen! Have you ever, Lena? It looks like the sky just poured out of those mountains."

"Over there." Bart pointed to a sandy shoreline not far from their vantage point. "That looks like a good spot for lunch."

The riders let their horses pick their way along the rocky trail to the edge of the lake. Evan slipped quickly from his saddle and offered Lena his assistance. She ended up needing more than just a hand. As she swung her right leg over the cantle, her petticoat snagged. She very nearly performed a painful and embarrassing head first dismount onto the shore. Evan caught her about the waist and gingerly untangled the troublesome skirts from the saddle.

Evan led the horses up the bank, leaving Lena to appreciate the view.

Lena had but a moment to reacquaint herself with solid ground before Jessie was at her side, seizing her hand and tugging her to the shoreline while Bart and Evan unloaded their saddle bags. "Isn't it perfect?"

Lena had to admitted she'd never seen anything quite as lovely and serene. The pristine lake, its mirrored surface reflected blue sky, rimmed with a halo of evergreens. Speechless, she stood at the edge of the lake, looking across to a rising hill of towering green pines and gnarled cedars. Everywhere in this wilderness was that strange juxtaposition of beauty and danger. Like the magnificent elk they'd seen earlier, she was at once both entranced and terrified.

Jessie soon bounded away to help Bart with the horses, leaving Lena alone on the shoreline.

Lena turned at the sound of heavy footsteps in gravel.

"Didn't mean to scare you." Evan stopped in his tracks a few feet away.

"I'd heard that there were magnificent mountains out here, sights unlike anything I'd seen, but this—this is beyond my imaginings."

Evan simply nodded, gazing out across the water as she had been, in silent appreciation.

The lake lapped at her toes, enticing and playful. "It's so lonely and yet so wonderful. It makes me feel as if we are the first people to discover this place since the creation of the world, untouched and unspoiled as it is, almost as if we were standing at the edge of another world. Have you ever thought of the tragedy it would have been had you never come here, Mr. Hartmann, if you'd never seen these mountains or this lake as we see it now?"

She watched him nod as he slipped his hands into his pockets.

She shook her boot free from the wet sand and found firmer footing higher on the shoreline. Staring at the sand on her boot, she recalled a walk she'd taken with Miranda along the shore of Lake Michigan. Was it just last summer?

Miranda's face suddenly arose from Lena's memory, specter-like, the child's eyes filled with wonder at anything new and delightful. This place, Lena thought, would have made her dance with giddy pleasure.

"I think my life would have been greatly diminished had I not come across all those miles. It was loss that brought me, but I think there is so much to be gained here." She stood quietly, her hands clasped before her, her breath coming in steady cadence, her breast rising and falling to a rhythm slowed by her surroundings.

Lifting his hand to shield his eyes from the sun, Evan tipped back his head to follow the path of an eagle skimming across the lake to land on a snag a few feet away. Lena mimicked him.

"Is that a bald eagle?" Lena asked breathlessly.

"They seem to like this place. I've never been here without spotting two or three."

The sound that came from the great bird's mouth didn't match its majestic stature. Lena turned a quizzical expression at Evan. "He sounds more like my chickens than the way I imagined an eagle should sound."

"I've always thought they sounded as if they were laughing."

Jessie called out, "Bart wants to take us on a hike along the shore. Coming?"

Lena answered, "Of course, wait for me!"

Bart and Evan took turns introducing the two women to the birds and animals that dared to make their presence known. Between them they pointed out no less than a dozen birds and as many small mammals which made the lake their home. Evan explained that in the summer months many more species of birds could be found nesting in the valley, but many had already started a southward flight to more hospitable winter climates.

Lena frowned at that, noting that once again the man had emphasized his point of winter's fearful approach. She stepped into the lead as the four approached a wide beach bordered by a clearing in the woods. Gold aspen leaves fluttered in the wind at the edge of the taller pines. "Why, this meadow looks as if it had been cleared of trees."

Dropping the saddle bag with their lunch inside, Evan nodded to her. "It was about four years ago. A man by the name of Jenkins thought it might be a good place for folks in Hailey to come and camp or fish. He had a mind to clear a road too."

"How interesting! What became of him and his idea?" Lena asked, thinking of her hopes for more visitors to these mountains.

"I think I heard he became ill and couldn't manage on his own. Don't remember the whole story. I can't say I'm unhappy that it didn't work out. It would have spoiled the place."

"But why? There's so much wilderness here, surely one small corner of it would not have much impact on anyone. You begin to sound a bit like a hermit, Mr. Hartmann."

"Not a hermit, ma'am. I just know that people have a way of pushing out the wildlife and changing a place forever."

Lena surveyed the acres of pines stretching as far as she could see, the placid lake with its many coves, the bounty of open space, and tried to imagine how it would be possible to push back such wild terrain. "But surely there is space enough to allow people to come here to enjoy this, if even for a brief time. I could imagine people from the cities back east traveling west on trains for the express purpose of spending a few weeks relaxing in all this splendor. I can't imagine that you or I could stop that."

"Oh, I imagine you're right about that. I didn't say we could. I'm just pointing out that we humans have a way of spoiling things, trying to tame what isn't meant to be gentled." Evan did not back down from his opinion, apparently having thought about it for some time.

Lena could see no reason to argue with the man so she asked brightly of Bart and Jessie. "Wouldn't this make a perfect place to have our lunch? I'm famished!"

There were no arguments on this point, so the men dropped their canvas bags at the edge of the clearing under the aspen grove. Bart and Evan eagerly unpacked lunch while Jessie and Lena spread the blanket on the grass within a wide beam of sunlight. Between bites of bread, cheese, and ham, the conversation turned to Tom Sawyer's picnic with Becky and the adventure they'd shared in the cave. Because the conversation was often infused with laughter, any wildlife they might have observed was frightened away by the commotion, including a single brown bear who'd caught a scent of ham. Had he not, the picnic would have ended quite differently.

With all crumbs consumed, Bart turned his attention to the serious task of fishing. Jessie perched on a rock near where Bart stood with fishing pole in hand, staring intently at a dark portion of the lake where his line disappeared into the water.

Her legs tucked under her skirt, Lena sat primly in the shade at the edge of the blanket. She felt full and content, physically and mentally. Evan rested with his back against a tree, face nearly as peaceful as she felt. "Mr. Hartmann, you said that you had planned to purchase a ranch for raising cattle and horses. May I ask if that is still your plan?"

Evan pushed his hat back on his head and turned a sleepy eye to her. "I've been studying on it. My mind's not made up."

"I see." She didn't press him for more, sensing a reluctance beneath the surface. Privately, she marveled at such an undertaking. How would the man do such a thing without help? But then, hadn't she taken on a similar risky enterprise?

The tranquil setting made it impossible for Lena to keep her eyelids open. Her head began to nod. Giving in, she lowered her head onto her arm and let the quiet and warmth lull her to sleep. The dream carried her away through gentle meadows filled with bird song and gurgling streams where bear cubs scampered along the shoreline and wonderful beasts she'd seen only in books roamed the hillsides. Large hulking animals as well as the smallest rodents appeared as tame as though they'd stepped from a painting of the peaceable kingdom. And she was not afraid.

Lena, still traveling within the dream, heard a familiar voice and turned, delighted to see Miranda running down the hillside to Lena's open arms. Oh, the joy of seeing the child alive and happy in this place! But in a moment the dream shifted from the pastoral scene to a frigid landscape. Lena was still running toward her, but everything changed in an instant. Miranda's face still glowed with happiness, the child apparently unaware of the danger looming behind her. Lena tried to run to her, calling as she did, urging the girl to make haste. With horror, she saw her feet encased in great blue blocks of ice.

Lena lifted her eyes to the white peaked mountain behind the child. A thunderous roar and a crack exploded on her senses. She clasped her hands to her ears calling more urgently to the child. Behind Miranda, a wall of white rolled like an ocean wave down the mountain directly toward her. Miranda turned toward the sound, then looked back at Lena, a look of surprise on her face before the wave overtook her. A hand grabbed Lena's shoulder, pulling her from the path of the snow. She awoke screaming. Someone was kneeling beside her.

"Miss Sommer, please wake up." Evan's brow was creased with lines of concern, his hands rested on her shoulders as though he might have been shaking her awake.

She sat up, throwing her arms about her, feeling the cold she'd only imagined, but the sun still bathed the blanket in light and warmth.

"Here," Evan pulled off his jacket, wrapping it around her shoulders. "You were dreaming. Are you all right?"

Embarrassed, Lena found it difficult to look at Evan. In her imagination, the dream replayed the scene of the wall of rock and snow rolling down the mountain. Was that the way it really was—an avalanche? How terrifying! But why Miranda? Lena squeezed her eyes shut, remembering the accident, the helplessness she'd felt seeing the child pinned beneath the carriage. There should have been something someone could have done. But no, no one could. A wave, not of snow, but sadness threatened to capsize her calm ship of emotions.

Evan touched her shoulder. "I'm all right. Thank you." she said, but her shaking hands betrayed her.

Then Jessie was kneeling beside her. "You okay, Lena? That was some scream. I thought a bear had crept up on you."

Feeling more awkward than ever at all the attention, she rose to her feet to prove she was quite in control. But she stumbled when she tried to take a step. Evan caught her elbow to steady her. "Bring that canteen, Bart." He guided her to a fallen log where she willingly accepted his help to sit. Now three pairs of eyes were on her. How silly of her. How weak she must look. She was not weak. But she couldn't deny that she was shaken. The dream had felt so real, firing every nerve ending.

Jessie knelt in front of her. "Maybe the sun was a little too strong on her head."

"Could have been the altitude," Bart chimed in. "We did come up a bit from Sawtooth City."

"I'm conscious, you know! You don't have to speak about me as if I weren't sitting right here." Her sudden rush of irritation pushed back the images that had shaken her. Anger could be useful after all.

Evan offered no opinion aloud. He had his own, but it also brought with it a whole hat full of questions. He'd heard her shout the name Miranda, and he put that together with Lena's comment about coming here because of a loss. But he didn't know if Miranda was her sister, her friend or, worse, her child. It wasn't his business, he knew, but it troubled him nonetheless. She was carrying a whole wagon load of grief, and carrying it alone, in a place that could swallow a person up with loneliness.

"Let's get packing. We want to be back in Sawtooth before nightfall." Evan picked up his bag and started back the way they'd come, leaving Lena in Jessie's care along with his unanswered questions.

CHAPTER 15

GAMBIT snorted a protest as Evan cinched up the saddle for a second time. "Ah, quit your belly aching! You and I both know you were holding your breath when I cinched that saddle the first time." Evan patted the bay on the rump before turning to pick up his saddle bags. Before he did, he blew on his hands to warm them against the frosty morning air. "Getting colder every day." The horse snorted and stomped his front hoof as if in agreement. "You'll be fine. You'll be warm in a bit when I take you out for a run."

Evan was hopeful of finding more evidence of a quartz vein, so when the shift foreman told him he wasn't needed, he made plans to explore north of his claim. He turned at the sound of a small rustle of fabric. A woman's head, her eyes squinting into the dark interior of the stable, stood just inside the livery.

Vicki's voice called out softly, "You in here, Evan."

"Sure am." Evan stepped around his horse, making himself visible to the girl. "What you doing out so early?"

Vicki stepped farther into the livery, pulling the thin wrap close to her neck. "I was hoping to catch you here. Didn't want to go to the boarding house. Might embarrass you in front of that nice lady who runs it."

"Now, when did I ever make you think I was embarrassed to be seen talking to you?" Evan crossed the space between them. Towering over the petite girl, he scowled at her. "You know me better than that."

"Maybe." She touched his sleeve in an oddly restrained way, her eyes suddenly shining, more alive than he'd seen them since before his brother's death. "Evan, they wrote! Well, my mama did, anyway."

Evan covered her pale hand with his own. Her fingers felt like ice. "Your family wants you back!" He surmised it from her expression. He laughed, heart suddenly light. "I told you that they'd change their minds when they heard they had a grandchild."

She squeezed his arm and shook her head. "Well, my mama does, that's for sure." Vicki released her grip and pulled a letter from her waistband. "She said she was afraid I was dead when she hadn't heard from me in so long. I... I never really thought she'd forgive me for running off with John the way I did. But she wants me to come home, Evan! Home!"

Evan nodded, a satisfied grin spread wide across his face. "And there should be another freighter coming up in a week or two. I'm sure he'll be glad to take you back down the mountain for the fare."

The shining light suddenly paled in Vicki's blue eyes and she frowned. "That could be the problem. Mama told me my Pa won't pay for me to come home. If I can get there, he said he'd take me in."

Evan ground his teeth. How could a man do that to his own flesh and blood? All he said was, "That's hard."

"I have a little saved up, thanks to Naomi and the girls too. I can get down the mountain, but not sure I'll have enough to get me all the way home on the train. I'm not even sure what tickets cost." Vicki seemed to shrink before him, looking far younger than her makeup and costume made her appear.

Evan gripped her shoulders, easing that grip when he saw her wince. "We'll get you home, Vicki. I can help."

Vicki looked away, her cheeks flushed. "You've done so much already. I couldn't ask you."

"You're not asking me. I'm telling you. I'm making sure you are on that train home."

She looked up, choking back a sob. "I'll pay you back, Evan. Somehow, I will."

Evan shook his head. "Not looking for payback. You'd be my sister-in-law if Jimmy had lived. You're family, Vicki."

The girl fell into Evan's arms, sobbing into his coat, muffled words spoken into the fabric, unintelligible. He awkwardly patted her head and wrapped one arm around her. Somehow her closeness made him feel a sudden loneliness for his brother, a wound still open.

When the sobs slowed to noisy sniffles, Vicki pulled back, drawing her sleeve across her eyes. "I gotta' go. Rebecca isn't very good at babysitting." She chuckled. "She can't abide the smell of babies, she says. Too much powder and sour milk."

"I'm heading up to the claim today. Got some gold dust stashed there. I'll stop by the assayer's office and bring some cash over later," Evan said. He took her hand again. "Don't you worry. You'll be home for Christmas, you and Rebecca."

Vicki stopped at the door, her hand resting on the frame. "Evan, you're a good man. I hope God won't forget that when he's passing out favors. You deserve a few good turns for all those you've given folks in this lifetime." She turned quickly and hurried out the door.

For the better part of the day, Evan scoured the creek bed, going as far as a mile upstream and out of his claim onto land no one, as far as Evan could determine, had tried to pan. The color did seem to improve a half mile north of his claim. He'd see about staking a claim later. Right now, he wanted to return to Sawtooth and put some money into Vicki's threadbare pocket.

He found her making supper for the girls in the kitchen. She blushed when he handed her the small bundle of folded bills. Tears pooled in the corners of her eyes and she threw her arms around him. "This more than covers the cost of traveling. I'm certain of it," she said without counting the sum.

"I hope it is. I want you to buy yourself some nice clothes. Something...you know, different, but some things for the child too. I want you to go back to your mother and father with your head up. Look them in the eye and tell them about Jimmy if you think you can. I'd like to know he'd be remembered by the child's grandparents - as a good man."

"The child will know of her father. I'll make certain of that." She hugged him again, then stepped back, her hands still holding his arms. "And she'll know about how good her uncle is too."

"I'll talk to the freight runners and try to find out how much rail fare is back east." He tipped his hat and stepped into the late afternoon bustle of men looking to relax after their day's shift. He felt good. Maybe things were looking up. He'd been disappointed a lot lately by people and Providence. Just seemed the world had taken a wrong turn somewhere, or he had. Maybe he should be heading out of this town too. Starting over somewhere else might not be such a bad idea.

It was only a short walk back to the boarding house, one that led him through the better section of town, the houses owned by the merchants, the bankers, the mining officers, the privileged. He was halfway down the street when he heard a moan from the shadowed side of the street outside the house belonging to Matthew Jamison, owner of the largest dry goods business. Evan followed the sound to find the crumpled form half hidden by a chokeberry bush inside the picket fence.

"Here now. What's happened to you?" Evan squatted down to find a boy of about ten clutching his stomach and curled up in obvious pain.

"It's nothin', mister." The boy managed to whisper.

"Sure looks about as far from nothin' as one can get. Let me look at you." Evan gently rolled the boy onto his back, causing the boy to groan again. His face already showed a bruise growing on his cheek, his mouth oozing blood at one corner. "Son, who did this to you?"

The boy tried to pull away, attempting to stand. "I... deserved it. Should 'a known better," he mumbled.

"Son, no one deserves a beating. You look like you ran into a gang of trouble." Evan could see the boy's face better now. "I know you, don't I? You're Tom Andrew's boy, Daniel. He works on my shift. You know me? Evan, Evan Hartmann."

The boy's eyes still clouded by tears, squinted up into Evan's face. "Yeah, I know you. You brought my pa home when he got so liquored up last month down at Naomi's place. You shouldn't have brought him home. He did more damage there than he would'a if he'd stayed in town." Evan saw the boy's attempt at a scowl, but the muscles of his face contorted in pain as he did.

Evan cringed. He knew the man had a reputation for brutality. He just hadn't witnessed it. "Are you sayin' your pa did this to you?"

"No. I ain't sayin' who or why," Daniel growled.

"Will you at least let me help you home?"

"Better not." The voice changed to one of resignation.

"I'd like to help, if I could. If your pa gave you a lickin' I'll try to talk to him."

"No!" The boy's voice came as a wail. "I told you it wasn't my pa."

"I'm not sure I can believe you."

The boy screwed up his face giving Evan the thought that he might be about to cry. "Okay, I'll tell you, but you gotta promise not to talk to my pa!"

Evan frowned at the promise he didn't wish to keep. But the boy was in trouble. He needed to talk. "All right. Then tell me."

"Old man Jamison has a daughter my age. We like each other. At least I think she likes me, too." Daniel groaned as he forced himself into a sitting position. He looked up at Evan with fire in his eyes. "I made the mistake of walking her home one too many times. This time as I was heading home, three boys from school jumped me. They wore masks like they were famous bank robbers or somethin'. They told me to stay away from Angela if I knew what was good for me. Then they beat me. Told me they'd do worse if they caught me on their street again." The boy sagged back against the tree.

"But I'm guessing, in spite of the masks, you knew who they were. Am I right?"

"Of course. Stupid, if they thought I wouldn't."

Evan knelt beside the boy, considering his options. If he took the boy home looking the way he did, he might get a worse whipping at the hands of his father. What he wanted to do was knock on the doors of the bullies who'd done this and give them the whipping they deserved. That really wasn't an option that would do anyone any good.

"Daniel, I can't leave you here. I just can't. I live a few streets away. Let me take you there and clean up your face at least. Maybe you can slip into the house and avoid your pa for a few days until the bruising clears up. What do you say?"

Daniel looked up at Evan with old eyes, sighed heavily and reached a hand for help to stand.

Half carrying the boy the two blocks to the boarding house, Evan's anger simmered inside with each groan. Judging from his cursory assessment of the boy's wounds, he suspected that at the very least the boy had a few broken ribs.

He'd always been enraged by bullies and he'd seen his share. When others gave in to their size advantage, he found a way to get them to reconsider their intentions. Sometimes it took no more than a quiet word or even a steady, meaningful look, eye to eye. Only once had he given in to the temptation to *educate* the bully with physical means. It'd worked, but it had sickened him when it was over and he stood triumphant over the boy, his own fists bloodied. Never again.

Evan entered the kitchen through the back door where Lena and Jessie were setting the table for dinner. He had to grab the boy's collar and pull him into the room before he bolted back the way they'd come. Daniel stood there, sullen, with eyes daring anyone to speak to him.

Mouth open, Lena froze with a plate in each hand, her eyes darting from Evan to the boy then back again. Evan spoke quickly, "Boy's name is Daniel. Got himself into a tussle." He released the boy's collar and looked down at him, not quite friendly in his expression. "Daniel, say hello to Miss Sommer and Miss Leach."

Daniel looked at Lena with a squint from his good eye. "Howdy," he mumbled.

"Oh my! You poor child!" Jessie was the first to move, kneeling before the boy with her apron already dabbing at the remnants of grass still encrusted in the drying blood on his cheek. Daniel flinched, pulling back. Evan effectively kept him in place by returning his hand on the boy's shoulder.

"Let the woman help you." It wasn't a request.

Perhaps because Jessie was well-acquainted with her own brothers and their rough and tough childhoods, she seemed least affected by the boy's appearance, knowing what needed to be done even before Lena could react. "The teakettle has some hot water. I'll poor some in a bowl so we can clean up those cuts."

Lena took a tentative step toward Daniel, her face awash with sympathy. "Maybe we should take off that jacket and give it a good dusting too."

The boy pulled more aggressively against Evan's restraining hand. "Don't need help takin' off my clothes." He threw a look at Evan and shrugged off his jacket. "Here!"

Lena cast a puzzled look in Evan's direction as she took the coat from the boy's stiff arm. "I'll just dust it off a bit."

Jessie carried a bowl of steaming water to the table, pushing the plates out of the way as she did. "Now, Daniel, you just come on over here. We'll have you patched up in no time." She waved him over with a towel in her hand. "Come on. I won't bite ya'."

He shuffled across the room and sat stiffly on the chair she'd offered him. Jessie wasted no time cleaning the boy's wounds, grimacing along with the boy each time her actions hurt him. Lena placed the boy's jacket on his lap, then stood quietly to the side watching Jessie expertly handle the boy's cuts.

Lena frowned. "I wonder if we shouldn't call in a doctor. That cut over his eye looks deep. Shouldn't he have a few stitches? I never asked, but I assume you have a doctor here."

Without meeting her gaze, Evan shook his head. "Don't have one. There's one down in Ketchum I hear, but he'd be the closest. Heard one was over in Snowberry, probably Silver City, but they're both a couple of days' ride. We tend to our own stitching up here."

"I wouldn't go to no doctor, anyhow!" Daniel said, jerking away from Jessie and jumping to his feet. "This ain't that bad."

Evan turned the boy to face him, touching his chin, turning it side to side. "No, think it'll heal fine. As long as it's clean, you'll have yourself a nice little scar to make you look tougher when you face those bullies again."

Lena looked up at Evan with a horrified expression. "You mean he was attacked by more than one boy? That's beastly! Why? For goodness sakes why would they do this?" She drove her hands to her hips, incensed. "We should report this to—the authorities! I assume we have some legal authorities here." She scowled at Evan as though the lack of legal authorities were somehow his fault.

An amused twitch pulled at Evan's lip. "Well, ma'am, we did a year ago, but seems we're a bit short on the law here too."

Lena threw up her hands, grabbing the bowl from the table. She stalked to the sink. She slammed it down on the counter, turning with a dishtowel twisted in her hands. "Well, the least we can do is get the boy to his parents so they can try to find out who did this."

"No!" Evan and Daniel said it simultaneously.

Lena, mouth agape, stared at them as if they'd gone mad. "Why forever not?"

"It's complicated," Evan said after a space of four heartbeats.

"Well then... Well, can I offer you something to eat, then?" Evan sensed her temper simmering just beneath the surface of her reserve.

"He'd probably better get on home..." Evan started.

"Sure!" Daniel moved to a seat where an empty plate begged filling. "He won't be missing me, if that's what you're thinkin'. Probably won't be home for hours."

Lena exchanged a look of some triumph with Evan before turning to the stove.

"Well, I guess that's settled," Jessie said as she cleared the table of soiled rags. She winked once at Evan before heading out into the main room of the house to call the men to dinner.

Seeing the boy, bruised as he was, shoveling food into his mouth at an amazing rate, raised only a few eyebrows. Everyone knew, or had at least seen, Daniel around and they all knew his father, so no questions were asked. Conversation flowed as usual as though the boy had always been in company with them.

When the meal was over and Daniel rose to his feet to leave, Lena intercepted him. "Daniel, I want you to know that you are welcome here anytime. I serve dinner at five o'clock. No exceptions. That understood?"

Daniel didn't smile, but he gave her a long appraising stare before answering. "Yes, ma'am. Thank you."

Evan picked up the book from the shelf and settled himself in the same chair across the hearth from Lena's favorite seat. "So, where'd we leave off?" He knew of course, but it gave him amusement to hear Jessie practically retell the previous passage with such animation.

"'*So, nobler than the rest was her attire; A crown of ruddy gold enclosed her brow.*'" Jessie quoted word for word, then flushing she poked her elbow into Bart who was chuckling quietly beside her. "Well, I remembered it, 'cause it was so lovely."

"Thank you, Jessie, now I know where we begin tonight's reading. Hope you'll pay better attention tonight, though," he teased.

Lena let her muscles unwind, a half-finished scarf that she was knitting lay untouched in her lap. She was growing to like watching Evan read as much as listening to his voice. Both were equally expressive. When he spoke of the black knight, his brows would knit together in a most fierce expression, while his descriptions of the lady softened his features in a most pleasant fashion.

She had read the book once before, but when Evan read one of the passages that she'd memorized years earlier, she sat with lips parted, spellbound by its lyrical romanticism, as though she had never heard it before. He brought the words to life.

"*I have sought but a kindred spirit to share it, and I have found such in thee.*"

Evan read the words haltingly, glancing up and meeting Lena's eyes, holding them for a moment before he continued.

Lena feeling the unexpected warmth in her cheeks, dropped her gaze to her lap. *A kindred spirit.* Was that what he was?

CHAPTER 16

As Lena pushed back the curtains, the view from the bedroom window revealed a transformed world. Frost encased every hedge, fencepost, and tree with gossamer robes of shimmering ice. The sun rose, a thin orb of pale butter against a light blue sky. She stood there mesmerized until she heard Jessie stirring awake.

She pulled another pair of stockings from her drawer before heading down to the kitchen with its promise of warmth. Shivering, she kindled the fire to life. It would be a good morning to bake some biscuits and keep the fire burning for warmth.

Looking a bit out of sorts, Carrick and Donal arrived in the kitchen a bit later than usual. They explained that they'd been bumped from their shifts again, so they offered their strong backs to Lena in exchange for the week's board. Since she'd come up with an idea to move the chickens closer to the house for the winter months, she welcomed their help.

As soon as breakfast was cleaned up, she met them outside and explained her desire to build a lean-to off the back porch. As they spoke, great puffs of frozen air rose from their lips. The brothers had some additional ideas of their own and motivated by the prospect of losing the hens to frostbite and the subsequent good food they enabled, the two brothers set to work.

Despite the air that chilled her lungs, Lena lingered on the front porch looking out over the sparkling landscape. The railing displayed a gallery of fairy ice sculptures. Chicago had its fair share of ice, but she'd never had a chance, or perhaps had simply never taken the time to appreciate winter's craftsmanship. She hovered her open palm as near the railing as possible without touching the delicate ice crystals. Eyes level with the railing she watched as the ice melted beneath radiant heat from her hand.

Down the road leading to town, Evan rode Gambit, leading another horse. How odd. Why would he return so early?

"Good morning again, Mr. Hartmann. I thought you were heading up to your claim this morning."

Evan tipped his hat, causing his black hair to tumble forward onto his brow. He pushed a lock to the side as he answered. "I am, ma'am." He leaned casually forward, his arm resting on the saddle pommel. "Was looking at all God's beauty this morning and thought to myself that you might want to ride out a bit and see it better. It's mighty pretty up on the ridge." With a casual wave of his hand, he gestured to the mare. "I've got your favorite little pony saddled. If you're interested, that is."

Lifting her hand to shield her eyes against the sun, she could see the little mare she'd ridden up to the lake. Standing next to the giant bay, Gambit, she looked more like a filly than full grown. She looked behind at Carrick arguing with Donal about some small detail of coop construction, then back at Evan, a smile tipping the corners of her lips.

"I think I'd just get in the way of Carrick's construction plans if I stayed here." She slipped her quickly numbing hands into the pockets of her apron and nodded. "Yes, Mr. Hartmann, I'd be pleased. If you'll just give me a few moments, I'd like to change into something more appropriate."

"By all means." He sat up and drove the hat back onto his head, a grin dropping years from his face.

Lena tripped through the front door and up the stairs to her bedroom. Running to the large chest of drawers belonging to Mr. Nash, she rummaged through the clothes until she found something suitable. A few minutes later, she stood in the middle of the room, squinting into the dusty mirror. She shook her head at her reflection. "What would Miranda say if she could see me now."

Evan stood up from the porch step as she returned, a weathered, wide-brimmed hat perched precariously on her curls. If the grin dropped years from his appearance, the impish grin that spread across his face upon seeing her attired in a man's pants and oversized jacket made him look a mere boy. "That's right sensible clothing, Miss Sommer. Mr. Nash would be pleased to see them put to such lovely use."

"Shall we ride out? I'll have to keep moving if I don't want to freeze." Lena stepped to Rosie's side and delighted Evan by pulling herself into the saddle quite handily. "My, that's much easier with pants."

"Indeed it is, ma'am."

Evan could have said far more to prepare her, but he remained characteristically mute. He'd understated the beauty by a mile. The route they'd taken had managed to keep the mountain vista a surprise until they'd made a turn in the trail that opened out onto the snow-covered range. Lena did not even attempt to restrain her reaction. She gasped, bringing her gloved hand to her lips.

Evan gave her a moment to take it in without spoiling the experience with words. Gambit tossed his head impatiently, following with a snort and heavy stamp of his hoof. Evan knew the bay expected a chance to run. Patting the big stallion's neck, he whispered, "Later, boy."

As sun warmed the air, the icy coating melted from leaves and branches. Plops of ice and water struck the leaf-covered ground sounding like gentle rain.

"What's the river below us?" she asked.

"Those are the headwaters of the Salmon. She travels a long way through some mighty pretty country."

"I've never seen anything quite like this. Breathtaking is a word I've used for many things from dresses to concerts, but I never truly understood the word until this moment."

Lena appreciated the man's patience with her constant queries but thought to ask another. "May I ask you a question?"

"Guess, you just did," Evan said wryly.

She paused, catching his meaning a second later, and smiled. "I know. I mean another one, about the boy, Daniel."

"Oh yes, Daniel. I didn't give you much explanation, did I?" Evan said.

"Did his father beat him? I've been thinking about that poor child going home to another beating."

Evan patted Gambit's mane. "Not last night, he didn't. That was the work of some town bullies." He shook his head. "If he ever tells me who they were, I'll have a talk with them."

"I see. Does he have a mother?"

"No. She died a few years back. Childbirth, I think."

"Oh. Seems so many here are orphans of some fashion, either by choice or fate." Lena ran her fingers down the reins, braiding them.

"Are you? An orphan?" Evan asked.

"That seems a strange thing to call myself now that I'm an adult. Doesn't a person stop becoming an orphan when they've grown? I lost my parents when I was seventeen. They had a great influence on my thinking, my interests. They owned a bookstore, one that specialized in rare books and first editions. That's why I recognized your book to be such a treasure. You said that your mother received it as a gift."

"Yes. When my father suffered a stroke, she worked hard to support us as a tutor."

"Do you mind my asking? You read brilliantly. Surely, that's the result of something more than reading with your family in the evenings."

"My mother saw to it that I applied to college. She hoped I'd read law one day, as her father had once."

Lena leaned forward, peering at his face shaded as it was by his broad-brimmed hat. "Really?"

"Didn't finish. Family matters caused me to change my plans."

"I see."

They sat in silence, the horses nibbling at dry grasses around their feet.

Evan shifted in the saddle. May I have a turn at the asking?"

Lena smiled her answer.

"Who's Miranda? You were screaming her name the other day at the lake."

Lena stiffened. Turning her face from him, she answered slowly, "She was the little girl to whom I was governess in Chicago. I cared for her for eight years."

"Eight years is a long time," Evan said.

"A lifetime."

"Don't think you can call yourself selfish if you gave some of your best years to raise someone else's child."

She turned to look at him, her brown eyes clouded. "Guess I don't see it that way. I'd give them again just to be with her and watch her grow, laugh with her, cry with her. The time went so quickly."

Evan reached across the space between them and placed his hand on hers. "I'm sorry to have made you cry. We do seem to have all left a part of ourselves behind. Maybe that's what draws most of us here. Everyone hoping to make a new beginning."

For a moment, Evan thought she was about to say more about those days she'd left behind and then he saw her pull away, her vulnerability shielded once more. He dropped his hand to his side. Looking to the distant range, he noticed the gray clouds amassing over the peaks. "Looks like something's moving into the valley. We better be getting you back."

Lena simply nodded.

"Would you like to handle Rosie on your own? I'm certain you can. She'll just follow Gambit if you let her."

"I think I can manage. Thank you, Mr. Hartmann."

He wished he could change her habit of calling him by his last name as she insisted on doing. Why did it always sound like a dismissal when she said it? As if there were unspoken words. *That will be all Mr. Hartmann.* It rankled him. Which, he realized, was why he probably used her last name while everyone else called her Lena. He turned in the saddle, slowing Gambit's pace. "Would you consider calling me Evan, like the others in the house?"

She gave him a mild smile. "Yes."

By the time they arrived at the house, morning's thin silver clouds had turned dark and moody. Lena drew her jacket close to her neck as she handed Rosie's reins to Evan. As she stepped up onto the porch something soft brushed her cheek, then again the light feather touch of a snowflake landed on her nose. Looking up, she saw white flakes floating ever so gently from the pale sky.

Evan said, "First snow. Might see a foot of it on the peaks by morning."

"Here as well?"

"Not likely. Too soon I think. This looks like just a dusting." Gambit shifted restlessly. "But it's just the beginning."

CHAPTER 17

"SORRY, Miss Sommer, we sold the last bag of flour this morning."

Lena surmised that the skeleton-thin woman behind the counter of Jamison's Dry Goods was more annoyed than sorrowful. The woman avoided looking at Lena, saying curtly, "You'll have to check back next week. We're expecting one more freight delivery middle of the week."

"Well, that seems extraordinary," Lena said. "Flour is a staple."

"Exactly. Whole town is stocking up for winter, has been for weeks." The woman's irritation brewed on her brow in a cluster of deep lines. "Is there anything else?" Lena felt she'd been dismissed.

"Well, no, I suppose I'll just look around for a while. Can you deliver the items I requested that you *do* have?"

"When we can get out your way, we will. Oh, and Mr. Jamison is only accepting cash now, no more credit."

In contrast to the gloomy shopkeeper, the shop bell tinkled a merry greeting as the door opened to admit two formidable looking women not of Lena's acquaintance. From their similarly pinched and sour expressions she doubted she'd wish to encourage one. The shopkeeper acknowledged the two women with a stiff smile. "Mrs. Miller. Mrs. Sanderson. Be with you in a minute."

Lena retreated from the shopkeeper's scowling face. "Please tally my purchases. I'll be happy to make my payment in cash. I just want to look at your boots." She nodded politely to the two women as they eyed her with open curiosity.

Again, the cheerful bell tinkled and a petite woman, dressed modestly in clothes appearing too large for her, entered somewhat hesitantly. The shopkeeper gave her no greeting, but did sniff loudly enough for the snort of disapproval to reach Lena. The other two customers took in her appearance, stiffened their backs and turned away from her.

Whispers changed to low conversation between the two women. "Just seems like anyone can shop here. Maybe we should be taking our business down the street to Mr. Baker's Mercantile where they might be a bit more particular about their clientele."

Mrs. Miller asked, "Mary Beth, does Mr. Jamison know you allow her kind to shop here with respectable women?"

Mary Beth, the shopkeeper, looked befuddled, her eyes darting from the girl to the older women expecting her response. She drew herself up to her full height and seemed to understand the need to reassert some modicum of control over her establishment. "Well, now..."

Mrs. Miller glared at the poor woman, her tone imperious. "Well then, I should like to speak with Mr. Jamison myself. Will you tell him to pull himself out of his office immediately? I'm sure he'll make time for us."

"Now no need for that, Mrs. Miller." Scurrying around the counter, the shopkeeper approached the younger woman with a rapid click of heels across the wood floor. "Young woman, what is your business here?" The question was far from a polite inquiry.

The poor girl shrank before this storm of hostility. "I was just looking for some traveling clothes. I didn't think..."

"Obviously!" Mrs. Miller scoffed, still maintaining her distance from one she obviously deemed beneath her station.

"Excuse me!" Lena said, closing the space between herself and the young woman. "Is there a problem? Isn't everyone allowed to shop here?"

"Not her kind!" the shopkeeper snorted. "You're new here so you don't know the way of things I suppose, like ordering for the winter early and *who* to associate with."

"You mean a woman in need of clothing? So am I. If she has the cash, I would suppose her purchase would be as welcome as mine would be. These are hardly prosperous times for any of us."

Mrs. Miller gave an ugly laugh. "I know you, *Miss* Sommer. I wonder how it would affect your position in this town as a business woman if it were known you keep company with women of her sort."

Lena lifted her chin a fraction of an inch and met the woman's venomous gaze. "I would not wish to associate with anyone who thought it was decent behavior to refuse another human being the kindness due them." Lena noticed Mrs. Miller's expression transform from smug to apoplectic.

"She told you herself that all she wishes to do is purchase an item of clothing." Lena pressed her lips into a tight line, considering her response. "In regards to my business.

Anyone in need who came to my lodging house would be given shelter, no matter their social status. She's offering to pay for merchandise so she should be allowed to do just that."

A man's voice boomed out across the room from the open door at the back of the shop. "Well, then you don't know how business is done here." Mr. Jamison stood with hands crossed over his generous belly. "And this is my business so I can refuse service to anyone I please."

Lena knew she must look as appalled as she felt inside. After a long awkward moment, she pulled her gaze from the man and looked at the cowering young woman beside her. With a slight tremor in her voice, she said quietly, "Perhaps you'd care to accompany me to the store down the street. Perhaps those running that establishment might be more enlightened as to the battle this country has just fought for equality to all."

Jamison shouted after her, "Good luck getting Baker to help you."

"Oh, and Mary Beth, please cancel my order. Good day." Lena took the young woman's elbow steering to the door. The shop bell tinkled merrily as they stepped outside.

Lena wasn't certain who was shaking more, the girl or herself. A block away and she finally pulled up to let her lungs catch up to her racing heart. The crisp air brought some relief to her heated cheeks. "I am so sorry. You didn't deserve that!"

The young woman pulled away, her eyes lowered, hands twisting her cloth purse. "I should 'a known better. I'm sorry you got involved."

"Nonsense! I chose to speak up. I couldn't live with myself if I didn't." Lena could feel the eyes of other's watching them. Her anger kindled anew. "Come with me! We'll try Mr. Baker's store. I didn't see many items of clothing here, anyway."

The girl pulled back, her face awash with anxiety. "Oh no! Please, I just want to go home now. I'll make do."

Lena took the young woman's trembling hands in hers. "You need some traveling clothes, yes?"

"Yes, ma'am. I'm leaving Sawtooth for good, me and my little girl. As soon as the next wagon comes in, I plan to be on it!"

Lena heard the resolve in her voice. "You have a child. How wonderful!"

"You wouldn't approve ma'am, if you knew what I... did for a living."

"Well, I'm not all that perceptive, I suppose, but from their rude remarks I think you might work above one of the saloons. Is that right?" Lena didn't wish to cause the poor woman anymore embarrassment. If she spoke truthfully, the woman might feel less cause for shame. Besides, the woman had said she was leaving town. Perhaps she was leaving the business as well. She reasoned that she deserved a new beginning as much as herself.

With a sudden flash of inspiration, Lena found the solution to their dilemma. "I have a wonderful idea! But first we should introduce ourselves, don't you think?"

The woman managed to pull up a faint smile and nodded. "I'm Lena Sommer and as you may have heard, I manage the lodging house at the edge of town, close to Beaver Creek. Do you know it?"

"Oh yes! My friend... She stopped short, biting her lip. "I know the place. My name is Vicki."

"Well then, Vicki, now that we are properly introduced, I'd like to invite you to my fine dining establishment and offer you a cup of tea and maybe even a scone if the men left any this morning. Won't you come with me, please?" Lena watched as indecision worked its way across the woman's face from her pinched brow to her uncertain smile.

"I don't know...You heard them. It could hurt your reputation if I were seen in your company. I should just go." She tried to turn but Lena still held her hands firmly.

"What those women think matters not the least to me, Vicki. If someone is going to judge me by the people I choose to spend time with then they are people I'd rather not know as friends. So, I insist!" She grabbed Vicki by the arm and towed her away from town and back to the house.

As she did, a question rose to the forefront of her thinking. Would her previous employer have agreed with the women in the shop? Her reputation would surely have been ruined as a proper choice for a governess had she kept companionship with 'ladies of the evening'. Surely, that was just one of the changes transforming her perspective over these past weeks.

The thought came to her that that moral superiority displayed by the privileged women of Sawtooth City did not factor in the possibility that except by the grace of God, they too might find themselves in the ranks of those shunned. Lena felt a cold shiver run up her spine as she contemplated the fine knife edge of survival she walked by choosing to stay here.

They entered the house through the front door, so they caught Jessie unaware and in quite a flustered state. She'd been fuming at Carrick all morning for disturbing the hens so much with their hammering and sawing that the *ladies* weren't laying. Jessie calmed down enough to exchange polite introductions with Vicki.

"Vicki is going home! She's in need of some traveling clothes and I thought that between the two of us we might have just what she needs." Lena watched Jessie's face to test the value of her suggestion.

Jessie enthusiastically endorsed her idea by hugging the young woman. "This should be fun!"

"I have a lovely shawl that would match the color of your eyes." Jessie rummaged through a drawer and pulled out a knit scarf the pale blue of an icy winter sky. She skipped across the floor, wrapping it around Vicki's neck. "See? It's perfect for you!" She took a step back and clapped her hands with glee. "How beautiful it is with your eye color! See Lena?"

"But I think you need some sturdy traveling attire as well." Lena pulled an elegantly tailored brown morning coat and matching skirt from the closet. Holding it near the window, she appraised it; looked at Vicki and then held it up to her. "It will need to be shortened of course. But I think it suits you. What do you think, Jessie?"

"It's lovely! And you'll turn not just a few heads when you step off the train." Jessie grinned.

Lena saw a shadow flicker across Vicki's face. In it, she saw a glimpse of the darkness in this woman's short life and how it threatened to overshadow her future. Lena's heart ached for her. She could read in the woman's eyes her self-doubts. She laid out a high collared lace blouse and kid gloves to complement the suit. Who said silk and fine tailoring couldn't be armor? "These will do nicely, I think."

The next moment Vicki's head was buried in her hands, great sobs shaking her small body. She sagged onto the edge of the bed. Through gasps for breath, she managed to speak a few words at a time. "I... can't take such... nice things. I don't deserve..."

Closest to her, Jessie wrapped her arms around the woman. "Now, you stop that talk. No one deserves nothin' when you think about it. I surely don't deserve my Bart. And I'm guessing you don't deserve a lot of the bad things that have happened to you, neither."

Lena stood apart, watching how easily Jessie knew what to say, how to give comfort. Without hesitation or fear of being too bold, she spoke her mind. Lena knew how to comfort a crying child. She'd done that enough, but even with Miranda, whom she adored, she knew she'd always held back a full demonstration of her affections. The child was not hers after all. It wouldn't have been proper. But, oh, how she wished she'd told the child how much she meant to her!

Lena did the only thing she knew to do. "Why don't we all go down to the kitchen and have a cup of tea. Are there any biscuits, Jessie?" Lena began to fold the clothes into neat piles. "You two go on ahead. I'll catch up as soon as I've found something suitable for Vicki to carry these in."

Jessie took a firm hold of Vicki's hand, chatting with her as though they'd known each other for years, leaving Lena alone. Lena stood before the mirror holding a rose-colored jacket, remembering when she'd worn it last. She and Miranda had visited a tea shop overlooking Lake Michigan two summers past. It had been a magical day, filled with laughter and surprises, a street musician had serenaded them, a sweet lady selling flowers had given Miranda a bundle of violets.

Lena lowered the jacket, reaching up to touch the silver brooch with its ruby eye. It winked at her from the tarnished mirror against the wall, the patina marring the reflection. Her hand drifted to her face, touching the fine lines at the edge of her mouth. They weren't wasted years. She'd served a purpose in someone's life. Surely, she'd made a difference in the child's brief life.

"Lena, the water is hot. Are you coming?" Jessie called from the bottom of the stairs.

"Yes, just a minute." Lena turned from the mirror and its distorted image, adding its restoration to a long list of chores. She knelt by the bed, pulling out a small satchel just right for carrying extra clothing for the trip ahead.

"Did you know that Vicki has a baby girl? Oh, I can't wait to meet her!" Jessie poured tea into Lena's cup.

Vicki appeared more relaxed after a cheerful dose of Jessie. Lena sensed that it would be best to keep their conversations to the present. "So when do you leave? I thought I heard that the freight wagon is expected next week."

Vicki nodded, placing her teacup back on its saucer as though it might shatter in her hands. "Yes, ma'am. I'm going home." A smile tipped her lips. "Ever since my husband died, it's all I've wanted." She cast her glance back to the contents of her cup. Perhaps she thought she'd said too much. She rose to her feet, with a suddenness that rattled the teacup she'd so carefully set down. "I'd best be getting back. My little girl will be wondering what's become of me."

Lena picked up the satchel, handing it to Vicki. "I've added a few other items that might come in handy. But there was one more thing I'd like to do for you, if you'd allow it." She hesitated seeing that every word seemed to cause the woman more discomfort. "Please?"

"You've been so kind. I can't." She took the satchel, voice thick.

"I'd like to buy a few clothes for the child, if I might. You said she was three months old?"

"Yes, next week. But you've already helped me. Why would you?"

She smiled at Vicki and said, "I just want to. Please accept that I want to do this?" How could she tell the woman that she needed to do this? She needed to be extravagant with her affections for a stranger as she'd not been with her familiars.

Vicki gave another shaky smile. "That would be nice. My little girl could use a few things." Her cheeks flushed again. Lena read it as an indication of shame. Lena's throat constricted as she felt her own sense of shame welling up. Her shame came not for what she'd done but for what she hadn't done.

"She hasn't got much more than a night dress and a thin little day dress. So, yes, ma'am. That would be a kindness. Thank you." She turned to the door then, as though to stay longer would be too painful. "I can't go with you to the store, can I?"

Lena knew she was not asking her permission but stating a fact, one reinforced by today's experience. Lena kept her pity well veiled. "Don't bother yourself about those old hens one bit. Trust me to select some items and I can bring them to you."

Vicki chewed her lip, evidently still fighting an internal war. "There is a back door to our house. You can get to it down the alley off Mill Street. I usually cook supper around four in the afternoons. You can find me there most days. If not, one of the other girls..."

Before she could open the door, it swung inward, followed by a cold gust of wind and the towering figure of Evan Hartmann.

Evan looked as startled as they. "Vicki!"

"Hello, Evan. I... Miss Sommer and Miss Leach have done me a great kindness. They gave me some traveling clothes for the trip home." Her expression softened as had her voice.

"Well, that's fine, Miss Vicki."

Vicki looked back at Lena and Jessie, her face less tense. "Thank you, again." And she was gone.

"So how do you think they know each other?" Jessie lay with the covers pulled snugly to her chin.

"I'm sure I don't know," Lena answered in a small voice as she climbed into the massive bed next to Jessie.

"This isn't a big town. I suppose there might be any number of ways they'd be acquainted." Jessie persisted.

"Yes, any number of ways." Lena rubbed her feet together to warm them, wishing Jessie wouldn't pursue her thoughts. She had certainly resisted the urge to follow the same path of thinking for hours.

"Maybe they met at the cafe or at some town dance or..." Jessie's voice trailed off as she obviously realized how limited the respectable possibilities were. "I mean I'm sure there's other ways he could have known her."

Lena thought her choice of wording telling. He had indeed known her in some way. She rolled over on her side facing away from Jessie. "Goodnight, Jessie."

"There used to be a church, you know. Maybe..." Jessie sighed heavily. "Suppose not. But that's not so bad is it? I mean if he did... you know, *know* her?"

"Jessie, I really don't want to think about it."

"All right. But I still think he's a nice man. And if we can be kind to Vicki, we should be kind to Evan too, don't you think? Even if... you know."

"Good night, Jessie."

Jessie sighed again, fussing with her pillow.

Lena squeezed her eyes shut, willing herself to sleep. She knew Jessie was correct. Justice should be blind. If Evan had known Vicki in the biblical sense, she shouldn't judge him any more than she judged Vicki. And it shouldn't matter. She had no claim on the man. But it did matter to her. It mattered a great deal, coloring her impression of the gentle, well-read man she'd come to know these past few weeks.

Still, she was not ignorant of the weakness of men where women were concerned. And perhaps Jessie was right after all. Maybe there was another explanation for their familiarity. A man should be presumed innocent, shouldn't he? She squeezed her eyes tight, white spots swimming beneath her eyelids. *Go to sleep, Lena. Go to sleep.*

CHAPTER 18

DETERMINED, Lena walked to Main Street and the Baker Mercantile the following afternoon. Although she was a bit nervous about delivering her gifts to Vicki, the idea of selecting baby clothes thrilled her. She could recall similar visits charged by her employer to find some item of clothing for Miranda. Oddly enough, the girl had favored yellow and not pink. So Lena made a game of finding a new shade of yellow with every purchase—canary, sun-kissed, banana, lemon. She would always deliver them to the child and they'd play a game to name the unique shade she'd discovered.

The shopkeeper at the mercantile knew nothing of her previous day's adventure down the street, so she was courteous and solicitous. Although the selection was considerably limited to what she might have found in the shops of Chicago, she did manage to find a cozy flannel nightgown with yellow print, and two dresses, one pink and one pale blue, and a warm yellow blanket with matching knit bonnet. At the last minute she pulled from the shelf, a cloth doll with a cheerful embroidered smile, adding it to the pile.

"Shall I deliver these for you?" the shopkeeper asked.

Lena stared at her for a moment, tempted by the suggestion, but quickly realizing the awkwardness that would pose for both parties, she quietly refused the offer. "No, thank you. I'll take them with me."

Lena was aware of the shopkeeper's attention to her while wrapping the items she'd purchased. Lena sensed her curiosity, but busied herself looking at boots and shovels, anything that would keep her too far away to be asked questions she cared not to answer.

"Here you are, then. Someone is going to be very pleased with your gifts." She smiled encouragingly.

"Yes. I hope so." Lena took the parcel and quickly made her escape with a hasty, "Thank you."

Lena knew the street Jessie had described, but she'd never visited the area. Women of her background and breeding just didn't. She cringed thinking of her hypocrisy. She was no better than those stodgy old serpents back in the mercantile.

Biting her inner cheek, Lena strode down the alley with more confidence than she felt. A sudden burst of men's laughter startled her. Her pulse quickened as did her steps. Relieved, she found the door she sought. Knocking lightly, she waited, trying to steady her breathing. This was ridiculous. Why was she so anxious? She heard heavy steps. A latch lifted on the other side of the door.

A slender woman with heavy rouge and bright red lips opened the door. "Can I help you?" Though the words were courteous enough, the tone was overly polite. "We don't give to charity." There was a definite smirk to those ruby-colored lips.

"I'm here to see Vicki. I think she's expecting me."

The woman's expression did not change at the news, her dark eyes scanning Lena from top to bottom. "She's not here."

"Oh." Lena clutched the parcel to her breast, sensing the simmering hostility, wondering if this was anything like what Vicki had experienced yesterday. She, too, wanted to run.

"Who's there?" A woman's voice called out from the room. "Who is it, Katie? Trouble?"

"No, no trouble, Miss Naomi." The woman kept Lena skewered in place with her eyes, her tone cold.

A shuffling of feet and then a hand reached around the woman to open the door wider. An older woman stepped out peering at Lena, her eyebrow cocked with a question.

"I just brought a few things for Vicki's child, something she can use on the trip." Lena said, focusing on this woman, who seemed slightly less hostile to her presence.

The woman's eyes shifted to the parcel clutched in Lena's hands. "For the child, you say. She told you she was leaving Sawtooth?"

"Yes. I met her in the shop. There was some trouble. I just wanted to help." Her throat felt oddly constricted as if her collar were too tight.

The younger woman blew out a snort and turned her back on Lena. The older woman gave her a half smile, almost solicitous in its delivery. "Don't mind Katie. We've had enough dealings with the female do gooders of Sawtooth to last us a good long while. I'm Naomi. I run this place."

Lena's instincts warred with her embarrassment. "I'm Alena Sommer. I just..." She seemed to have lost the ability to speak. Lena pushed the package into Naomi's hands, taking a quick step back at the same time, stumbling on the step. "I'm sorry to have troubled you. If you'd just give this to Vicki, I'd be grateful." She spun away and hurried down the alley. She moved through the streets like a blind woman, putting as much distance between herself and the dirty alleyway as quickly as she could without running.

Brushing tears from her cheeks with the back of her glove, vision clouded, she nearly ran into Ely coming out of the bank. She put up her hand, stopping herself in time to avoid the collision, excusing herself, eyes averted.

"Miss Lena?"

Looking back, she recognized the kind face of her friend and the tears sprung fresh to her eyes.

Ely hurried to her side and took her arm in his. "Here, let me walk you home. There, there." He patted her arm as they walked.

Lena felt mortified by her emotional display in public and kept her head ducked, pulling her hat low over her face. "Thank you, Ely. I'm glad you came along when you did."

"What is it? Can you tell me or would you rather not? I will not be offended either way." His gentle tone did not help to strengthen her stoic resolve. Instead, his kindness weakened it.

"I don't mind talking to you, Ely. Of everyone I know, I think I could talk to you." She grabbed his arm tighter.

"I am glad you feel such."

She told him of meeting Vicki, of the harsh, unkind treatment she'd received from the mouths of the ladies at the shop, explaining how she and Jessie had found her some clothing for her journey. She hesitated and Ely looked over at her.

"And today?"

"Today, I purchased some clothes for the poor woman's child. We both knew that for her to go to the shop would be a bad idea, so I went alone."

Ely searched her face when she pulled up mid-stride.

"It was just that those ladies were so brutish and cruel! They might have simply spat in her face."

Ely made a sound deep in his throat, akin to a growl. "I don't have much use for the likes of such, putting others down to feel better about themselves."

"They didn't even know the woman, or anything about her circumstances. Her husband died, Ely, and she turned to.. .what she does to survive."

"Is a shame, it is. It is not uncommon, even back home. But sometimes there's family that can help out."

"Well, that's just it. She's leaving Sawtooth with the child to go back home. She deserves a chance to start over." Lena felt her face grow warm as she thought of the woman's liberation from a life she obviously didn't want for herself or her child. She felt again the indignation of the women's bigotry, her passion stirring.

"So, why the tears, Miss Lena? You tried to help."

Lena looked away, the passion fading as she recalled the angry face of the woman barring the door. "They hated me, Ely. They didn't even know me, but they loathed me for who I was and what I represented to them."

Ely shook his head slowly, patting her arm again as he led her down the street. "Guess you learned how the girl felt, didn't you?"

Lena gripped his arm even tighter. "Exactly! Ely, that is exactly it! I wasn't just another woman to them. I was a loathsome do gooder, someone who sits in judgment.

"Guess prejudice works a two-way street."

With her back to the road while taking down the day's laundry, Lena missed seeing Vicki walking up the road from town. Vicki called out to Lena, causing her to turn with a clothes pin still held between her teeth. She pulled it out, allowing her lips to spread wide in a smile at seeing the baby perched on Vicki's hip.

"Oh, you brought your little girl!" She dropped the laundry into her basket and called to the house. "Jessie! Come out and see Vicki's baby!"

Vicki had already wrapped the child in the yellow blanket Lena had given her. Little more than a single blond curl poked out of the well-swaddled baby. Jessie ran down the steps, clapping her hands the entire time. "Oh, I do love babies! Let's see the dear."

Without hesitation, Vicki passed the child into Jessie's outstretched arms. She touched Lena's arm. "Thank you for the sweet gifts. I'm most grateful to you."

Why shouldn't she willingly share with someone less fortunate? It shouldn't come with thanks, she thought. *I was doing what I should do.* She was grateful that Vicki, at least, did not seem offended by her gifts. And yet...

"Vicki, I believe I owe you an apology." Lena held up her hand, interrupting an imminent interjection. "Please believe me, I am honestly so pleased that I could help, but I think I may have been just as thoughtless as those foolish women back in the shop." She took a deep breath, letting the shame drive her relentlessly toward truth. "When I came to your defense, gave you those things, I think I was doing it for selfish reasons—making myself feel somehow superior in my charity. And that, Vicki, is just as awful as what those ladies said to you." Lena swallowed past the knot in her throat, taking Vicki's delicate hand in hers. "I'm sorry. Please, forgive me."

Vicki's soft hands tightened within her grip and then wrapped about Lena's wrists as she pushed herself up on tiptoe to brush a soft kiss against Lena's cheek. "Thank you," she whispered. "I'd almost stopped believing people could be so decent."

Folding back one edge of the blanket Vicki revealed the cherub face of her child. Rosy cheeks made her appear to be in perfect health. She could have been the child of anyone, privileged or not. Lena basked in her innocence. She moved closer, reaching for the child's chubby fingers, admiring their perfection. "Look how beautiful, Jessie. She's a perfect angel."

"And look at those eyes, Lena. Have you ever seen a shade of green just like those?"

Lena's breath caught as the child locked eyes with her, green eyes a stunning shade of emerald. Pieces suddenly fit together. Her mouth went dry. She felt suddenly tired, so very tired.

"Would you like to hold her, Miss Sommer?" Vicki asked.

"I...Yes, of course." Lena forced herself to ignore the knot forming in her stomach, the suspicions. Hadn't she just admitted her bigotry? She took the child into her arms, touching the downy softness of her skin. She was perfect. She smiled into the baby's laughing eyes, Evan's eyes, feeling suddenly so very old—and foolish.

"We heard from a man who came in from Ketchum yesterday, the wagon should be in town next Wednesday. The baby and I could be home in just a few weeks if we can catch the train out of Hailey in time." Vicki's eyes glowed with real happiness.

In spite of the heavy sadness weighing upon her heart, Lena smiled. "I'm happy for you, Vicki. I feel quite sure your family will fall in love with your little girl. She's charming." She passed the child back into Vicki's arms. The younger woman pecked another kiss on Lena's cheek and one on Jessie's before turning back to the road leading to town.

Jessie yelled out, "Maybe we'll come and see you off."

Vicki answered but neither Jessie nor Lena heard her words.

Jessie picked up the laundry basket and tripped up the stairs.

Lena sank down on the front step, feeling she'd learned far too much about herself and the world at large in such a short span of time between morning and afternoon of this single day. For years, measuring herself against others less tolerant, she'd thought of herself as a kind and good person, even generous. It occurred to her that she'd been using an imperfect measuring stick.

For the first time in two days, she looked up, really seeing the snow encasing the peaks of the Sawtooths. The recent storm had added feet, not inches, of snow on those high mountains, just as Evan had said it would happen. A sudden wave of sadness brought her to her feet, glaring at the mountains and their old men, stone faces.

It occurred to her that if her life were a dramatic play, she might shake her fist at the mountain in defiance. But she did not. Instead, she walked across the length of the porch and dropped down onto the chair she'd made into her bed on that first night. As she did that night, she pulled her legs up beneath her wool skirt, hugging her knees.

Once again, she found herself taking assessments, counting the costs. Everything worth having comes at a cost. She reminded herself that she was lucky she'd not given her heart to the man. He interested her, but there had been no promises, no unspoken understandings. He'd offered friendship. What had changed? Nothing, really.

Chuckling to herself, she realized that she must appear as broody as the mountains. She rose to her feet, striding to the porch railing. Her fingers wrapped tightly around the sturdy post and she lifted her eyes to the mountains. Her brow relaxed, a wan smile returned to soften her features.

She had no intention of moving from here, any more than the mountain might pick up and relocate to the other side of the river. She had no desire to go back east, to the life she'd lived there. She couldn't, even if she wished.

If winter came with the fury of which she'd been warned, then let it come. It would certainly be an adventure. If she survived the winter months, she might even be allowed to purchase the house and at last have a hearth of her own. This wasn't the time to count the odds of her success. It was the time to plant her feet firmly on the path she'd chosen.

Evan scooped out a measure of grain to add to Gambit's feed for the night. "You looked pretty good out there, boy. Jimmy might have been right about you after all. A stable of foals from you might be just the thing to secure a place up here as a supplier of fine horses." He wiggled his fingers under the stallion's mane, finding his sweet spot.

Lifting the saddle bag from behind the door, he slung it over his shoulder and headed up to the house. The heft of the bag testified to the dust he'd found that day. He smiled. There was still some hope that the claim, and the new one he hoped to secure farther up the stream, would yield some profit. Maybe he'd be able to locate a tract of land suitable for running cattle and horses, one he could afford. With those optimistic thoughts running through his mind, he found the sight of Lena asleep on the front porch particularly heartwarming. He took the steps quietly. Her voice stopped him. He hesitated, hand on the doorknob.

"Mr. Hartmann."

"Evan, remember? Sorry to have disturbed your sleep. You looked so comfortable there."

She pushed her hair back into the bun at the nape of her neck, adjusting her skirts about her legs at the same time.

"Taking advantage of the warmer temperatures today. We called such days Indian Summer."

"Yes, ma'am. Often that way here too. Usually means there will follow a particularly bad string of winter storms." Evan regretted sharing that news. She'd shown him before how little she favored his attempts at forecasting. She'd see soon enough without his becoming the constant harbinger of bad news. He cursed himself for letting his good mood loosen his tongue.

Lena rose to her feet and folded her arms at her waist. "I see that you were correct about the last storm. There's more snow up there in the crags. You seem to be quite good at predicting weather conditions, Mr. Hartmann."

Although her words were gracious enough, there was a chilliness in their delivery. Could this have something to do with Vicki? Was that the reason for her coolness? He felt a twinge of protectiveness toward his young friend. But having learned what Lena had done for the girl, his esteem for her had risen. Maybe he was just misinterpreting. Mood greatly dampened, he left her standing there alone staring up at the white capped range.

CHAPTER 19

THAT evening Lena handed the second volume of *Ivanhoe* to Evan, giving the excuse that her throat was a little sore. He settled himself in his usual chair while Lena disappeared into the kitchen.

"Oh yes, we stopped last night at this wonderful passage. Then we all got carried away with a discussion about its meaning." He laughed lightly, then repeated the lines. "'*He that does good, having the unlimited power to do evil, deserves praise not only for the good which he performs, but for the evil which he forbears.*'"

Bart summed up the passage in a few words. "We all are pretty rotten folks, except for rare moments when we choose to do something selfless, which ain't that often."

Jessie passed him an incredulous look.

"Easier to kick a man in the teeth than give him a hand up out of the mud." All eyes turned to Carrick who had given his unique and succinct summary. "What?"

"You! You been listening," his brother said, surprise evident in every feature.

"Well, yeah. What 'ya think I've been doin'?

Jessica flapped her hands at the men, shushing them. "We already been down this path! Let's get on with it. I'm worried about Rebecca. I just know she's gonna' get her heart broke."

"Who loves who?" Bart asked, his face a blank.

"Why she loves Ivanhoe, of course!"

"She does?" Bart asked.

As Evan listened to their banter, he couldn't help but smile at the transformation in this house of men in just a few short weeks. Where most nights they all closed themselves into their rooms and fell into their beds in exhaustion, now they were engaged in conversation, laughing, joking, at times even *debating*. It occurred to him that men just didn't behave this way naturally. Lena had drawn it out of them and in the process knit them together, almost, he thought, like family.

While the banter continued, Evan watched Lena emerge from the kitchen and without turning her face to the group quietly slip upstairs. He wanted to call after her, sit her down, and explain what exactly Vicki was to him—but a very stubborn part of him rankled at the thought of being forced to defend his innocent friendship. He'd done nothing wrong and if she would so quickly judge him, then what value was there in her opinion, feckless as it was?

For the next few days, the skies remained clear, the temperatures mild—mild enough to finish insulating the chicken coop and chop more wood. Lena made a trip into town to try two more shops in hopes of locating some staples like flour and sugar. Each time she was told the same thing. They were waiting for the next shipment from Ketchum.

Walking through town she passed far too many men lounging around, men who were hoping for the mining company to work out their difficulties back east and restart work in the mine. She also overheard one man talking about word he'd received about new discoveries farther north in Stanley Basin. He went on to suggest it might be a good time to head up before the word got out.

She slowed her pace in hopes of hearing more of their conversation but they'd stepped into a side street, their conversation trailing with them. An unpleasant churning in her stomach made her wish she'd stayed at the house and sent Jessie out on this fruitless mission. At the sound of someone calling her name, she turned. From across the street, she saw Evan and Daniel emerging from the bakery. Daniel clutched a large paper bag and wore a wide smile. He called to her again. "Miss Sommer, come have a sweet bun!"

Hesitating for just a moment, she crossed the quiet street to them. She needed something to lift her spirits. "Those look delicious!" She removed her glove, accepting the confection.

"The baker is closing his shop today and is selling everything half-price! We made out pretty good, Mr. Hartmann and I. Good, ain't they?" Daniel took another bite, giving her a perfect Tom Sawyer grin with sugar-sprinkled lips.

It was a priceless sight and one that made her forget her stress of moments earlier, including this new bit of information about the bakery closing. "Perhaps I should buy some for the men. Is there anything left?"

Daniel said, "Oh yeah! Plenty! Why I bet he baked enough to feed half of Sawtooth!"

That made her wonder if he might be willing to sell a little of his flour rather than tote it along with him. "Hmm. I think I should have a talk with the baker."

"Do you need any help?" Evan asked after he'd swallowed down his last bite. "The boy and I could tote some things back to the house.

She considered his offer. Choosing reason, she accepted. "Can you wait for just a minute? I'll know if I could use your help after I speak with the baker." She took a step to the door, then suddenly turned back." Why aren't you in school, Daniel?"

Daniel's grin spread even wider. "Ain't no more school, miss!"

"*Isn't*, Daniel, there *isn't* any more school." She blinked. "For goodness sakes, why not?"

"The teacher is packing up to leave with the Jamison family. They're all heading to Boise City. Guess Mrs. Jamison has had enough of the cold. I'll miss that girl of theirs though. She was sweet on me. I just know it." He stuffed half of the next bun into his mouth, looking mournful.

"I heard that Mrs. Jamison was yearning for a bit more society life than Sawtooth can offer," Evan added.

"But why take the school teacher?" Lena asked.

"Well, I think the Jamisons were paying most of her salary, and with them leaving..." He shrugged.

Lena stood there a while longer mulling over this new bit of news, hoping the recently consumed pastry would not further disturb her nervous stomach. She turned back to the shop, calling back over her shoulder, "I shouldn't be but a moment."

As it turned out, the baker did indeed have two, twenty-five-pound bags of flour and one whole and one partial bag of sugar he'd rather sell than carry out with all his other goods. So, she enlisted Evan's and Daniel's help to carry them.

"Would you like to stay, Daniel, and help me with a few chores? I'll fix you a nice lunch in exchange for your time."

Daniel looked back at Evan, who nodded. "You can come up to the claim with me another time. Go on. Miss Sommer probably needs your help more than I do." He left Daniel in the kitchen with Lena and her list of chores.

Lena put the boy to work covering the vegetable garden with straw and cleaning out the hen house again. Both chores she'd put off too long. Daniel surprised her later in the morning by chopping a substantial stack of kindling for her to keep at kitchen door where it would be sheltered from the snow.

For all his hard work, she rewarded him with a slice of ham on fresh baked bread. Jessie had gone a bit mad with all the flour on hand and baked an extravagant pile of sugar cookies. Lena sat across from him with a cup of coffee and one of Jessie's plate-size cookies.

"How long have you lived here, Daniel? Seems you know your way around very well." Lena waited for him to swallow a sizable bite of sandwich.

"Hmm... It was the same year my mama died. So that'd make it..." He looked up at the ceiling, obviously doing some challenging mental math. "That'd make it three years past, about the same time as Mr. Hartmann I guess. Lots of folks started driftin' in about then."

"Where'd you live before that?"

"Oh, here and there, mostly where the gold's showin' yellow. We've been in Nevada and over Boise way." He took another bite of sandwich. "This is real good, Miss Sommer, but I can hardly get it down fast enough. Those cookies look even better! No offense meant to your cookin'."

A smile hovered at her lips. "No offense taken."

"It ain't bad driftin' around like we do. I get to take in some pretty sights, and most times I don't have to go to school like I did here." He scowled before taking a long drink of water. "But it wasn't so good for Ma. She came down with consumption. It was bad. That was the first time I met Mr. Hartmann."

"Oh?"

"Mmm." He reexamined the ceiling. "That must have been over a year ago, I guess. Yup! Late spring." He fell to his sandwich again as if forgetting his life history stories. Lena watched him, hopeful he'd come back to it without her asking.

"He's kind of weird." He pushed his plate away and looked over at Jessie, cutting apples for a pie. "Can I have one of your cookies now, Miss Leach?"

Jessie answered by placing the full plate of cookies in front of him. "I told you before. Call me Jessie or call me Hey, but please don't call me Miss Leach. I can't tolerate the sound of that name."

Daniel looked chagrined and passed her a crooked smile. "Okay. Hey, I thank you for the cookies."

"You scamp!"

He closed his eyes and took a bite of soft sugar cookie. "That's *real* good!"

"Daniel, you were saying something about Mr. Hartmann being, ahem, *weird*."

Jessie looked over her shoulder with an amused expression.

"Oh, Mr. Hartmann! Yeah! So, when my ma was ailing, and my pa was all twisted up about it, Mr. Hartmann came over and chopped us a whole season of wood. You know he did that even when he was working at the mine. Pa would come home from work only after spending a few hours over on Mill Street. But Mr. Hartmann would come to our place and chop wood."

Lena gripped her cup tighter. "Is that so?"

"It's the honest to God truth."

Jessie swung around from the counter giving the boy a stern look. "Daniel! I don't think your mama would want you usin' the Lord's name in vain like that!"

"Sorry, ma'am. It's what I hear's all."

"That's an interesting story, Daniel. And I'm sorry for the trouble you've had, losing your mother like that," Lena said.

The boy stared at the plate of cookies for some time. "Things ain't the same."

"Are you all right?" Lena feared she might have stirred up sad memories.

"Fine, Miss Sommer. I was just thinkin' how much I'd like to have another cookie, but I think I might die if I did." His voice was so mournful that Lena nearly laughed aloud, but she managed to stifle it by taking a drink of cold coffee. Jessie snorted without restraint.

CHAPTER 20

O N the morning of Vicki's departure, the sun came out in glorious golden rays, melting the last remnants of the snow that had dusted the trees and rooftops the night before. With glistening eyes, she turned to her friends, hugging each in turn. Make-up smeared the tear-streaked faces of Naomi's girls as each took turns hugging the baby and kissing her for good luck.

Evan stood to her side waiting to help her into the wagon. His mouth had set itself into a grim line until Vicki turned to him. She waited quietly before him for a moment, then reached her arms about his neck, pulling his face close to hers. She whispered something then kissed his cheek before releasing him.

Naomi passed the child to Evan after he'd helped Vicki into her seat. Evan held the child for a moment longer, then handed her into Vicki's arms. Vicki looked up at Lena and Jessie standing at a distance. They exchanged waves of farewell. Then with a smack of reins, the wagon started off with a lurch. Vicki grabbed the seat with her free hand, laughing as she did. The wagon wove up the hill out of town leaving those behind to make their way home at a slower pace.

Lena brushed a tear from the corner of her eye while Jessie sobbed beside her. Lena pulled a handkerchief from her pocket and handed it to the girl. Jessie blew hard.

"I'm so happy for her. And I'm so sad too! Isn't that peculiar?" Jessie managed between sobs.

"I think that's not so peculiar, Jessie. The world is full of paradoxes." Lena watched as Evan walked away in the direction of the livery.

Jessie blew her nose again."I wish I could understand some of those words you use, Lena. You're too smart for me."

Lena looked over at Jessie's red nose and puffy eyes and looped her arm through the girl's. "I'm not too smart for you, Jessie. You've got smarts I could not even hope for."

"Really?"

"Yes. You have people smarts. You understand people better than I ever could. You also have something even better. You have a giant heart of compassion. You just seem to know what to do in almost every situation." Lena pulled on her arm, leading her back toward the house and chores they'd abandoned so that they could see Vicki off.

"But you're book smart. That's something I'll never be." Jessie sniffed, but the spring was returning to her gait.

"Book smart doesn't mean much out here, does it?" They walked together in companionable silence, enjoying the last days of moderate temperatures, strolling like school girls.

Jessie gave Lena's arm a little shake. "Did you know that Evan paid for Vicki's trip home? I heard one of the ladies mention it. I think that just proves what Daniel was sayin'. Well, maybe I wouldn't say he was *weird,* but he is different. I know you don't want me to be a match maker, but you two *should* get together. I just think you were meant for each other. You're both book smart and kind." Jessie looked over at Lena. "Are you listening to me?"

"I heard you, Jessie. But you're wrong about Mr. Hartmann and me. I think you have read his kindness toward me as something more than it is. As you said, he is a thoughtful person."

"Maybe you aren't so smart after all!" Jessie tugged at Lena's arm, then poked a finger in her ribs, forcing Lena into a smile.

As they passed the livery, she couldn't keep from stealing a glance through the open doors. Evan stood just inside, stroking Gambit's nose, appearing to be engaged in conversation with the stallion. She forced herself to look away. What was the word she'd thrown at Jessie? *Paradox.* Yes, Evan's character was paradoxical to her. How could a man of such obvious compassion turn his back on his responsibility to care for his own child? It just didn't make sense. There had to be another explanation. There had to be. But what were the odds of two people having such astonishingly unique eye color?

"Come on! We've got work to do." Lena picked up their pace, hurrying them past the livery and back up the hill.

After a full day of working at his claim and coming home with little to show for his efforts, Evan walked up the porch steps with slow weary steps.

"You look exhausted, my friend."

Evan looked in the direction of the voice, seeing Ely sitting on the front porch bench, a cloud of smoke drifting about his head.

"Ely, never knew you to be a man to smoke." Evan shuffled over and sat beside him, groaning as he took a seat.

"Oh, I enjoy my pipe from time to time. Usually when I have things whirling around in my brain that will not settle right."

Evan chuckled softly. "Had a few of those times myself."

With light quickly fading from the fall sky, the temperatures plunged. But neither man seemed eager to leave the comfort of the porch and the view of the mountains.

"So what unsettles your brain, my young friend?" Ely asked.

Evan didn't answer right away. It wasn't his way. "Tough time for folks."

"*Ja*, surely is that." Ely sucked on his pipe and blew out one perfect ring. "Now, I know it is not my business," he paused to blow out another ring, "but it is troubling to me, so I speak of it."

Evan looked at Ely with an even gaze. "I'll help if I can."

"I hope you can. It is just this. I have noticed that you and Lena are not as friendly these days as you once were."

Evan pulled a hand across his face. "What am I to say?"

Ely shook his head slowly, puffing quietly on his pipe. "I am sorry. It is none of my business. You do not wish to talk of it. I understand."

"We're not unfriendly."

"No, I have poked my large nose in where it should not be," Ely wagged his head.

"She is a fine woman."

"*Ja*, she is, very fine."

"She's smart."

"*Ja*, very smart, well-educated too, I think."

"Yes."

"And very kind."

"Yes, kind," Evan said, an echo.

"*Ja*. She is an attractive woman too," Ely said. Evan felt Ely's eyes upon him.

"Yes, she is."

"*Ja*, and she is opinionated."

"Very," Evan said through thin lips.

"*Ja*, opinionated, like others I know." Ely took in three quick puffs.

Evan turned a narrow-eyed gaze at him. "Are you trying to say something?"

"*Ja*, maybe." Ely rubbed his chin thoughtfully.

"Ely, you don't understand. She has a very bad opinion of me."

"And you know this?"

"She hasn't said anything, but..."

"You have made a reasoned assumption," Ely agreed.

"Yes, a reasoned assumption," Evan parroted again.

For several moments only the sound of Ely drawing on his pipe broke the late afternoon silence.

"I think she has assumed that I am the father of Vicki's child." Evan sighed and slumped back against the chair.

Ely pulled the pipe from his mouth and turned to face Evan. "Have you corrected this assumption?"

Evan stroked his hands down his pant legs. "No."

Ely said nothing.

"If she judges my actions without knowing the truth, I don't think she is the kind of woman I would want to know better." Evan met Ely's eyes, then looked quickly away. "Am I wrong?"

"*Die welt befindet sich in einem Chaos,*" Ely said.

Evan looked at him, confused. "Sorry?"

"This is the fault of the world, *ja*. People rush to judgments. People become angry. People war." Ely sighed heavily, dropping his hand holding the pipe to his lap. "It is none of my business, but I think you make a big mistake not to talk to this woman and tell her the truth. You did a very fine thing, Evan Hartmann. Our friend, Lena, deserves to know that truth."

Evan sat back again, feeling an inexplicable tightness in his chest.

Ely brought the pipe back to tuck securely between his lips, a frown deepened the wrinkles on his brow. "There is one more thing that I will say."

Evan wasn't certain he wanted to hear anymore advice, even from his friend, but he met Ely's dark eyes, waiting.

"You are very good at thinking of others." Ely took a look drag on his pipe, his eyes closing for a moment. "Perhaps, you need to think more of yourself. How many months has it been since your brother died? Five? Six?"

"Seven." Evan felt his throat constrict in that uncomfortable manner he'd grown to expect with memories of Jimmy.

"I must wonder if you have made any plans for your own future. I think we both know that this place is dying. Dreams die too. New dreams come to take their place, sometimes better ones, *ja*? Have you allowed yourself to dream again, my friend?"

Evan felt his face tense, his hands already clenched in his lap.

Ely broke the awkward silence, setting down his pipe. "Ah, but it is not my business." He reached over, patting Evan's leg as if he were a child to be comforted. "I am sure you will work this out, *ja*?" Without further words, he rose and left Evan there.

A moment or two passed before Evan laughed aloud, the heartiest laugh that had come from him in a very long while. He felt good, the way he did after a discussion with his father as a youth, cleansed and set back on course by a good scolding.

Lena resumed her seat by the fire that night, but Evan lingered near the back of the room. It was as if they'd regressed to when they'd first all come together.

Lena noticed that Jessie seemed agitated, fidgeting with her blouse and winding strands of her hair around her finger, while Bart, sitting beside her also looked somewhat uneasy. Lena lifted the book from her lap. Locating her place, she began. She'd only been reading for a short time. The line from the book read simply, *"'Certainly,' quoth Athelstane, 'women are the least to be trusted of all animals, monks and abbots excepted.'"*

"Don't you dare look at me like that, Bart! I didn't mislead you! And yes, I'll marry you, right now if you want!"

All eyes turned to Jessie as she stood red-faced, yelling at Bart.

Bart waited for a heartbeat as he seemed to take in the words. Then he leaped to his feet and threw his arms around Jessie, lifting her off her feet as he did. "You will?" He turned to look at those around him. "You heard her! She said she will!"

Carrick was first to launch from his chair and slap Bart on the back. "Congratulations!"

Donal flanked Bart, planting a second resounding slap on his back. "Took you long enough to make up your minds."

Lena wrapped her arm around Jessie. "You kept that decision pretty quiet."

Jessie lowered her gaze, suddenly and uncharacteristically shy. "Well, we've had to make a change in our original plans. Bart thought we'd be settling here for a while, but the mines..." She looked up at Lena with a painful expression. "I'm so sorry."

Lena turned to face the girl, her hands resting on Jessie's shoulders. "Why? Why would you apologize? You're getting married!"

"But we'll be leaving... leaving here and you. I hate leaving you alone and I don't want to say goodbye to you." Tears welled up in Jessie's eyes. "You've been like a sister to me. At least I think you have. I never had one, but you're what I'd imagine my sister to be like."

Lena drew the girl into her arms. "I know exactly what you mean. You've been the same for me. I can't imagine these past few weeks without your bright smile and that wonderful laugh." The words made the truth suddenly clear and tears sprung to the corners of her eyes at the thought of losing Jessie's sweet encouragement every day. She hadn't realized how much she'd come to depend on the girl.

Evan reached for Bart's hand and shook it gravely. "I want to wish you and Jessie the best."

Bart's face was suddenly somber. "Guess we might as well tell you the rest of our plans then. Maybe you all should take a seat."

Jessie slipped from Lena's embrace and sidled up to Bart, slipping her hand in his.

"Well, the mining folks up at the office don't seem to be able to make up their minds about what they want to do with this mine we've all been workin'. So we decided it might be the best to head out of the Sawtooths now before the heavy snows and get on down to Ketchum or Hailey where I can find work."

Jessie broke in, "Then after a year or so, once we have a bit of cash, we'll cross on over to Oregon."

"My brother has a bit of land there and has been after me to come out and help him work it."

"They've been building a new house for their growing family, and they want us to move into the smaller one they built when they first settled there." She squeezed Bart's arm. "We'll have a house of our own, just like we dreamed."

Ely voiced the sentiment they all felt when he said, "*Ja*, and we will miss you two. Won't be the same. And who will you have perform the ceremony? The preacher left this summer."

Jessie skipped to Ely's side and hugged his arm. "Why you, of course!"

"Me?" Ely chirped.

"Yes, you talk pretty and you are by far the wisest of us all. That makes you a good stand-in for a preacher."

Evan asked the next logical question, "And when will this wedding be?"

Bart grinned. "This weekend."

"Two days," Lena said, her voice soft. "Not much time to prepare."

Bart nodded and said, "We can't waste any time. Want to be heading out with two other families leaving next week. Feel we'll be better off traveling with folks, in case the weather turns bad, you know?"

"I suppose we could've waited to get married in Hailey by a *real* preacher, but who would we invite? We want you all to be with us when we stand up." Jessie, face aglow, looked around her at the friends she'd made. "Besides, I might need someone around to hold me up so I *can* stand up."

As the laughter died away, a deeper realization settled on Lena. They weren't just moving out of the house; they were leaving the valley completely. She turned to the kitchen, hiding her expression from the happy couple. "I think I should make us all a pot of cocoa. This is cause for celebration." Her words did not match her tone, but she hoped no one detected the disparity.

Alone in the kitchen she gripped the edge of the sink to steady herself. If only she'd had some warning. Why was she so blind these days, failing to see the obvious truths around her? She pulled herself erect again and rummaged through the cupboard for the can of cocoa. Where was it? She felt a sudden flash of anger. "Where is it!"

"I think I saw Jessie put it in the cupboard over there." Lena spun at the sound of Ely's voice. He was pointing to the other side of the room. "Over there," he said again.

She took a sharp breath and walked quickly to the cupboard. It was there as he'd said. With shaking hands, she pulled it from the shelf and returned to the work counter, working quickly now, afraid to stop and allow her mind to dwell upon anything other than her task.

Ely began to take cups from the shelf, placing them near the stove. He watched her silently then said, "You are sad, *ja*? It is all right to be sad."

Lena measured the sugar into the pot. She reached for a measuring scoop and dropped it.

Ely retrieved it before she could stoop to pick it up. She met his eyes, seeing there the compassion she didn't wish to receive in that moment. "Thank you," she said tersely.

Ely took her hand. "Why are you afraid to let your emotions show? You are a woman. You are allowed."

She pulled her hand free. "I am sad. Yes. I will miss her. Yes." Her voice faltered. "I am angry too." She turned back to the counter, dumping great scoops of cocoa into the pan.

"Angry?"

She spun on him again. "Angry! *Ja*!" To stop her trembling hands from showing, she shoved them into her pockets.

"You are angry at Jessie?"

"No!" She said it louder than she intended. "Of course, not!"

"Then who are you angry with?" Ely pressed.

"I don't know—God, maybe?" She covered her face with her hands, feeling the hot sting of tears against her palms.

Ely sat before her, looking up into her covered face. "It is none of my business, I think. But I will stick my large nose where perhaps it is not wished."

She turned from him, stirring the pot, attempting to quiet her emotions.

"Does this have anything to do with our friend, Evan?"

She stopped stirring, feeling her shoulders tense. "Why would you think that?"

"I have watched you grow cold toward him these past few days. It is clear that you are not pleased with him."

Hands clenched, she turned on him again, her eyes clouded by unshed tears. "You're right, Ely! This *is* none of your business!"

Ely stayed seated for a moment longer, then slowly rose to his feet. "*Ja*, you are right, Lena. I told you that I thought as much. Please forgive an old man." He started for the door.

"No! Wait!" Lena rushed up behind him clutching at his jacket sleeve.

He turned, his face calm and soft, lined by his years. There was no judgment in his eyes, not even an indication of offense. "I wait, Lena."

"I'm sorry, Ely, truly sorry. I shouldn't have said that. I know you just want to help, but you can't. This isn't something a soothing tune can resolve. I..." She looked at the floor, struggling for words without exposing her heartache, her unreasonable heartache. She felt so abandoned.

"But Lena, perhaps I can."

She shook her head, looking up at him with a small sad smile. "I don't think so."

He watched her for a long moment, then held his hand out to her. In her remorseful state, she took it. "May I tell you a story?"

She cast her gaze to the stove. "Well, I think..."

"It will be short. I promise."

"All right." She sat on the long dining bench and Ely shuffled to her side to sit next to her.

"In the old country, my home, I had a dear, dear friend. From childhood, he was my best friend. We were both musicians, violinists. We shared a room. We were both very poor. Everyone was. It was springtime. I remember the lilacs in bloom outside our window. A letter came from my aunt, my mother's sister-in-law. It was an answer to prayer." He leaned close, whispering. "It contained a good deal of money that would pay for many months of rent. My uncle had sold an instrument belonging to my mother, you see. And because she had passed on, he sent it to me! Wonderful, *ja?*"

Lena nodded once, wondering at the story's relevance.

He smiled. "I showed it to my friend, Edward. He was excited too, and we decided to go out and celebrate our good fortune. Oh, and we did! Then we came home, and I put the envelope of money on the table near the one comfortable chair in our little room. The next day when I went to take some money from the envelope to pay our landlady the rent, what do you think?" He waited a half minute, then answered his own question, "I will tell you. The envelope was gone, just vanished."

"Oh no."

"Oh, *ja*!" His countenance fell. He drummed his fingers on his knee for a moment. "This is the sad part of the story, Lena. I thought my friend had stolen the money. I knew he played a violin that was not his. He was making payments on it, you see. I thought that he had used the money to pay off his violin debt. I even accused him to his face of this awful thing."

"And did he?"

Ely's face fell even farther. His eyes dimmed briefly. "No, Lena, he did not. But because I assumed the wrong thing about my friend, our relationship, which had been so dear, was broken."

"How do you know he didn't take the money?"

"He told me he did not."

"But he might have been lying to you."

"But my friend had never lied to me in all the years we had been friends, not once. I should have known he did not lie to me then. But I was angry, oh, so very angry. I assumed the worst."

"Still, you don't know that he didn't take the money," Lena insisted.

"I do. I do know. I stayed in that little room by myself for two more years, two lonely years. It was not until I was moving all my items to another house that I learned the truth that makes my story such a sad one."

"And what was that?"

"I was not a very good housekeeper. You may not choose to believe that now, seeing how fastidious I am. But as I was moving my comfortable chair, what do you think? An envelope fell out from beneath the cushion. It was *the* envelope, the one I accused my dear friend of stealing. And sadder yet, I never saw my friend again, so I could never tell him how sorry I was for not believing him."

Lena touched his arm. "Oh, Ely." She sat back studying him for a moment. "But what does that have to do with me?"

"Lena, I think you have assumed wrong things about our friend, Evan Hartmann."

Lena pulled back.

"Wait, please, and let me finish." Ely lay a restraining hand on her arm, imploring her with his earnest eyes. "Did you ever think of any other explanations for Evan's kindness to the young woman, Vicki?"

"Ely, I really don't..." Ely closed his eyes but kept his hand on her arm, keeping her from rising to her feet.

"You knew that Evan had a brother, *ja*?"

She didn't respond to his question, but her shock must have been obvious. "A brother?"

"He was killed last spring. It was an avalanche, a terrible thing. Jimmy's body was only found this summer when the snows melted. Evan changed after that. He became more solitary, spending more time at their claim."

Questions and answers pressed in from all sides. Lena felt the breath pushed from her lungs.

"He is changing again, Lena. You've done that. You've changed him." Ely squeezed her hand.

Lena met his eyes, seeing him indistinctly through a veil of unspilled tears.

"Have you ever considered that it is Evan's nature to help those who need it?"

She found her voice, but it sounded strange to her ears, small, as though from far away. "Yes"

"Did you ever consider Jimmy and if *he* knew Vicki? He did, Lena. He knew her very well."

She sagged. Her mouth went dry. Her stomach tightened. She opened her mouth, then closed it again. She couldn't meet Ely's steady gaze any longer, so she looked away before asking, "And were his brother's eyes green like Evan's?"

"Ja." He released his hold on her arm and she stood, hitting the table with her thigh, causing the mugs to rock. Walking stiffly to the sink, she felt her stomach rolling, wanting to be sick.

"Sometimes things are not what they appear," Ely said quietly.

"I never thought... I should have... given him the benefit of the doubt. I judged him even when I knew him to be..." She turned to look at Ely, hot tears searing her cheeks. "Oh Ely, I really am no better than those women at the shop who judged Vicki. I'm such a hypocrite!" Her temples throbbed. She pressed her palms to the side of her head.

Ely pulled her hand away, holding it between his delicate artist's hands. "We all are, Lena. We all do these things, but there is yet time for you to take back your cold anger and replace it with the warmth you once showed him. He needs it."

She shook her head. "But Ely, what could I possibly say?"

"You will know. But you must say *something* before it is too late and your friendship cannot be mended. Do not make my mistake."

Jessie burst through the door, all brightness and joy. "Can I help?"

Lena brushed at her tears with the back of her hand and managed a strained smile. "Of course you can. I've probably burned the cocoa."

CHAPTER 21

A WAKE, staring at the beams overhead, Lena suffered wave after wave of painful remorse. If only she could be physically sick and purge herself of this feeling of vileness. Jessie's hair tickling her neck was just another reminder of her shortcomings. Jessie had never made assumptions, or at least hadn't allowed them to dictate her actions.

At least she hadn't given voice to her ugly thoughts. But Ely knew. Somehow, he'd surmised from Lena's behavior what her black heart had held against Evan. And if Ely knew, then Evan might have arrived at the same conclusion. Rolling to her side, she buried her face in her pillow and groaned. All the while he was demonstrating true charity, she was thinking him a brute, capable of casting aside his own child.

"If I have a little girl, I think I'll name her Alena Rowena," Jessie said softly.

Lena rolled over. Jessie lay there smiling at her, gathering the freckles on her cheeks in a bunch as they so often did. "You're awake!"

"And so are you," Jessie observed. "I heard you groan just now and you've been tossing like a ship on the sea. That's poetic, isn't it? Guess *Ivanhoe* is rubbing off on me."

Lena couldn't help but smile even in the midst of her anguished thoughts.

"What do you think of the name?" Jessie asked.

"Alena Rowena? It does have a nice rhythm to it. I like it. But what if you have a little boy?"

"Well it won't be Ivanhoe. That just sounds silly. Ivanhoe Long. No! Definitely not!"

"You could call him Cedric," Lena offered.

Jessie rolled onto her back, looking thoughtful. "No. But I think Evan sounds nice. Evan Long."

"Too short. How will you let him know how much trouble he's in if you call out, 'Evan Long, come here this instant!'"

Jessie laughed and threw herself onto her side, propping her head on one hand. "So, now that Bart and I have made the decision, how about you and Evan? We could make it a double wedding!"

Lena groaned again, pulling the pillow over her face. "You're hopeless."

"What's wrong? You're acting very strange, Lena."

Lena pulled the pillow from her face. "Am I a terrible person?" It was a ridiculous question, and she knew it as soon as she'd given voice to it. Who would answer, yes, to such a question, even if it were true?

"Silly, of course not!" Jessie poked her in the arm. "Why would you think that?"

Lena longed to make Jessie into a priest so she could confess her black heart.

"I definitely think that Evan doesn't hold that opinion of you." Jessie poked her again.

Lena sat up and swung her feet to the cold floor. "I need to cook something!"

"Now?" Jessie sat up, clutching the quilt to her neck. "It's surely after midnight!"

"I'm going to make you a cake for your wedding. We have plenty of flour, sugar and even enough eggs. You go back to bed and dream nice dreams of Bart and Baby Rowena."

"Baby *Alena* Rowena." Jessie corrected, slipping back beneath the covers.

As she entered the darkened kitchen, streams of moonlight flowing through the bank of windows reflected off the polished planks of the dining table. She stood in the dark, looking out upon the shadowed landscape. For the first time, the view did not thrill her as it once had, and the looming presence of the house around her felt less welcoming. She lit two lamps and set them on the wide windowsill, their light magnified by the glass window, pushing back the shadows. Pulling *Mrs. Parloa's New Cookbook* from the shelf, she began to leaf through it.

It felt good to do something. Doing was always preferable to worrying. But as much as she concentrated on devising a cake she'd never made before, thoughts continued to creep into the corners of her conscious mind. She rehearsed a hundred apologies, imagined his response, and dismissed them all. The problem, she realized, was that she'd never actually accused him of anything. How would she bring up the subject without making things worse? Maybe she could just change her attitude and be kind to him again.

The eastern sky brightened, bringing the forested ridge line into silhouette. Lena had succumbed to fatigue. Evan found her slumped at the table, head resting on her arm. Smiling, he watched her for a few moments, grabbed a biscuit from the tin and slipped out the back door without waking her.

An hour passed before Jessie appeared. Standing with hands on her hips, she kicked Lena's toe, startling her awake.

"What?" Lena blinked hard and wiped drool from the corner of her mouth. She focused on Jessie's face. "What time is it?"

"Time we were making breakfast for the men." Jessie continued to stare at her with a distinct look of disapproval. "You've been down here all night?"

Lena stretched her back and groaned a little, rubbing her neck. "I have. Look in the pantry."

Jessie crossed to the pantry, letting out a squeal of joy as she saw the cake, two layers high, sitting on the shelf. "Oh, it's sweet! Lena, you're a dear!"

"I thought we could decorate it today. Together. I found a recipe and instructions for making sugared flowers." Lena yawned. Shuffling to the stove, she retrieved the kettle.

Looking out the window and seeing the line where sunlight bathed the mountain brought her fully awake. It was later than she'd thought. She threw a quick glance at the wall clock, confirming the lateness of the hour. "Oh my! We need to be quick about breakfast today. The men will be in shortly."

Jessie began taking pans from the cupboard, "Well, we'll be one less for breakfast. I saw Evan ride out early."

Lena looked over sharply, started to form a question, then stopped herself. Flour covered her hands as she stood staring down at the snow-like surface of the counter. She did not look forward to a day of rehearsing apologies as she had throughout the night. Waiting only prolonged her anxiety.

For the remainder of the day, Lena busied herself with cleaning the main room to make it spotless for the wedding the next day. Together the women spent the morning decorating the cake, experimenting with the icing recipes and techniques. The laughter and camaraderie helped to quiet Lena's overactive mind for a while.

After sharing a lunch of cold ham and their dwindling supply of cheese, Lena led Jessie upstairs. Jessie sat on the bed brushing her hair while Lena rummaged through one of her trunks. With a satisfied sigh, she pulled out a lace-trimmed veil. Jessie slapped her hands over her mouth, a little exclamation of surprise slipped out between her fingers.

Lena held it up. "It was my mother's. I'd never have purchased anything so elegant for my own wedding, such as it was to be. Somehow it would have seemed frivolous, but I brought this with me. Sentimental reasons, I suppose." She looked over at Jessie's youthful face, glowing with hope and promises. "I'd be so pleased if you wear it for your wedding, but only if you wish to."

Jessie took the veil in her hands and lay it on the bed beside her. With gentle strokes, she traced the delicate weavings of lace along the border. She looked up with glistening eyes, then leaped to her feet, throwing her arms around Lena. "Oh, Lena! I'm going to miss you so much!"

Lena pressed into the girl's embrace, feeling unworthy of her affection. "I'm so happy for you, Jessie."

Jessie pulled away, reaching for the veil and holding it to her breast. "I'm happy for me too!" She skipped to the dusty mirror and placed the veil over her golden tresses. "Who'd have thought, Jessie Leach would ever find such a match!" There was a tone of pride in her voice as well as awe.

"Bart is a wonderful young man, and it's so clear that he loves you. I think it was very sensible of you to wait and get to know each other first." Lena perched at the end of the bed, watching Jessie adjust the veil over her brow to allow a curl or two to peek out from beneath the beaded headpiece. "So does this mean you like the veil?"

Jessie turned to Lena, eyes shining. "I love it! Thank you, Lena. Do I look like a bride now?"

"Jessie, I've never seen a more beautiful one in my life!" Lena reached up and pulled the edge of the veil over the girl's shoulder. Her voice softened, and she whispered, "Truly, Jessie."

By late afternoon, the windows sparkled, the polished floors reflecting all the added sunlight. Lena and Jessie put their heads together and planned a simple meal for the wedding day. Since both, thinking quite practically, knew their efforts would only be to please themselves they'd decided against any fancy recipes from Mrs. Parloa. They planned to enjoy the day somewhere other than in the kitchen. So, they'd invested their time this afternoon in preparing everything for the following day.

All the while Lena busied herself cutting meats and baking fresh bread for tomorrow's sandwich plates, she kept watching the trail leading out from town. As soon as possible, maybe even before Evan had come into the house, she wanted to be rid of this weight on her heart, one way or the other. Nothing would spoil Jessie's wedding day.

Shadows stretched long across the brown grasses. Lena near to the point of biting her nails, a mortal sin where her previous employer was concerned, collapsed on the front porch bench. As anxious as she was to speak with him, her fatigue and loss of sleep from the previous night overtook her. In mere moments, her head sagged onto her chest and her body slumped against the side of the chair.

What awakened her was the squeal emitted from Jessie's lips as she bounded quite noisily out the front door and down the steps. Rubbing sleep from her eyes and attempting to pull them into focus, Lena followed Jessie's trajectory across the lawn to where Evan stood holding a petite mare by her halter.

"Oh, it's the little bay from the livery!" Jessie cried as she ran up to Evan. "She looks so much like my dear little Sugar."

Evan's grin spread ear to ear. "I know. Bart told me."

"Is she yours?" With her face buried in the little mare's mane, her words muffled.

"Nope."

Jessie declared with utmost confidence. "Oh, why forever not! You should buy her straight out! She'd be a good addition to your breeding stock. I feel certain,"

Lena watched from the edge of the porch, noting the suspicious grin on Evan's face.

"Well, I'm not sure the owner would sell her to me, that's why."

Lena detected the mischievous glint in his eye.

Jessie pouted. "That's a shame. Look how sturdy she is! My grandpa would have invested in her. He knew good horse stock when he saw it."

"Well, I'm sure you're right. But I still don't think I could convince the owner to part with her. Shame, I guess."

Evan's poorly restrained grin exploded into an open-mouthed laugh before he offered the reins to Jessie. The girl looked up, a puzzled expression written on every feature.

"She's yours, Jessie! Here, take her for a walk."

Jessie's eyes went wide. "Mine?"

"She's my wedding gift to you."

Lena felt oddly isolated in that moment. This was not the first time she'd stood apart from Evan and the recipient of his affections, watching from afar, on the outside looking into the heart of the man. Twice she'd seen his actions for what they were, honest compassion expressed with deeds not words. Once she'd wrongly judged him. Today she couldn't.

"Evan! Are you serious? Mine?" First Jessie threw her arms around Evan's neck in that natural way she had of expressing herself so freely without concern for social propriety. The next she was hugging the mare with equal enthusiasm. "Oh, you dear thing! You dear sweet thing!" She glanced back over her shoulder at Evan. "What's her name?"

"Well, there's one we call her, but I suppose you could name her whatever you want," Evan drawled.

Jessie took a step back, then looked back at Lena, motioning her to come down the steps. "Come Lena! Come see her. Can you believe it?" She grabbed Evan's arm again, shaking it. "You dear man! Thank you!"

"She's a tiny little mare, isn't she? She seems just perfect for you." Lena approached the mare and Jessie with slow steps, reluctant of encroaching on Evan's enjoyment of Jessie's delight.

"Oh, she is! What do you think I should name her, Lena?"

"Well," her eyes shifted for a moment to catch Evan's quiet face. A heartbeat later, she said, "Well, if your first baby girl will be named for Rowena, your little mare could be Becky, I suppose."

Grabbing Lena's arm, she said, "For both books!" She threw her arms about the mare's neck a second time. "Yes! Becky! I'm going to walk with her a little. We girls need to have a talk." She led the mare along the creek behind the house, leaving Evan and Lena alone.

"Does Bart know of your gift?" Lena asked, for lack of anything else to say.

Evan kept his eyes on Jessie and her new mare until they disappeared around the house. "Yes. I asked him if he thought she'd like the mare." He turned back to face her, the smile gone from his face. "He's at the livery, picking out a saddle."

"I suppose you helped with the purchase of that too?" She recognized the tone of sarcasm in her voice and hated it. Resentment? Was she jealous? Of Jessie for being worthy of the gift or Evan for his generosity to give it?

Evan watched her in that quiet way she was growing to understand as his habit when thinking. She paled at its intensity, the appraisal within it. Or was she simply projecting on him her personal habit of judging people's thoughts and actions so harshly? She felt wretched.

"Yes. Bart and I have been friends for a bit. Gave the saddle to him. Seemed a nice thing to do."

Of course, it was. The remorse of the past twenty-four hours came rushing back, pulling her conscience back to where Ely had left her last night. Speak to him, he'd said. But how? She opened her mouth but none of the rehearsed words came to her tongue. Her mouth went desert dry, throat constricted.

"Well, I think I should go down and settle up with the livery owner. Seems she's happy with the girl." He started down the road to town in his natural ambling gait.

"Mr. Hartmann. Evan." Lena heard her voice as something apart from herself.

Evan turned.

"I've been wanting to talk to you." She blinked, praying for some measure of intelligibility, her mind so befuddled as it was couldn't possibly form a sentence.

"Okay. I'm listening." He folded his arms in front of him, looking formidable and unapproachable.

She took a calming breath, shoving her hands into the pockets of her skirt. "I... made a terrible assumption a few days ago." She couldn't help herself from studying his eyes, hoping to see some encouragement there. Nothing. She tried again. "The young woman, Vicki. She's a sweet girl."

"Yes, she is," Evan said, his expression still flat.

"Her child seemed a dear thing as well." Lena knew she was stalling, searching for the right way to express her humiliation.

"She looked a lot like her father," Evan said steadily.

Lena felt her chest tighten. Was he helping her? It would be like him, she thought. Wasn't that what Ely had said about him? He liked to help those in need. Was he seeing her need just now, to be understood, to confess her lack of charity?

"Evan, I judged you without knowing the truth." Each word that she uttered seemed to lift weight from her soul, even though she knew he must surely hate her for them. She wanted to be rid of this awful feeling of guilt. The next four words came more easily than she'd expected. "I am so sorry."

Daring then to meet his gaze, she saw a flicker of expression breaking through the mask. She couldn't read it as much as she tried.

Evan nodded then. "Thought it might be so."

Oh, how she longed in that moment for him to smile on her, to pour out that compassion she'd seen him spill out so generously on others. "Will you—can you find it in your heart to forgive me?"

His gaze shifted, barely imperceptible, to her feet and back to her face, as though taking all of her into account. She felt she'd been weighed and found wanting. The next words he spoke were unexpected and painful beyond what she felt she could bear.

"'... trial moves rapidly on when the judge has determined the sentence beforehand.'"

She recognized the sentence at once. It was from *Ivanhoe* and it was aptly spoken. She was guilty of trying him and she had set herself as judge as though she were Lady Justice herself. And Evan, having studied the law, knew the ugliness of her crime. She had not presumed his innocence as the law would require. She felt her stomach sour.

The compassion in the man must have known the sincerity of her apology. He took a step toward her, his hand reaching out to steady her.

Lena wanted to run, but her feet felt encased in ice. He touched her elbow, his hand supporting her, *encouraging* her. Was he forgiving her?

He took one step closer, until she could see the small lines at the edges of his lips and the deeper ones around his eyes, testifying to the many smiles that had carved them there. His presence enveloped her. "I can forgive because I've been forgiven. Can you forgive me for my arrogance? The way I bullied you when you first arrived and assumed you hadn't given any thought to your choice to stay here?"

Lena's lips parted, but she was too startled to speak. He was asking *her* forgiveness?

He continued, "I thought your decision was made thoughtlessly and out of pride. But I was wrong. Ely corrected me on that point, but I never apologized." He took one step closer until she could feel the warmth of his breath on her cheek. "Can you forgive me?"

She felt as though something had pushed the air from her lungs.

Misunderstanding her silence, he said, "I'll give you some time to think on it."

He gave her then the gift she'd envied, his smile of compassion. But there was something subtly different about it, something deeper. The warmth of it made her forget the coolness of the approaching night. And then he turned, the warmth swept away with him as though a shadow had passed in front of the sun, blocking its rays.

As he strode down the hill, he called back over his shoulder, "I'll be back for dinner." His tone was bright and light. With a sudden revelation, she knew that he'd not only forgiven her, he'd forgotten the offense.

CHAPTER 22

FOR the second night in a row, Lena couldn't sleep. Instead, she found herself creating math problems from the beams in the ceiling. Multiplying the number of beams by two, then dividing them by fours and fives. While it didn't change the number, she'd counted each sleepless night, it kept her mind from wandering too far to places she didn't wish it to go.

Somewhere between the time Jessie's quiet snores had commenced and the crowing of the solitary rooster, she fell into a restless sleep. Six hours later, Jessie shook her the rest of the way to full consciousness, her face alight with anticipation for this, her special day.

"Wake up, sleepy head! It's my wedding day!" She announced it as though she hadn't been proclaiming it with the regularity of a grandfather clock all the previous day.

Lena stared up into Jessie's face, deadpanning a lack of comprehension. "Wedding day? Is someone getting married?"

"Oh, Lena!" Jessie slammed her pillow on Lena's face and leaped from bed, obviously heedless of the cold floor beneath her bare feet. "What do I do first?"

"We could maybe sleep another hour." Lena teased, while keeping the covers close about her neck. Only a blush of pink peeked above the eastern hills.

"I couldn't possibly sleep." She hugged herself and spun on her toes, curls flying about her head like a golden halo. She let her wild spin carry her onto the bed, tumbling next to Lena. "Do you think Bart's awake this early?" She brought her hand to her mouth, giggling. "I'll know tomorrow, won't I?" Lena couldn't help but laugh with her, the infectious nature of her joy could not be fought off.

Lena rolled over to regard her dear friend—how brief their acquaintance and yet how deep was their bond. "Jessie, don't ever change. No matter what happens. Don't change, ever."

Jessie tossed her head to the side, meeting Lena's gaze. "Oh, I don't think I can promise that. Everybody changes. You know that. You've changed."

"How? You've only known me a few weeks. Surely, I'm not that different."

"You are, though. You're far less stiff and proper. You used to never walk around barefoot, even here in the bedroom. You don't even wear your corset every day like you used to do. And you laugh more. And you're really funny when you want to be." She appeared to be warming to the topic of Lena, The Transformed. "And you don't get so angry with yourself about burning the biscuits or leaving the clothes too long on the line when the dust blows up, or letting the stove fire burn too low."

Lena wondered at that. She didn't feel any closer to being like Jessie with her kind heart and generous nature. And she certainly wasn't any younger or more attractive than when she'd arrived.

"But *you're* perfect, just as you are. You don't need to change," Lena said, her tone serious.

Jessie sat up abruptly, sniffing the air. "Do you smell that? Someone's cooking bacon! Why that wonderful man! Bart is making us a wedding breakfast!" She leaped from the bed for the second time, quickly pulling on her skirt and blouse. "Come on, Lena!"

With a little less enthusiasm, Lena pulled herself from beneath the covers and made the bed, pulling on her clothes well after Jessie had bounced out of the door. She tidied the room, putting a few of her personal items into a small leather satchel she used for her trip west. Tonight, this cozy bedroom would become a honeymoon suite for Bart and Jessie, and nothing Jessie said in protest could change her mind. Bart's room would be just fine for her until the couple left later in the week.

When Lena arrived in the kitchen a short time later, she was surprised by the presence of not only Bart but Ely and Evan working at preparing a much larger breakfast than either Jessie or Lena had planned. She stood in the doorway, feeling a bit awkward until Evan greeted her in that easy way of his and invited her to slice some potatoes for frying. With the multitude of hands at work, breakfast was prepared in short order. By the time Carrick and Donal walked in, the table was groaning under the weight of a lavish breakfast of fried potatoes, ham, bacon, eggs (in lesser supply), and rolls, generously sprinkled with sugar and cinnamon.

In far less time than it took them all to prepare it, the feast was dispatched. Evan groaned as he pushed his plate away from him. "Don't let me eat another bite until tomorrow."

Ely helped himself to another cup of coffee and asked, "So when is this wedding to commence? I'm ready."

Carrick and Donal said nearly in unison, "So are we!"

Jessie laughed. "Well, that's fine for you all, but some of us have some change of clothing to perform."

Lena added, "And there are the dishes to which we must attend."

Evan rose to his full height and stretched his arms above his head. "Well, that sounds like something I might be able to handle." He looked quite intentionally across the table at Lena. "That is, if you could use the help."

Trying to hide her surprise, she smiled hesitantly. "Of course, I'd welcome your help."

Jessie giggled. "So formal, you two."

Without a reply to her jibe, Evan began to collect dishes from the table and carry piles to the sink. Lena scrambled to her feet and heated water for washing while Carrick and Donal left the house to take care of outdoor chores. They were still refining their chicken coop construction, more often arguing than working out their design flaws. Ely retreated upstairs to work on his wedding speech. Bart walked down the hill with Jessie to check in on her new mare, Becky. That left Lena and Evan alone in the kitchen.

While Evan seemed as pleasant as he had been before their misunderstanding, Lena felt something had changed. The kindness he showed her seemed impersonal. She could have been anyone, a street urchin, an ailing widow, a penniless girl. He was kind because it was his nature to be kind, not because of any quality she exhibited or he desired. That realization was almost as painful as the idea that he might never forgive her.

The table was cleared, and the dishes stacked by the time the water was heated. She began to pour steaming water into the bowl they used for washing, but her hands were trembling again and the boiling water splashed onto her hand. She yelped in pain, dropping the kettle in the sink.

Evan immediately grabbed her injured hand and placed it in the rinse bucket of cool water. Lena blinked back tears, from both pain and embarrassment at her clumsiness. She tried to pull away from his grip, but he held her hand firmly under the water.

"You need to keep your hand there for a while. That could be a nasty burn and it might blister if you don't cool the skin," he said in that calm manner that defined him.

Lena grimaced at the throb in her hand, nerve endings screaming in protest. But as his closeness overrode the urgency of her pain, she felt her body relax against him. His arms wrapped around her. Both his hands gripping her wrist firmly as he held the injured hand beneath the water.

His chest pressed against her back, she detected a change in the rhythm of his breathing, a quickening. His breath tickled her neck, sending a shiver along her collarbone. Her heart fluttered wildly. Surely, he must have heard it, felt it. For a moment, she felt she was falling, but there was no fear of the sensation, only wonder. Then he stepped back as he released her hand, taking with him the warmth as he had once before.

She remained as she'd been, her back to him, afraid he'd see the effect he'd had on her. At last, his voice oddly husky, he said, "You'd better see if you have some clean cloths to wrap your hand. Go on upstairs, I'll finish here."

Once the door was closed behind her, she fled up the stairs to the bedroom. Closing the door to her room, she stood with her back to it, tears streaming down her cheeks, falling onto her blouse and skin. She moved to the window as if wading through water. A brisk wind blew back the curtains, and she took in deep, gasping breaths as though she'd been drowning.

Surely love didn't feel like this—this terrifying suffocation. If this was love, she wanted nothing to do with it—this agony of heart and body. This did not match with any poems of love she'd ever read. Those poets lived for this? How could someone want something that tore at their insides this way?

Her mind raced against her heart as she struggled to make sense of her feelings, to find a rational explanation for what had just happened. Her reason told her in a clarion voice that his actions were a natural response of his compassionate character. He'd seen her in need and rushed to assist her; nothing more had happened. The rest was her own jumbled emotions twisted by lack of sleep.

And yet... Could he feel something more for her? Her frantic mind looped back on itself, refusing to be disassociated from her heart. She laid out all the facts like numbers in her ledger. Struggling to comprehend the full picture, she tried to look at them dispassionately. But how could she? This heart-pounding, gut-wrenching emotion could not be sorted out by reason. Reason had betrayed her the moment he touched her.

Even as she recalled the rhythm of his heart and warmth of his breath on her neck, her voice mocked her. She was looking in a mirror reflecting a face of arrogance and hypocrisy. She wasn't Jessie, with a heart for everyone. She wasn't Vicki, who'd dared to love even after being so wounded by life. It hurt, oh, how it hurt to view herself as someone so unworthy of love such as she desired from a man such as Evan Hartmann.

Throwing herself onto the bed, she covered her face and wept.

For the third time in a row, Jessie awakened her. She felt a hand on her shoulder, gently shaking her, a dip in the bed as someone sat. "Lena? Are you all right? Evan said you injured your hand. Let me see it."

Lena sat up, stiff from muscles tensed for too long. Her eyes felt itchy and hot, her skin too tight.

Jessie took Lena's injured hand, cool fingers gently coaxing her blistered palm open, clucking at the angry burn like a mother hen. "Let me put some cream on it and wrap it up for you."

"It was a silly accident. I was careless..." Lena explained, her voice trailing off.

Jessie dipped a finger in a sharply herbal scented salve, dabbing it on Lena's palm. "What is it, Lena?"

"It's nothing. I'm just sad that you're leaving, that's all," she lied, poorly. She always had.

The younger woman tipped her head to one side, studying her. Lena dropped her head to avoid her eyes. "Lena, you aren't telling me the truth. I can see it as clear as I *can't* see myself in that mirror!" She tucked her hand beneath Lena's chin and lifted her face. "You're in love, aren't you?"

Too weary to turn away, Lena simply closed her eyes.

"It hurts, doesn't it? Love can be like that, you know. Or maybe you don't. Have you ever been in love, Lena?"

Lena pulled her face away from Jessie's hand. "I don't know. I liked a boy once in school." It sounded so childish.

Jessie shook her head. "That wasn't love. Does it feel like your insides are going to eat you up? Like you're starvin' and you can't find anything to fill up the ache?"

Lena turned her gaze back, searching Jessie's face for any sign of teasing. But she wasn't. Jessie knew. "Maybe a little. I know that whatever this is hurts worse than anything I've ever felt before."

Jessie smiled and drew her friend into her arms. "Lena, you love Evan. He's a fine man, worthy of a good woman's love."

Lena pulled back. "But that's the problem, isn't it? I'm not good enough for a man like him." Tears again. How could she have any more to cry?

"Lena, that's crazy talk! Why would you think that?"

"Because it's true."

Jessie shook her head, looking more like the mother-of-the-bride at that moment than the bride. "Do you love Evan?"

"I don't know. I haven't known him that long. We haven't talked that much. How could I?"

Jessie held Lena by both shoulders, like part of her wanted to give her a good shake. "Do you *love* him?"

"If it means, do I have trouble breathing when he's around, or have difficulty expressing a sensible thought, or can't sleep for thinking about him—then, yes, I guess I do."

"Why was that so hard?" Jessie asked, a smile pulling up the corners of her mouth.

"Because it's all so impossible."

"Stop that! You're tired and you aren't seeing things clearly. You love him and I think he loves you."

Lena closed her eyes, remembering his hands on hers. She remembered then that hers had not been the only hands trembling.

"Well, I'm glad we have that settled!" Jessie stood and walked to the chest of drawers, pulling out a simple cream-colored dress with lace at the neck and cuffs. She twirled, holding it in front of her, a smile, warm and lovely, decorating her honest face. "Help me get myself ready for a wedding?"

A little more than an hour later, Jessie walked down the stairs, dressed in cream and lace, the veil falling in graceful folds about her shoulders. Lena followed behind wearing a silk dress the color of a winter sky. Bart stood waiting at the bottom of the stairs, gripping a bouquet of yellow tufted grasses, a few sprigs of cascading golden birch boughs, and the last of the season's white yarrow. Jessie stopped at the last step, chin up. Bart, absolutely stupefied, stood gaping, bouquet threatening to spill apart in his slackening grip.

"I think you mean to give me those flowers, Bart."

Dreamlike, Bart drifted forward, flowers extended. Then, inexplicably, he drifted back to his original spot and resumed gaping.

"Bart, I think you mean to take my arm now."

Bart ghosted forward, offering the crook of his arm. Jessie hooked it and joined him on the ground floor. They stood, shoulder to shoulder, unmoving. Lena could hear the clock ticking in the kitchen.

"I think you mean to marry me now, Bartholomew Long."

Brief though it was, Lena had never witnessed a wedding so beautiful, nor so true, as that of Bartholomew Long and Jessica Leach, held in the bright main room of the last boarding house in Sawtooth City. Their wedding procession took them down one short hallway, serenaded by a single violin played by their unofficial officiate. The brothers stood like soldiers at attention in front of the hearth, both exceptionally well scrubbed. Ely waited for them at the end of the room, back to the windows, violin beneath his chin and an ancient fraying Bible beside him on the windowsill.

Evan met the 'procession' as they entered the room, falling in place a pace behind Bart, even with Lena. The four stopped before Ely, the afternoon sunlight flooding through those wide windows. No stained glass or marbled cathedral could have compared to the subalpine backdrop for this humble mountain ceremony.

When Ely passed his violin to Carrick and took up his Bible to speak his piece, Lena could have sworn she saw a corona of gold glint across the couples' heads. Jessie stood with her simple bouquet in one hand, her other twined with

Bart's. They spoke their vows as if in a waking dream. Everyone's faces shone in their reflected joy. It was one of those rare, perfect moments.

And then, finally given permission to kiss his bride, Bart stalled.

Jessie gave his tie a little tug. "Mr. Long, I think you mean to kiss me."

Bart blinked, looked down, and gave his arm a vicious pinch. Upon finding himself indeed awake, he laced his fingers behind her head, tangled in her hair. "Mrs. Long, I mean to kiss you an *awful* lot."

And he did.

With the chairs pushed back, and the floor opened, it would have been impossible to resist the call of a dance. Ely removed his jacket and began a tune, more familiar to the dance halls than the concert halls of Europe. Because there were only two women to make partners for the men, Lena and Jessie were soon perspiring despite the cooler temperatures. Carrick and Donal were exuberant dancers, seemingly more at ease dancing solo than with a partner, but both women persevered and did their best to keep up with the pace of the Irish brothers.

Mercifully, Ely slowed his pace, allowing the women to catch their breath. Bart approached his new wife, looking almost shy, and danced her around the room while their friends looked on. Lena rested at the side of the room, sitting on the arm of her favorite chair, watching them glide about in a circle, unconcerned about those watching them. They were in a world apart.

So entranced by the sight of these two people at such a moment of beginnings, she didn't hear Evan's approach. He gently touched her shoulder, and she turned. Without a word, he extended his hand to her, and she took it, bandaged as it was. "Maybe we both ought to try our off hands. It'll make it interesting." They switched hands before he led her into the open space with her good hand held firmly in his.

In one smooth movement, he pulled her into the dance. His hand at her waist held her firmly so that no step came unanticipated, turning her in perfect unison with his own steps. She had danced before but never like this, as though she and her partner were one entity, not two. In mere moments, she became a part of the dance, the music, the joy, the hope. She was an extension of him as he was of her. As the tempo quickened, Evan pulled her closer, giving her no opportunity to stumble.

Too soon, it was over. He held her for just a moment longer than necessary, and then stepped back, smiling with those emerald eyes. She had no idea in that moment if she were smiling or simply staring up at him. Heedless of this magic, Jessie broke the spell by calling out to the men, "It's time for cake!"

For the remainder of the afternoon, while the others talked of ordinary things and plans for the future, Lena could think of little else than this puzzle that was love. She joined in the conversations from time-to-time but found herself awkward where once she had been the one to lead their discussions and draw out their ideas and thoughts. And at all times, she was aware of Evan's presence, noticing details about his mannerisms and small habits, the way he pulled at his eyebrow when he was thinking, and the way he laughed with his head tossed back, the lock of black hair that persisted in falling over his left eye.

As evening approached, Lena accompanied Jessie upstairs to pick up her bag of clothing. She kissed Jessie lightly on the cheek and closed the door softly behind her. At the bottom of the stairs, Lena found Evan standing quietly waiting for her. Without a word he took her bag from her hand. He stopped outside Bart's room and took a quick look inside, then turned back to her, pulling the door closed behind him. "I think you might be more comfortable in my room. I don't like to be critical of a person's personal habits, but, well, let's just say Jessie has her work cut out for her. I might not be much better, but at least I do my laundry regularly." He let out that laugh which seemed to travel up from his feet.

"Are you quite sure? I don't want to put you to any trouble," Lena said, feeling suddenly shy with him.

"Just give me a minute to clear out my things and make sure it's respectable enough for a lady."

He put down her bag and opened the door to his room at the end of the hall. She could hear him rummaging through drawers before he emerged a few minutes later with his clothes tucked up under one arm. He picked up her bag with the other and took it inside for her. "It's a bit bigger than Bart's room. I think Nash intended two men to bunk here."

There were windows on two walls, making the room feel larger than it really was. And she could see that he was right in saying he was a neater person in his habits. Counters were free of clutter. The bed was neatly made, and no clothes lay scattered about. She knew that he couldn't have cleaned this much in the few minutes he'd taken in the room.

"This will be quite nice, thank you, Evan. You can have your room back this weekend." Saying it made her feel that wave of sadness roll over her again. Jessie would be gone within the week.

"It will be hard on you," Evan said. There was that compassion again, coloring his voice and eyes. But this time she felt that perhaps they were really meant for *her*.

"I think we will all miss them."

"Hmm." Still holding his clothes in a crumpled bundle, he leaned against the doorpost, looking boyish and awkward.

"Well, thank you, again." Lena clasped her hands before her, unwilling to meet his gaze. "It was a lovely wedding."

"Yes."

He remained in the doorway making it impossible for her to close the door. She brought her hand to her throat to touch the brooch.

He took a step back into the room, lay his hand against her cheek and brushed the top of her head with a kiss. "Goodnight, Lena."

He turned and closed the door behind him.

Lena remained there, looking at the closed door. A long moment passed with more sensations than reasoned thoughts vibrating through her body, before she whispered, "Goodnight, Evan."

CHAPTER 23

THE next two days flew by for Lena and all too quickly she was forced to say goodbye to Jessie and Bart. There were hugs given as they cleaned up breakfast dishes, hugs as they stepped from the house for the last time, tearful hugs as Jessie mounted up on her sweet Becky, and the final waves as the newlyweds followed their traveling companions' wagons out of town.

Walking back to the house with Ely, they talked of unimportant matters, a conversation of distraction from those things that weighed most heavily on their hearts. Upon reaching the porch steps, Lena hesitated, her throat tight as she looked up at the massive log pillars and well-crafted doors and windows, remembering seeing it for the first time with Jessie by her side. The young woman had imbued her with courage to enter that door.

Ely turned on the top step, looking back on her with a quizzical expression. "Did you forget something, Lena?"

"No. I was remembering something. I was remembering why I came here; what I wanted." Thin rays of November sun stretching out from the eastern range, warmed her face and the land for perhaps the last time before the winter staked its claim. She didn't know what those grey clouds, hanging dark and heavy over the peaks, meant for her future, but she knew she must hold on to Jessie's optimism and courage. Jessie had said she was changed. Perhaps what awaited her would change her yet again. She hoped it to be true.

That night as the men sat around the table, the two empty seats suppressed their mood and inclination to talk. With the dishes cleaned and put away, Lena couldn't bring herself to sit by the fire as had become her custom. Instead, she pulled Nash's bulky winter coat from the hook and left the familiar hearth to stand on the porch. The air had a bitter edge. She pulled the collar up and shoved her hands into her pockets.

She wandered to the chicken coop where the hens had gone to roost hours earlier. At the sound of her footsteps, a few hens warbled at her, bringing their heads out from under wing. She bent to look in on them, perched on Carrick's roosting sticks. She tried imitating their contented trills, watching their bright black eyes winking at her.

"That's not half bad, you know." She straightened and spun around, seeing Evan smiling at her from the porch. "Did they answer?"

"I was waiting to hear if they did. I think you interrupted them."

"Looks like the boys did a good job on the coop. Ingenious design. Don't think I've ever seen one quite like it before. Did they split logs for that thing?"

Lena looked back at the rambling chicken house and the run that stretched nearly the width of the house. "I think they might have become a bit carried away with their project."

He chuckled, "I've seen cattle barns less sturdy. You could shelter goats in there if you wanted. They'd give you milk next spring too."

"Hmm, that might be a very good idea."

He strolled around the corner of the porch and settled himself on the long bench that afforded the best view of the valley and river. He slid to the side, allowing her plenty of space to sit beside him. She hesitated for just a moment before joining him, pulling her skirts close to her legs, shielding them from the biting air.

They sat in silence for some time, their breaths coming in small puffs like the smokestacks of the steam engines that had brought her west. How far she had come! Staring out into the descending darkness, she began to notice drifting white flakes, visible in contrast to the pines. "It's snowing!"

"Seems so."

A little knot tied itself up in her stomach. "How long will it take them to get to Ketchum? Do you think they are there yet?"

He must have heard the concern in her voice. "Oh, I would expect they're pretty close to it if they aren't already there."

"You don't think the snow could have blocked the pass?"

"I wouldn't worry, Lena. The worst part of the trip is closer to this end of the trail. Remember coming over the summit just past Galena?"

She shivered remembering the precipitous drop along that portion of the route. "I do. In the fall, I thought it lovely. I wouldn't want to see it now."

He smiled. "Probably not. But they should have been well past that before this snow moved in. Bart's pretty savvy about traveling up here. That's why he encouraged the other families to move out today instead of later in the week as they'd originally planned. He'll take good care of Jessie."

His easy speech and relaxed manner gave her assurances she needed, and she breathed a sigh. She decided to enjoy the beauty of the snowfall rather than worry. "This is a beautiful snow. I've seen at least three different types since I've arrived. But these cotton ball flakes are my favorite. Will there be much of it by morning?"

"Not likely. This is a passing storm, hardly a storm at all. Just rain that got a bit uppity."

He had that silly little half-smile on his face. Unlike Bart, Evan's jokes rarely elicited laughs, but he continued to try all the same. She liked that quality.

"Uppity snow?" Lena said flatly.

"You know what I mean." He looked disappointed. "Rain turns to snow when it's cold enough."

She continued to stare at him, feigning incomprehension.

"Snow is prettier than rain. Can't you imagine rain wanting to be admired like snow?"

The more he tried to explain his poetic imagery, the more ridiculous it sounded and the more humorous. She couldn't restrain her amusement any longer and burst out laughing.

"Well, I'm sorry if I'm not Sir Walter Scott." He attempted to adopt an insulted expression, but the smile lurked just at the corner of his eyes.

"Uppity snow?" Lena covered her mouth as she broke out in another bout of laughter.

"I think it was humorous," Evan said.

"Oh, it was! It most assuredly was!" Her laughter dissolved into a hiccup, then another, followed by another.

"What's going on? The house is like a tomb tonight without Jessie and Bart. If you two have found something amusing, I think we'd all enjoy knowing of it." Ely peered out an open kitchen window.

"Oh, it's nothing. Lena just insulted my sense of humor that's all."

Lena tried to say something but hiccupped loudly instead.

"If I didn't know better, Miss Sommer, I would suspect that you have been drinking strong spirits," Ely said.

"I...*hic!*.. .have not! But I *am* freezing out here." She jumped to her feet as another hiccup gripped her diaphragm. "I'll make some cocoa for everyone."

"We still haven't finished the chapter we started when Jessie and Bart made their marriage announcement. It's not too late. I'll read a chapter while you make the cocoa," Evan said.

"Only if you... *hic!*... read loud enough so that I can hear you in the kitchen." Lena led the way into the house as more snow began to fall.

"What are you yelling for?" Carrick asked after Evan had read a paragraph of *Ivanhoe*. "We aren't deaf, you know."

Lena stuck her head out of the kitchen, a wooden spoon in her hand about to drip chocolate on the floor. "He's reading so I can hear, Carrick. Let the man alone if you want some hot cocoa and leftover cake."

Donal leaned over to Carrick and whispered, "There's leftover cake? Did you know there was leftover cake?"

"She probably hid it knowing how much you eat."

Evan peered at them over the book with one raised eyebrow. "Are you two finished? May I continue now?"

"Oh, sure," Donal answered.

Late that evening, Lena peered out the window at the still falling snow. "This isn't a storm?"

Evan shook his head. "Not by a long shot. When it turns into a storm, you won't have to ask."

That knot in her stomach returned as she watched snow piling atop the wood cutting block and dusting the pine boughs nearby where light spilled out from the house illuminating the steps and closest trees.

Evan drew closer, looking through the window pane to her side. "But I suspect the creek will show some frozen edges tomorrow. Pretty soon there won't be much use in my going out to the claim. The ground will be hard as granite."

"That's difficult to imagine."

"But you lived in the Chicago. I'd have thought you would be used to such things as frozen ground and ponds."

"It's a little different in the city, and that's where I've lived most of my life. It's not the same, as you've pointed out to me on a number of occasions."

Evan looked thoughtful, then stepped back from the window. "I'll be leaving before breakfast in the morning. I have some work to do at the claim. Just wanted you to know."

"I could make something for you to take with you if you like," Lena said.

"Don't want to trouble you. I'll manage," he nodded to her and gifted her with a warm smile. "Goodnight, Lena."

"Goodnight, Evan."

After climbing into Nash's large bed, she was aware of just how cold the winter would be without Jessie beside her for added warmth. But she felt her absence in other ways as well. The two often talked for an hour or more until one or the other fell asleep. The absence of her chatter made the entire house seem colder than it had been when she was here. She wrapped the quilt tighter to her body, tucking in the edges under her legs.

Still, the day that had begun with such sadness, with farewells and tears, had ended with less of the despair she'd feared would overwhelm her. There was still companionship with the men of the house, discussions and laughter. She wasn't alone, not really. And there was still Evan. He truly seemed to have forgiven her.

Moonlight reflecting off the fallen snow cast a strange blue light upon the ceiling. The snow had stopped, the sky clear again. She tried to imagine Jessie and Bart, now settled into their temporary home in Hailey. She knew that Evan was right. Bart would take good care of her friend.

She would need to keep very busy. Despite what Evan had said about managing to find something to eat, Lena resolved to get up early and prepare something for him. She might even have time to pack a lunch. Maybe, she mused as her mind grew comfortably fuzzy at the edges, maybe she could coax a smile in exchange. She imagined that she could live quite happily on a steady diet of Evan's smiles.

As she began to drift off to sleep, she realized for one brief, lucid moment, that she was no longer cold.

CHAPTER 24

JESSIE and Bart had been gone for one week when a letter arrived at the boarding house carried by a young boy Lena recognized as one of those who made odd-job deliveries around town. Such a rare occasion as receiving any correspondence deserved her full attention, so she waited until she was seated at her desk to open it. The message was brief. Thomas Baxter, Mr. Nash's attorney, wished to meet with her at her earliest convenience.

Initially, she thought he might have received word from Nash's sister regarding her wishes for disposing of her brother's property. As she reread the letter, she felt more certain this was not the case or he might have referred to his desire to share good news with her. Good sense told her not to put off the requested appointment, so changing into her more business-like wool tweed suit, she started off to his offices that afternoon.

Mr. Baxter greeted her warmly at the door to his office, offering her tea and taking the time to make small talk concerning the weather. After giving her a chance to take at least a sip of her tea, he opened a small file on his desk. "Miss Sommer, you seem to have been managing the boarding house quite well for someone with limited experience in this business."

"Thank you, Mr. Baxter, I hope that I have. I've certainly endeavored to that end." She gripped her teacup to steady her hands.

"I wish that I could tell you that I've received communication from Mr. Nash's sister, but that is not the case. Honestly, I would have been surprised to have heard from her so soon. I'm not sure..." He hesitated, fingering the papers in front of him for no apparent reason. "Miss Sommer, you must have heard the rumors concerning the mining company's financial difficulties. No doubt, you are aware of merchants selling their businesses and leaving our small community."

Keeping her countenance as placid as she could, Lena nodded and said, "Yes, Mr. Baxter. But I am attempting to provide lodging for those still employed. There are also rumors of Eastern investors who are willing to pump life back into the mines."

Baxter placed his hands upon the desk, lacing his fingers together. "Yes, I have heard those as well. The truth is, I must take all of this information and place it before Mr. Nash's sister and allow her to make an informed decision. I cannot in good conscience suggest that she keep the property. If the town continues to fail, in a very short amount of time the property will have little or no value. Likewise, I cannot, in good conscience advise you to attempt to complete this transaction as we discussed some weeks ago. Neither one of you will benefit."

Pulling her hands back into her lap and out of sight, she straightened her spine. "Mr. Baxter, when I came to you, I did not seek your counsel. I do not wish to be rude, but I do not do so now. Mr. Nash and I corresponded for many months and in those letters he explained to me the risks of operating a business in a boom town. He also detailed his reasons to believe that this type of business could outlast many others. He believed that this unique area will one day draw visitors who are attracted to the vistas only found here as does Yellowstone."

"But Miss Sommer, such events could be years away. One must employ lobbyists in Washington and have roads that make it easy for people to come here, advertisements."

She could hear the near pleading tone in his voice, but she persisted. "I want to try, Mr. Baxter. And I cannot see how my staying here will not be preferable to Miss Nash than having the property simply fall into decay."

"But there are men who would pay for the lumber in the building, and if we were to sell the property this spring she might recover some of her brother's investment before the elements destroy it."

Lena sat back in her chair, calculating, reconstructing her carefully thought out plans. Mr. Baxter rose from his chair and walked around the desk to stand before her. "Miss Sommer, I just don't think you see the problems clearly. I know it's difficult to give up a dream."

"If I were to give you something as a down-payment, would that help?"

"Have you heard what I've said?" He sounded weary.

"Yes. Would you try to convince Miss Nash to wait until spring and give me the time to come up with what she feels would be fair payment?"

He shook his head. "I just don't think..."

Lena took off her glove and brought her hand to her throat. Unfastening the silver brooch, she looked at it for only a moment before extending it to Baxter. "I know this isn't much, but it is solid silver and the stone is a genuine ruby. I was told it was valuable. It may have more sentimental value than monetary, but it is the best I can do at the moment. If I cannot pay the remainder come spring, I'll go."

"This is really that important to you?"

"Yes."

He looked at her for a moment longer, a heavy sigh and then, "The other reason that I needed to see you so quickly is that my wife and I are leaving in a few days to spend the winter in Hailey. She's had enough of freezing temperatures. I was hoping to convince you to travel with us, but it's obvious that you've made up your mind to see it through." Looking at the brooch in his hand once again, he said, "I'll ask Miss Nash. Since in a few weeks it will be difficult to get word to you or anyone up here, you probably won't hear from me until spring. So, feel free to stay in the house and I wish you the best. It won't be easy."

"I know. I've been warned many times." She gave him a wry smile as she rose to her feet. "Seems everyone is quite knowledgeable on the subject of weather."

He took her hand lightly in his, his face suddenly solemn. "It is not a thing to take lightly. Many have done so and have suffered terrible consequences as a result. I don't wish to frighten you, Miss Sommer, but look to the mountains and heed the warning signs. Lay in supplies." Then he led her to the door, holding it open for her. "You have a great deal of what my father would have called 'spunk', I hope you have the tenacity and perseverance to face this winter." He leaned forward, a hint of a smile peeking from beneath his mustache. "No pun intended."

Stepping into the hallway, she gripped his hands. "I will always be indebted to you for this opportunity."

He shook her hand, holding it for a moment more. "I hope I will not regret my decision and my sentiment does not turn out to your misfortune. Should you change your mind about staying, there are three families traveling south the day after tomorrow. I'm sure we could find room for you."

She nodded, while a tremor of doubt shivered down her legs. Meeting his eyes with a level gaze, she said, "Thank you, Mr. Baxter. I wish you safe travels. And I will see you in the spring."

Stepping from the building onto the main street of Sawtooth, she felt far less confident than she had just sounded upstairs in Baxter's office. But she squared her shoulders and lifted her chin. Out of nervous habit she brought her fingers to touch the brooch that was no longer there. The finality of her decision struck her, not just the surrendering of the brooch but her refusal to accept the man's offer to leave the mountains.

She pressed her lips together into a thin line. This was what it meant to be the captain of one's own ship, she supposed. Whether one was a ship captain or an inn keeper, the weather could always be an issue. Storms came into people's lives in a multitude of ways. If she must face a storm to become an independent woman then why shouldn't it be this one?

Lena wasted little time shedding her suit and putting on a sensible skirt and blouse, exchanging her more fashionable boots for the sturdy ones she'd purchased at the dry goods store. She glanced into the tarnished mirror and tucked her loosened strands of hair back into the bun at the nape of her neck. Leaning closer, she touched her cheek, squinting into the dusty reflection. "Lena, where has your ivory complexion gone? You look more like a weathered frontier woman with those ruddy, sun-burned cheeks." She shrugged and made a face at herself before heading downstairs to finish her morning chores.

Her normal chores, those she and Jessie had been doing together, seemed to take far longer, considering there were two less people to care for. Sharing the work as well as conversation had made the work almost inconsequential. The laundry seemed mountainous, and the evening meal preparations onerous.

Ely arrived home before the others. Donal and Carrick had worked their shift today, much to their relief and Lena's, while she knew that Evan was up in the hills working his claim while the weather permitted. He might not make it back to share the meal with them, but she'd be sure to keep his dinner warm, regardless.

Looking weary, eyes red, she assumed Ely had been studying figures all day in the mining office. "Ely, you look exhausted. Have a seat and I'll brew a fresh pot of tea."

Ely sank onto the bench closest to the wood stove. "Is difficult time, new reports requested every day. The bosses are pushing to send some out this week to the investors back east. How many ways can one figure the same numbers, I ask them. But every day, there seems to be something else they wish to include. Look at my fingers, Lena, they are as black as the bottom of your kettle." He lifted his right hand for her inspection.

She examined his ink stained fingers, clucking sympathetically. "I've made your favorite dried apple pie for dinner. Maybe that will lift your spirits."

"You spoil us, Lena. But I am not complaining. If I had been blessed with children, I would have hoped for a daughter to be as kind as you." He pulled his pipe from his jacket pocket along with his pouch of tobacco.

"Here you go." She poured hot tea into a porcelain cup and then into a second one for herself. "A restorative cup of tea always sets things to right!" She lifted her cup, blowing on the steam, her face suddenly thoughtful. "Was that Jane Austen who said that? I'm not sure, but I think it is a correct assessment."

"So, what did you do today, besides make a pie for your good friend and boarder, Ely?"

Her afternoon activities had successfully distracted her from the disturbing morning meeting with Mr. Baxter. "There are more chores to do now that Jessie isn't here to share them. I kept busy." Somehow, she wasn't sure she wanted to share how she'd defied the man's advice, stubbornly holding onto her original plan to stay. If she spoke of them, she might have to reconsider those plans, and that was not something she felt she could afford to do.

"I thought I saw you from the office window this morning. Were you in town?" Ely walked to the stove and used a wick to light his pipe. Drawing rhythmically on the stem, he watched her through the tendril of smoke emerging from the bowl.

Lena sat back, giving Ely a narrow-eyed look. "Ely, you are a shameful busybody! Next, you'll tell me exactly where I went, because I suspect from your face you know quite well I was in Mr. Baxter's building."

"Really?"

"You know I was."

Ely returned to his seat near the stove, puffing energetically on his pipe, sending smoke signals to the ceiling. "Well then, what did the man have to say? Did he hear from Nash's sister?"

"Well, that's certainly direct."

"I'm an old man. I don't have time for beating around the tree."

"Beating around the *bush*, Ely."

"I don't have time for that either. What did he say?"

She sighed, fully realizing he'd persist until she repeated the whole conversation. "I can see you will not be satisfied with my telling you that he was simply concerned for my well-being."

"No." A puff of smoke left his lips to form a thin cloud between them.

As close as she could recall the details, she confessed them to Ely along with her refusal to join their group of winter refugees fleeing to the lower elevation of Hailey. The knot in her stomach grew as she relayed each detail of Baxter's arguments.

"Hmmm."

"I suppose you think I'm a foolish woman, too."

"I did not say that. I have a better opinion of Mr. Baxter, however. He seems to be looking out for your interests as much as for Miss Nash's financial well-being. I think I might like this man."

"But you agree with Evan that it's unwise of me to stay here," she persisted.

"Is that what you want me to say?" He pulled the pipe from between his teeth.

"I would like to know your honest opinion." She paused with the teacup halfway to her lips. "At least I think I do."

"Well then." Sticking the pipe back between his teeth he puffed away in silence for several moments, in which time Lena had emptied and refilled her teacup.

"There are many things to consider, *ja*? And life is full of risks, I think."

"Yes." She thought of the risk she'd taken simply getting on the train out of Chicago.

"It is a risk to go out the door every morning. One never knows what might be waiting there. One could be run down by a horse and carriage, or attacked by wild animals or choke on an apple, which you packed for lunch." He sat quietly looking toward the ceiling at the cloud of smoke circling his head. "Some risks are unnecessary, *ja*?"

Was he going to suggest this risk she was taking could and should be avoided? Probably. She braced herself for his next words.

"But sometimes risks are necessary because what happens at the end could be wonderful and not a catastrophe, *ja*? Or maybe the catastrophe is exactly what we need. I think we miss much in this life that could be waiting for us if we don't face those things that make us afraid." He paused a while, puffing with that serene expression she envied. "Perhaps the better question to ask is, what do you really want, Lena? Is it this house? Or is it something else, perhaps. Is it these mountains? Your independence? Friends? Family? So many things we poor humans desire from this life, *ja*?"

This was not what she expected from him, this philosophical thesis. "You should have written a book, Ely, on how to avoid a question."

He pulled the pipe from his mouth, then chuckled. "That is very good, Lena. But there is a problem with your question, I think. I cannot answer as to whether you are foolish in your decision because I lack the facts and figures to give you a good report. The mining company gives me many numbers to consider before I write their reports. I can tell them how much they are spending and how much they are making."

She rose and picked up Ely's cup along with her own. "I was hoping you would give me your advice, Ely."

Ely gave her a look that stopped her cold. "I have answered your question with a question. If you can answer that, then I believe you will have answered your first question."

CHAPTER 25

RISING early the next day, Lena settled herself at her desk, determined to write a letter to Jessie. She planned to ask Mr. Baxter to deliver it once he arrived in Hailey. As she picked up her pen, gazing out the window for inspiration, she saw Evan riding up the road leading Rosie. Laying aside her pen, she walked out onto the porch to greet him.

"Lena, I want you to take a ride with me. We won't be gone long. Think I can have you back by noon. Can you put on that old jacket of Nash's and some sensible pants?" His inviting smile pushed away all thoughts of letter writing.

"What do you have in mind?"

Evan leaned forward, resting his arm on the saddle horn, the smile touching his eyes with a merry light. "Why ma'am, if you're determined to become a frontier woman, I think it stands to reason you know how to shoot a gun. Have you?"

"Shot a gun?" Lena asked, incredulous.

"Shot a gun, yes, ma'am."

"Well, no. Do you really think it's necessary?"

Evan's eyebrow lifted at that. "Remember that cub you saw a few weeks back, the one you thought was so adorable?"

"Yes."

"Well, its mama or some other cub's mama, ripped the door off a cabin a little farther up the creek here. Started rampaging through the kitchen. No one was home at the time, so it didn't become the problem it could have. And what if something goes after your chickens? Are you going to throw a frying pan at a two-hundred-pound cougar?"

"I'll just be a moment."

"Wait!" Evan took a step to Lena's side.

"What? What am I doing wrong?" Lena continued to tilt her head with her eye on the sights of the Remington carbine, afraid to move her head from the position he'd recommended.

"You're doing fine, Lena. I just don't want you to hurt yourself with the recoil. It won't be as bad as the shotgun Nash has over the fireplace, but...well, here, let me show you." He moved her right arm farther back, adjusting the butt to touch her shoulder.

"But won't that hurt more?"

"Not as likely. Now just keep your eye on the sights and squeeze the trigger, nice and slow. And keep your feet a little farther apart for balance. Okay?"

Lena held her breath, trying to remember everything. She put a gentle pressure on the trigger, but it resisted more than she'd expected. The tensed muscle in her finger twitched, the explosion of powder rocking her back on her heels. She looked around at Evan with wide eyes and the faintest suggestion of a smile. "I did it!"

Evan nodded. "Yes, ma'am you pulled the trigger." He looked toward the target and she followed his gaze. "Next time, you want to try hitting the target."

Her excitement cooled a bit as she saw the can still sitting solidly on the rock. She swung back to him, the gun now pointing at Evan's stomach.

"Hold on!" Evan yelped and skittered to the side. He reached for the gun, gently redirecting the barrel. "Always assume a gun is loaded, which, by the way, it is."

"Oh. Sorry." She lowered the barrel, looking chagrined.

He gave her a reassuring grin. "Why don't you try again."

After going through half a box of ammunition, only three cans showed any damage. Lena looked over at him, her disappointment evident. "I'm not very good, am I?"

Evan drew his hand from his face where he'd been stroking it more steadily with every missed shot. "Well, let's just say the wildlife haven't much to worry them until you can aim a little better." He saw her expression fall a bit farther. "But, you'll probably be able to scare them off if you just keep firing—and the gun doesn't jam." The last part he muttered under his breath.

"Sorry." She handed the gun back to Evan.

"That's okay, really. You just need to keep practicing. Maybe go out to the creek behind the house and pick a log you can shoot at every day for a while." Squinting at the cans still sitting undamaged upon the rock, he added, "And maybe we should try the shotgun next time."

Arriving back at the house, Lena slipped from the saddle, looking far less awkward than she had on their first outing. Handing Rosie's reins to Evan, she asked him, "I know we haven't mentioned it for two weeks, but I would like to know something. Your opinion does matter to me. Taking me out today, to teach me to shoot, was that because you aren't opposed to my staying through the winter, as you once were?"

Evan fingered the reins for a moment before meeting her gaze. "Lena, you're a strong-willed woman. I'm not saying that's bad. It'll sure make the battle you're going to be up against easier if you are strong and determined about your decision. But what I said about the challenges, even to your survival—I still hold to those warnings. This isn't a friendly place for women alone—or anyone, really."

Gambit snorted his impatience, emphasizing with an irritable stomp of a foreleg. Lena lay her hand gently behind his soft ear and stroked him. She turned his words over in her mind, before saying softly, "But you haven't really answered the question."

Evan sat up straighter in the saddle, gathering the reins in his hands. "I'm thinking that this house is your gambit. You're willing to risk everything on keeping it and making a go of it here. I'm just trying to help you hedge your bet."

Lena stepped back as Gambit lifted his head, clearly feeling the soft pressure of the bit giving him the signal that they were about to move.

"I'll see you this evening. Got some things to do." With that, Evan turned the horse's head to the road back to town.

From the top step of the porch, she watched him go, a man so apparently comfortable in his skin and his place in the world. She envied him, envied his confidence in his abilities to do most everything that would ensure his survival in the world. Just by being a man, he had an edge on that survival, an edge she would never possess. She felt the sting of the disparity and her analytical mind sought for a way to enhance her odds. He'd called it a gambit.

She swung around, taking in the wide front porch, the spacious windows, the sturdy structure she'd claimed for her own. This permanence and stability was what she longed for when she'd first read of Mr. Nash's offer to join him in his endeavor. Was it worth the risk? Was it truly the answer to her longing?

The fading sound of Gambit's strong hooves beating out a steady rhythm with Rosie's quieter ones keeping a harmonious cadence beside him, drew her gaze back to the road. Evan's body seemed to flow with the stallion's movements, his rise and fall matching perfectly the horse's gait.

As the facets of her heart and mind struggled to align, she feared that no single gain would be enough.

Gambit's nicker reminded Evan that he'd not given the stallion his usual grain after their ride out that morning. "Sorry, boy. Think I'm distracted." He scooped a measure into the horse's bucket, then resting his arms on the stall door, watched Gambit wiggle his lips seeking out every morsel. Gambit looked up at him, grain and drool seeping from the corners of his mouth.

"So, should I have told her to leave, Gambit? Was it selfish of me not to?"

Gambit stared at him a while before dropping his head to seek out another mouthful of sweet grain, ignoring the question.

"So, you refuse to give an opinion too? Must be us men. We'll think it, but not say it, right?"

There was still no answer from the stallion, but the mare called out her disapproval of Evan's favoritism.

Shoveling another scoop of grain, Evan dropped it before the little mare. For just a moment, he could have sworn her look had an extra measure of scorn.

Evan raised a hand to his face to scratch at a day's growth of whiskers. As he'd stood before the mirror yesterday he'd reminded himself why a man grew a beard up here as he put the razor to the side, unused. Pride didn't keep away frostbite. Hefting Gambit's saddle, he went back to work setting his tack to rights.

The barn door creaked open, admitting a draft of cold wind, lifting and redepositing the loose straw strewn about the floor. Naomi, dressed in a man's canvas coat and sensible boots, entered, tugging a heavy scarf away from her face as she did. She looked smaller than usual, dwarfed in winter clothes too big for her petite frame.

"Naomi, what brings you out here?" Evan stood, stretching expansively. The tiny stool he'd been using while oiling and mending an old pack harness did not agree with his spine. He welcomed the interruption.

"Good morning, Evan." She threw a glance over her shoulder, lifting a hand to shield her eyes from the thin disk hovering high in the sky behind her. "Well, I guess I should make that, good afternoon."

"Were you looking for me?" Evan scrubbed the oil from his hands onto a dirty rag.

"Well you might flatter yourself to think so." Probably more out of habit than true flirtation, she arched her neck and winked at him. The next moment, artifice dissolved and her years suddenly showed in the anxiety creasing her face. "Truth is, you are a good sight at a time like this."

"What's going on?"

"I really thought the girls and I could hold out till spring, but things are bad, Evan. Have you seen how many wagons have been heading down that trail to Ketchum and Hailey? I just don't think we can stick it out. Truth is, I'm here about hiring a wagon, or buying one if I can't."

"What will you do?" Evan knew how much she'd invested in the house, losing it would be quite a blow.

"Start over, I guess. Sell it to them that wants it for the lumber and windows and such. Scrap is about all it's worth now."

"Hailey?"

"No, I think I'll go back to Boise City and take any of the girls who want to come along."

"That's a hard choice. Know you've put a lot into this place."

"Been thinking I might try a different line of work, you know? I've gotten pretty good at designing clothes and hats for the girls, since none of these fine shops will see fit to serve our kind."

Her tone held less bitterness than he would have expected in those last words. She just seemed to be reporting a fact. "So, you're thinking of setting up business in Boise? Certainly is a big enough town for it."

"Maybe at first, I'll just take in some mending, just to earn some respectability, you know. But later, maybe try my hand at the millinery trade. That's my fancy."

Evan searched her face, seeing a spark of hope flickering there, hope to start again. He gave her a warm smile, unable to resist pulling her to his side in a brotherly hug. "You're an amazing woman, Naomi."

She pulled away, swiping at her eye with a sleeve. "It's a long road from here to there."

He knew she referred to more than the road over the pass to Boise City. She'd have to navigate the wags and busybodies who would try to pry into her past. "Who's going to handle the wagon for you? You'll need something more than a buggy to carry all your things and a few passengers, I expect."

The crease between her eyes deepened. "Have to manage that, just like the rest of the details."

Evan pulled a hand to his unshaved face for only a moment, his mind already decided. "I'll drive you."

Looking up at him, Naomi's face could not have registered more surprise if he'd asked her to a church social. "You'd do that?"

Evan shrugged. "Why not? You surely need the help. You don't think I can manage the team?" He gave her a lopsided grin.

"Evan Hartmann, you know that ain't it at all." She stared at him for long thoughtful moments. "I never knew a man with a heart as big as yours. And I gotta' tell you, the idea of drivin' a team up and over that mountain about takes the nerves right outta' me." She twisted her hands together.

"Evan, I'd be grateful beyond words if you'd do that for us. Can't pay you much, but what I can, I will!"

"We'll talk about that later. Why don't you go on back and do your packing while I see about renting a wagon for you?" He turned from her as though everything was settled, but her voice called him back.

"Evan, you are the straightest man I ever knew. God in heaven must have known this ramshackle excuse for a city needed a guardian angel when he sent the likes of you here." She turned on her heel without giving Evan a chance to reply.

CHAPTER 26

As shrewd as Evan had become at horse trading, negotiating for a wagon was no great problem. Taking the time to test the pair of horses included with the deal took just a bit more time. He drove them down the trail toward the pass for a few miles before turning back to check how they handled streets. One was a bit more mule-headed than he'd prefer, but the price was fair, so he'd make it work.

As he passed along Main Street for the second time, Thomas Baxter flagged him down from in front of his office building. Evan pulled up the team, acknowledging the lawyer with a nod.

"You're just the man I was hoping to speak with today." Baxter said in an almost breathless tone.

Evan noticed the man's face seemed flushed, his manner uncharacteristically anxious. Evan stepped from the wagon so they could speak eye to eye. "What can I do for you, Thomas?"

"Don't know if you heard that Mrs. Baxter and I are heading out tomorrow." He pulled a handkerchief from his pocket and wiped his brow.

"No, I hadn't heard that. Sorry to see you go. Just leaving for the winter or permanent?

"Think it's permanent. We'll see what the mining bigwigs decide over the winter. Even then, I'm not sure I can keep my Amy happy here. She's determined her life is wasting away up here away from proper society. She hasn't given me a moment's rest since the first snowfall." He wiped his brow again.

"No peace in a house with a quarrelsome woman I've heard." Evan tugged at the harness securing the equally quarrelsome horse, looking for adjustments that might make him less so.

"So, I've been worrying about our Miss Sommer."

Evan looked over his shoulder at the lawyer, wondering about the man's use of pronouns. When did she become *our* Miss Sommer, he thought? "What about?"

"Well, I spoke with her yesterday about staying on here. Told her why I didn't think it was wise financially, not to mention all the other ways. I mean, I respect the woman. She's very reasonable and I know there's nothing more I can say to dissuade her. But, we are leaving, you see. And even though I invited her to go with us, she declined. My wife heard of it and she's been nagging me ever since to speak with her again."

Evan kept his attention focused on Baxter, imagining the conversation he'd had with Lena, picturing her sitting prim before him and completely unresponsive to the man's appeal.

"I was just hoping you might have more influence with her. Surely, she would listen to you. Nash certainly listened to your advice, seems he came to you far more than to me over the past two years."

Pushing his hands into his jacket pockets, he rocked back a bit on his heels. "Well, Thomas, you must know by now that Lena is a determined woman."

"That and more!" Baxter snorted. "She knows that I'll be advising Nash's sister to sell the property for whatever she can get for it. Lena's made an offer, even though she's not likely to be able to fulfill it if all her tenants move out." He reached in his pocket and pulled out another handkerchief, carefully unfolding it to reveal the brooch. "She gave me this as a token of her sincere intentions. I don't know what it's worth, but I knew I had to take it."

He recognized the brooch immediately. "Keeping that house seems to be more important to her than most anything else, as far as I can see. And I figure a woman's got as much right to a dream as a man. If she chooses to gamble for it, then I have to respect that."

Baxter seemed to study Evan as though trying to read more into his words. "Are you staying up here this winter? I thought maybe with your brother gone, you might not want to remain here. Saw you with the wagon, here, and was wondering if you were planning to pack up."

There was likely more to Baxter's innocently phrased question. That would be like him. Most men had more thoughts rolling around in their brain box than they allowed to slip between their lips.

"This is for Naomi and a couple of the girls. I offered to drive them down the mountain."

"Oh," Baxter mused. "Sounds just like something you'd do."

Evan scarcely acknowledged the remark, saying, "I've just been thinking. If you're leaving so soon, would you mind a little company on the trip? We'll add a little more color to the parade, but I'm sure the girls won't bother the sensitivities of the rest of the ladies traveling south." It was a dig he couldn't resist, giving the man a rueful smile as he said it.

"It's fine with me, Evan. I won't even mention it to Mrs. Baxter. By the time she sees who's following us, it'll be too late for her to object. Well," he reconsidered, "she'll *object*, but there won't be anything she can do about it."

"Thanks. If there's trouble with the weather, it'll be good to have company along."

Baxter came another step closer to Evan, his voice low. "But are you planning on coming back up the mountain?"

"You mean, do I plan on coming back to look after *our* Miss Sommer? Yes, I don't want her staying here alone any more than you do." He couldn't avoid casting a quick glance at the mountain tops as he added, "God willing, the mountain and the snows don't kill me, I'll come back."

A soft knock came on the door to Ely's office. Buried as he was in the newest stack of papers detailing the mine's production, he scarcely heard it.

"Ely?" Evan stood in the doorway with his hair brushing the top of the frame. "Can I trouble you?"

Taking off his reading glasses, he blinked blearily at Evan. "*Ja*, of course. Come in." He waved vaguely across the desk. "There's a chair over there somewhere."

Evan located the chair. Removing the small stack of papers camped there, he sat holding them on his lap.

"What is it that brings you? No, let me guess, *ja*? Lena."

"You never cease to disappoint me with your intuitive nosiness," Evan said dryly.

"Ah, I am right, *ja*?"

"Yes. Did you know Thomas Baxter talked to her yesterday?"

"*Ja*, she told me."

Evan frowned. "We aren't going to talk her out of this." Evan said it flatly.

"No."

"Will you stay?"

"I think the managers stay and that means they will want me too. So, *ja*, I will stay."

"That's good."

"And you? Will you stay?"

"If I can get back across the pass, yes."

"Where are you going?" Ely looked concerned.

"Naomi needs some help to get down with a few of the girls. I offered to drive them." He carelessly dipped his shoulder, as though it were a drive to the church social across town, not up and down a pass that had taken the life of his brother.

"Does Lena know?"

"I haven't been back to the house. Been helping Naomi load some things onto the wagon."

"She will not be pleased with this news."

"I have to, Ely."

Ely sat back, pulling the pipe from a plate atop a stack of papers and reaching into his pocket for the packet of tobacco. "Then you must."

"There's something else. You know the books, the four volumes of *Ivanhoe*?"

"*Ja.*"

"Lena says that they are valuable. Do you have any idea how much they might bring?"

Ely shook his head. "I do not know much about such things. Old violins, *ja*, I know something. I would think much depends on finding a buyer."

Evan scooted forward on his chair, catching a file that slipped from the stack as he did. "Lena spoke of a bookstore in Hailey. A man there deals in old books and first editions."

The pipe at last lit, Ely sucked in a breath of warm smoke. "Why is this important now?"

"Lena gave Baxter her brooch. Did you know that?"

"No, I did not. It belonged to the family with the little girl which died, *ja*?" He cocked an eyebrow. "Why would she do that?"

"He said that she gave it to him as a down payment."

Ely nodded, his eyebrows now knit together. "I see."

"I want to know if I can sell the books. Use the money to make a greater down payment on the house and ask Baxter to return the brooch to me." He waited to read Ely's reaction.

"It might work." Ely stared through the smoke cloud, eyes narrowing. "But this was a precious gift from your mother, *ja*? Are you certain you wish to do this?"

Evan hesitated no longer than a heartbeat. "Yes."

Carrick, Donal, Ely, and Lena stared at Evan with a range of expressions from disbelief to admiration, as Evan explained his intentions to drive Naomi out of Sawtooth.

"It is a good thing you do, Evan." Ely, aware of the plan, could say little more.

Donal leaned forward, his young face animated with interest. "You're driving all those pretty gals by yourself? Heck, why didn't they ask me?"

Carrick snorted. "You'd be the least likely fellow for that. Besides, this won't be any kind of pleasure trip. I surely wouldn't want to be up there with the sky as broody as it's been these last few days. I'd say you're a bit off your head to do it. Maybe if you were just going, but coming back? What's the chances of that?"

Evan scowled at Carrick. Carrick apparently caught the look and then the reason behind it. His eyes flickered to Lena's white face and back to Evan's. "But, then again, you are the best at handling a team of horses. None better, in fact." He threw a look at his brother. "Haven't I said that a hundred times. Look at that Evan! Have you ever seen anyone so knowledgeable with horses?" Into it now, he took his praise a little too far as he added, enthusiastically, "Why you could outrun an avalanche with a good team under your control!"

The scowl turned to a glare, louder than any words of warning. Carrick slumped, murmuring, "Sorry."

Donal, distracted, suddenly elbowed Carrick. "If Evan can go all the way to Hailey and still plan on coming back, we could sure make it to Stanley. We could leave next week stake us a claim, set up camp, nestle in all cozy and be ahead of the crowd coming in the spring!"

His comment made nearly as much impact as Evan's. Ely and Evan exchanged glances before even gauging the effect on Lena.

Carrick, quicker of wit than his brother, now appeared fully aware of the unspoken tension in the room. He gave his brother a narrow-eyed glare that stopped him cold. Donal, mouth agape, looked across the table at Lena. Her face was no longer visible, head lowered, staring at her hands.

"Well..." Carrick started, his gaze shifting nervously from Lena's slumped shoulders to Evan's furious glare. "Think I'll be turning in. I'll see you in the morning, I expect."

"But I haven't finished my pie." Donal whined until Carrick pinched his ear and gave him a look that brooked no argument.

"I'll just sit by the fire for a while. Think I could use a smoke." Ely carried his plate to the sink and slipped from the room.

"Lena..." Evan started.

"No, Evan, don't..." Lena took a shaky breath, and rose to her feet gathering the dishes still scattered about the table.

"But I want to explain," Evan tried again.

She stopped, the dishes all but forgotten, and met his eyes. "Evan, you're doing what makes you who you are. You don't need to explain. This is what you do, care for people in need. Just like you've cared for me when I've been in need, and cared for Jessie and Daniel, and Vicki, and who knows how many others before I ever met you."

"It isn't what you might think."

"Evan, I know that what you're doing for Naomi is done out of the purest form of friendship. Donal's a boy with a boy's perspective on women. I know that this is a good and selfless act of love."

She saw a sudden transformation in Evan's face in that moment, something unexplainable. In some strange and wonderful way, she felt he was really looking at her for the first time, not as an object of pity or someone in need of rescue. She wanted that look to stay in his eyes forever. She wanted not to be the one needing, as much as the one to be needed.

He reached out and took her hand, not as gently as he had before, but almost as though he were a drowning man reaching out for rescue. She looked at his hand enveloping hers with his warmth, the cold fear that had at first gripped her upon hearing his news, dispelled.

"I'm coming back. I promise."

Lena knew it was a promise he had no control to keep. Out of compassion and perhaps something more, he had given it as a gift. She gave him back the gift of her smile. "Do, Evan. Do come back."

CHAPTER 27

THE departure of the four wagons the next morning had a surreal festivity to it. A crowd of mournful looking men stood on either side of the street watching Naomi's girls climb into the wagon. And it was colorful, with the girls bedecked in bright scarves that fluttered from the collars of coats too big for them. They were the last to go, allowing the other families to precede them down the trail, just as Evan had promised.

Loud halloos followed them out of town and even along the road a quarter mile from Sawtooth. Men stood, hats in hands, waving as the wagon passed by taking with it all that gave their lives any measure of comfort, smoothing the harsh corners of their rough existence for a few moments every week. To most of these weary, hard-edged men, watching them leave was like watching the black clouds of winter bear down upon them.

Lena stayed back at the house, unwilling to watch Evan leave. Instead, she gave her farewell from the porch steps, holding back the tears pressing against her eyes. While a storm stirred a tidal wave of anxiety in her stomach, she would appear to those around her, calm and composed. She even smiled and wished him safe travels, then turned to the door.

Only after she stepped into the kitchen, did her composure slip and Ely was there to see it happen. No torrent of tears gave way her feelings. She was too afraid to yield to them. She leaned against the sink, her fingers white as she gripped the edge. Refusing to look out the window for fear of catching some last glimpse of Evan, she stared into the gray dishwater, speckled with oil and soggy bits of biscuits.

"He will come back, Lena," Ely said in his soft scholar's voice, the lilt of wisdom in his tone but not his words.

She knew there was no assurance in his statement, only wishful thinking, to imbue her with courage. Her voice eerily calm, she said, "I know he will try. I fear that effort will be his death."

She spun on him, her eyes glistening with unspilled tears. "I wish I'd asked him to stay out of these mountains until it was safe to return! But I'm a selfish woman, unlike Evan in every way." With the words spoken, she felt her composure eroding. Like a river bank in flood stage, her fears pounded at her reserve.

Expressionless, Ely let her speak without correction. His silence cut deep as she assumed his reticence to be a confirmation of her self-condemnation. In the silence of the room, where only the soft ticking of the wall clock offered an opinion on time's cruel constancy, she stood before him, feeling exposed, naked. Squaring her shoulders, she walked quietly from the room, closing the door soundlessly behind her.

She made her way like a blind person to the desk beneath the windows, touching the backs of chairs and tables along her path, those things in her life which were solid. Reaching out for the desktop, she leaned onto it with arms straight, finding support for her trembling legs. The view from the window called her out of the house, the suffocating stillness, and her self-focused fears.

Having yet the sense to take Nash's coat with her, she stepped onto the porch, wrapping herself in its rough cloth to shield her from the chilling winds. A pale sun broke through thin clouds, casting a patchwork of light and dark. Those high peaks, now thoroughly capped with snow, shone, as though stealing energy from the sun.

Following the path leading away from town, she wandered aimlessly. Her body felt heavy and awkward as she trudged the path angling near to the stream. A blue jay scolded her from a pine branch angled out high above the trail. She stopped, gazing up at the opinionated bird, with a less than friendly expression. "Why are you concerned about where I should walk? Don't you have better things to do?"

The bird, hopped along the branch, showing off his brilliant sapphire and ebony coat to best advantage, and squawked again.

"You should be busy, preparing for winter, like everyone else, or flying away to warmer places! Leave me alone!" Her voice rose in pitch.

He hopped to a lower branch, tipping his head to peer down at her, bouncing two and fro on the limb with a care for her remonstrations.

She felt he really might speak to her in a language she would understand. His black eye shone with a luminescence that could have been mistaken for intelligence instead of avid curiosity. He bobbed his head.

A laugh bursting from her lips surprised not only the bird but Lena with its suddenness and volume. In that moment, all the pieces of her life, the confusing events of recent weeks, the failed expectations, the whirlwind of emotions that had derailed her reasoned perspectives began to settle into neat little piles, like snow on cedar branches. It was not that she could make sense of any of it, not yet, but the knots that had tangled all these threads of her life were loosening. She felt her hands releasing their grip on the fear that had been governing her thoughts.

She was a fool when it came to expressing her love. She accepted that. But Jessie had told her she could change— that she was changing. She recognized little alterations, shifts of perspective toward herself and others, and they gave her what she desperately needed in that moment— hope.

From the branch above her, the blue jay squawked yet again. Lena squinted up at the bird and squawked back, waving her arms. Had she insulted him or wished him a good day?

Ely was gone all day and was absent for dinner as well. Donal and Carrick, sitting across from her were uncharacteristically quiet. Lena watched them with their heads lowered, shoveling food into their mouths, avoiding eye contact. She knew, and they knew she knew. With their plates wiped clean by the final slices of bread, they exchanged a quick glance.

Before Carrick could speak, Lena said, "So when are you two heading north? I assume it is still north to these new diggings you've been talking of." Her tone belied no hint of her feelings on the subject.

The two brothers exchanged surprised expressions before Carrick grinned at her. "Guess you can read us pretty well."

"Fairly well. You've both been afraid to look at me all evening. Besides, you already said that was what you were considering."

"We mean to leave tomorrow. Got our kits together and bought a couple of horses and a pack mule. Weather seems to be clearing some. We might get lucky and hit the trail in a lull between snows," Donal finished with that lopsided grin.

"We know a couple of boys who already headed up there today. We'll just trail them tomorrow," Carrick explained.

"It sounds as if you've thought it through then. I'll miss you around the hearth at nights, but I wish you God speed," Lena said levelly.

The boys stood almost in unison, both shoving their hands in their pants' pockets. "We'll be sure missing you too, Miss Lena," Carrick managed, his voice sounding strange.

"For sure, we'll be missing your cooking. Didn't think anyone on this side of New York City could bake an Irish soda bread the way you do."

Lena tried to memorize their features before they too, faded from her life. She wondered what Jessie would do. The fondness that had grown in her heart for them both welled up, and she knew. She stretched out her arms and wrapped them around Donal first, stepping back she saw his eyes glistening. She gave Carrick a stern look. "You will take care of this brother of yours. Make sure he doesn't get into any more trouble than you'd allow for yourself." She hugged him tight.

Both young men grinned at her, with a shyness she'd not seen in them. "Well, we'll be packing our things. Want to head out early."

"Sounds like a good idea. I'll pack some things to eat."

"Oh, don't bother, we'll be fine." Carrick said, but she saw Donal's face fall, indicating he felt quite the contrary.

"It isn't a bother." Lena laughed lightly, folding her arms in front of her in a fashion that showed she'd made up her mind. "Now, go pack your things. I won't help you with that."

Later that evening, as she sat before the fire, a book open in her lap, Ely opened the door, pursued by a brisk west wind. She looked at him and smiled. "You were working late."

"*Ja.*" Closing the door behind him, he gave an exaggerated shiver and shrugged out of his coat. "The bosses are keeping me busy."

"I see. There's dinner on a plate in the kitchen and the kettle is hot."

"Lena..." Ely started across the room, but she lifted her hand to stop him.

"Ely, it's all right. I'm starting to see the truth about myself. What I said was true. If you had been polite and tried to comfort me by denying it, you would not have been the true and good friend you are."

He stepped beside her chair, looking just a little older than he had that morning, his eyes red from the strain of reading too many numbers under too little light. "You say that you are seeing truth about yourself. So many never do, and I think that many of us see only small pictures of ourselves as others paint them for us."

Lena gave him a mild smile. "Still the poet. I think you have a gift for hiding your thoughts in beautiful phrases. I only understand parts of what you say."

Her smile must have reassured him that she was no longer upset because he continued. "It is just this, my young friend, the truth you claim to see is only part of the truth of who you are. We can all be better than we are. Only God can be perfect, and He knows Himself well enough not to expect the same of us."

"Now you are the theologian."

This time it was Ely who laughed. "No more than you, my friend."

She thought that a curious thing to say since she put her faith not in any powers beyond hers. But his next words took that question from her mind.

"Something brought you here for a reason," he said with no trace of humor.

She considered that for a moment, a bemused expression on her upturned face. "Of course. I had an agreement with Mr. Nash."

"No, Lena. Your work here is more than the running of a boarding house. You do not see that, do you?"

Bemusement slipped into full puzzlement. "I don't think I understand."

"That is the truth you do not yet see." He gave her hand a light pat and turned to the kitchen.

She watched him go, afraid to ponder his words. Her day's work had kept her from thinking deeply about anything, not her future, or the fate of her friends, or Evan. Until Evan returned that would become the routine of her day—work with her hands and deny her thoughts any fertile ground to replant the fear she'd expelled this morning. Closing the book, replacing it on the shelf, she turned down the oil lamps and retired to her bedroom.

Before dawn, Lena was up cooking, preparing food for the brothers' trip north. Packed away in a small box was enough for the day's journey, and to spare. As they strapped the last of their belongings onto the pack mule, she watched from the bottom step. Nash's coat seemed scarcely able to keep out the chill, and she resolved to search through his things for more warm clothing.

Ely stood beside her, his collar turned up to cover his ears, a wool cap resting above his bushy eyebrows. "It is cold this morning. This is good."

She looked at him for explanation. "Why would you say that? They're likely to get frostbite."

"But cold usually means clear sky, *ja*? Better cold, than snow."

Carrick stood by his horse's head and shook Ely's hand solemnly. He turned to Lena and tipped his hat before stepping into the stirrup.

"Don't forget what I said about taking care of Donal," Lena said, her smile broad and teasing.

"Oh, I won't. And I won't soon forget what Aunt Polly said to Tom Sawyer. 'Who knows, he may grow up to be President someday, unless they hang him first.'"

Lena's face reflected her surprise as she looked over at Ely, who was laughing aloud. "They were listening!"

"Of course they were. Perhaps you see a little picture of yourself painted by a hand not your own."

For the remainder of the day, no surface in the house was unacquainted with her dusting cloth. The evening meal was simmering on the stove and a fragrant pie baking in the oven. Now she was attacking the chicken yard, bringing extra bedding and feed. She heard running steps on the road to the house. The voice calling out to her was familiar. Turning, she saw the boy, Daniel, running around the corner of the house, his face flushed and pinched by worry. She rubbed her hands on her apron and stepped out of the enclosure to meet him.

"What's happened, Daniel?"

"Is Mr. Hartmann here?" The words came out in small explosions of breath.

"No." He didn't resist when she took his hand and led him to the porch steps. "Tell me what's wrong?"

He sagged against her, still trying to catch his breath. "It's my pa. He's bad sick."

Taking his hand into hers, she noticed how waiflike he appeared, his eyes lined with dark circles. Her heart ached for the child. She wrapped her arm about his narrow shoulders, gently pulling him close. "How long as he been ill?"

"Came home a couple of weeks ago not feelin' so good. He's coughin' a lot now, 'most sounds like his insides is gonna' come out."

"Have you been taking care of him by yourself?"

"Just me. Nobody else to do it since Ma died."

"You come into the kitchen and have something to eat while I gather a few things."

He put up no argument but followed her into the house, collapsing on the bench at the kitchen table, his head resting on his arms. Pulling out the remains of last night's meal, she placed it in front of him and put a fork in his hand. "Eat!" That's all she said before leaving the room to find some items she thought would be of use. Returning to the kitchen after only a few minutes, she found the boy asleep, the food barely touched.

Without waking him, she rummaged through cupboards for honey, cinnamon, and cloves, adding them to the lavender sachet she'd collected from her room and Epsom salts she'd seen on a shelf in Evan's room. Wrapping the food in a dish towel, she included that with the other items in her bag. The last thing she did was gently lay her hand on the boy's shoulder to wake him.

Startling awake, he looked up at her blearily.

"Daniel, let's go tend to your father."

Nearly gagging at the stench as she stepped into the small cabin, she brought the back of her hand to her nose. Looking around at the boy, she noticed that he seemed unaffected. As she moved farther into the darkened rooms, the rasping sound of the man's breathing sent a chill of memory up her back. It was how her father had sounded during the last painful week of his life. Swallowing down her fear, she avoided a heap of soiled sheets, as she moved to the side of the bed where Daniel's father took in shallow breaths, too weak to fill his lungs.

Within minutes, she knew that she would not be able to care for Daniel and his father here. She turned to the boy, taking his hand firmly in hers. "I need for you to run to the mining offices on Main. Do you know where they are?"

Daniel nodded.

"Find a man named Ely Beckert. Tell him that Lena needs his help right away." He started to pull away, but she pulled his arm back. "And tell him to hire a small buckboard from the livery and bring it here."

She released his arm, and he was off at a run, huffing out the door. Turning back to the man, she tugged him up into a sitting position. His body slumped forward, oblivious of anything but the need for air. Grunting with the effort, she held him there while she stuffed pillows and anything else she could find within reach to prop him upright. Only then did she place the back of her hand against his forehead, feeling the heat.

Stabilized in his sitting position, she walked to the cooking area, finding a skillet with the greasy remains of some meal from days past. She gritted her teeth, taking a finger full of oil onto her finger and returning to the bed with it. Knowing full well, that her efforts here were a pitiful replacement for what the man needed, she refused to just watch him suffer. So, she smeared a small amount of grease beneath his nose and on his exposed chest. Then wiping her hands on her skirt, she reached into her bag withdrawing the bottles of cloves and cinnamon. These she mixed into the grease on his chest and upper lip.

She reassured herself that once he was back at the house tucked into a clean bed, in a room with windows that might be opened, she could care for him more properly. And the sooner she could coax him to drink tea and broth, the better would be his odds for survival. In the meanwhile, she talked to the man, telling him about his son and his kindness to her a few weeks past.

The sound of hoof beats and wagon wheels on dirt brought her to her feet. She flung the door wide, grateful that Ely had taken her message seriously. "What can I do?" Ely called out to her even before he stepped from the wagon.

"It's Daniel's father. We need to get him home where I can care for him. Will you please help me move him?"

"Of course!"

It took the three of them to lift the man and carry him to the wagon. With more effort they managed to lay him in the back of the wagon, Daniel scrambling in with him.

With Ely's assistance, he was settled into Carrick's old bed. Between Ely and Daniel, the two even managed to bathe him. While they were busy at that task, Lena put together a soup, rich in garlic. But the boy's eyelids drooped as soon as he sat at the table and Lena nearly despaired of getting food into him. Ely lay a hand on her arm and said, "The boy's body needs more sleep than food I think. Help me carry him to Donal's bed."

The boy scarcely roused from sleep as Ely carried him to the room and tucked him in beneath the quilt. He never even stirred at the sounds of his father's ragged breaths. So, Lena stayed the night, slumped in a chair between them, waking from time to time to check on her patient. From time-to-time, she would pound his back when spasms of coughing took him, or apply more chest rubs. This time she used a less offensive mixture of beeswax with cloves and cinnamon. And whenever he stirred to consciousness, she forced him to drink tea or broth.

The next morning, Ely stuck his head inside the door. Daniel was still sleeping and his father resting. He found Lena in the kitchen, a plate of ham and eggs waiting for him.

"Lena, you must be exhausted, *ja*?"

She sat across from him, nursing a steaming mug. "Yes, a bit. I think he's breathing just a little better, but it's good we moved him here. I don't think he's turned the corner yet. Daniel may have come to us in time. I hope so."

Ely shook his head, chewing his meat while staring at her. At last he said, "You look very pretty like that, with your hair loose. You have nice curls."

Lena blushed, pulling her hair back and twisting it into a quick braid. "I didn't take the time...You needed breakfast."

Ely chuckled. "Thank you. That was very thoughtful of you. But you are a kind person."

She looked up, feeling neither thoughtful, nor pretty. Just tired.

"Little pictures, Lena. These are true too, not just those you draw for yourself." Ely winked.

For the remainder of the day, Lena set her task to getting food into both Daniel and his father, starting with a stack of pancakes dripping with honey for Daniel. Half-way through the stack, he slowed. "Can I have them for lunch please? Don't seem to be able to fit as much in my belly as I used to."

It made sense, and it saddened her. How long had the boy gone without sufficient food, let alone quantity suitable for his growing body? She was angry at herself as well as the townspeople who had looked the other way. But her anger with herself was greater. She should have seen it. Hadn't he dived into the food she'd put before him? So consumed with her thoughts, she'd missed the need of the child.

"Do you think you could get your father to drink this tea? Even if he doesn't, just hold it under his nose for a while and let him breath in the steam."

"I'll try." He took the mug in his small hands, walking carefully down the hallway trying not to spill the liquid. She watched him go, an idea weaving its way into her heart.

She hurried through her cleaning and joined Daniel in the bedroom with his father. The man had yet to rouse to consciousness. Lena feared that there was little else she could do but wait. Daniel helped her prop more pillows behind him and she showed him how to pat his father's back to loosen the congestion pooling in his lungs.

Taking a clean pillow case, she dusted the inside with lavender from a sachet she kept in her linens. She'd seen her mother do that for her father in those trying last days before he had succumbed to the pneumonia. They took turns forcing him to swallow sips of tea flavored with honey, cinnamon and cloves. Lena was impressed that Daniel managed the task more successfully than she.

As they shared a cup of steaming cocoa that afternoon before the kitchen's wood stove, Lena happily noticed a bit of color returning to Daniel's cheeks. She loaded a plate with sugar cookies and pushed them across the table to the boy, smiling at his delighted expression.

"You know that you're very good at this—taking care of your father." She blew on the steaming liquid.

"Since Ma died, I kinda had to." He reached for a second cookie, still chewing on the last bite of the first one.

"But, I mean, the nursing part of caring. You seem to take to it. Maybe you would make a good doctor." She watched as his eyes widened, then as quickly narrowed into a skeptical frown.

"Me?" He laughed around a bite of cookie and had to pick up a few crumbs that tumbled from his mouth.

"Of course, you. Why not you?" She put down her cup and took his to the stove to refill it. "We certainly need more frontier doctors and I've learned that you can be educated in two years before finding a doctor to take you on as an apprentice." She warmed to the idea as she talked. "And think how much a doctor is needed here. There are remedies and treatments they know that would keep so many more people alive."

Pushing the cup toward him, she took her seat, injecting a bit of challenge in her voice. "Why shouldn't you become one?"

He avoided her question by taking a gulp of his new cocoa, spluttering as it scalded his throat. "But I'm nobody. You have to be somebody to become a doctor, somebody smarter than me anyway."

Propping her elbows on the table with her fingers steepled before her chin, she tried to adopt a bit of Ely's philosophical air. "I think it depends more on what you want. If you think that helping people in that way is something you'd like to do, then nothing can stop you. And, anyway, who told you that you aren't smart?"

Daniel let out a soft snort at that. "How about everybody?"

"Maybe everyone you know is wrong, then. I think you show remarkable skills. You're patient with your dad, who can be difficult from what I've seen. You're a quick learner. And despite what everyone says, I think you're smart."

Taking another cookie from the plate, he nibbled it thoughtfully, his eyes focused on the ceiling. "Me? A doctor?"

"You won't have to stay here forever, or even follow your father around for the rest of your life. There's a world of possibilities out there. You just have to know what you want and try for it. Maybe you won't be a doctor but maybe there's something else you'll find you want even more. Just don't give up on something because you think *everybody* thinks you can't."

Squinting at her over his mug, he said in a voice sounding years older than his freckled face bespoke, "You're a good talker, Miss Lena."

She laughed at that, rising to her feet. "Come on, help me clean out the chicken house. You interrupted me with that chore yesterday and it has to be done."

After another simple meal of soup and bread, Lena cleaned up the kitchen, scarcely able to keep her eyes open. Carrying another cup of broth into Daniel and Tom's room, she was pleased to see Tom's eyes open, Daniel perched on the bed beside him.

"Mr. Andrews, you're awake!"

He mumbled something too soft to make out from across the room. Daniel interpreted for her. "He said 'thanks'."

"Well, he's very welcome. I brought some more soup. Maybe if your father is awake, he might take more of it." She handed the cup to Daniel, who blew on the surface and tested the temperature by taking a sip first. He grinned at Lena before offering the cup to his father.

After a few minutes, Tom Andrews sagged back against the pillows, eyes closed again.

"Do you think that means he's better?" The look on Daniel's face revealed that in spite of his father's treatment of him in recent months, the boy still loved him.

"I think it's a good sign." She took the cup from Daniel's hands and set it on the nightstand, then she perched herself on Daniel's bed. "I want to ask you something."

"Sure." Pulling up the covers on his father's sleeping body, he jumped onto the bed to sit beside Lena.

"Well, I've been thinking. You and your father have been living by yourselves for some time.. .and you've done a good job of keeping things together, but I was wondering if you might like to live here for a while. You could stay until your father was well and back on his feet again. You're a great help around the house, chopping wood, taking care of the chickens, and I'm sure there are a great deal more jobs we could find. How would you like that?"

Daniel did not look quite as enthusiastic as she'd hoped. In fact, he looked rather sad. At last he brought his head up. "This is a boarding house, Miss Lena. We couldn't pay ya' anything."

Relieved by his response, she lifted her hand to touch his unruly thatch of hair. "That's all right, Daniel. I wasn't asking you to pay for the room. It's empty and likely to stay that way for the winter. Besides, I already told you I had work for you to do. You'll earn your board."

Brightening at that, he said, "Well, sure it'd be fine to stay. It's warm here and plenty to eat."

"But there's one more thing that comes with the bargain."

He narrowed his eyes, waiting.

"I'd like to teach you some things that might help you later in life—after you leave Sawtooth."

"Teach! Aw, I don't know about that! Don't think I ever learned anything much useful in school here except how to get beat up for likin' a girl too good for me."

There was no restraining the smile that tugged at her lips. "I think you'd find the experience a bit different with me. But you have to *want* to try."

He stuck a finger in his ear and screwed it around for a while, eyes scrunched in serious consideration. "Suppose it wouldn't hurt too much to try. I would like to read more than I do now. Heard the teacher read a story once last month that she never got to finish, before she took off and left for Hailey or Boise, or wherever she was goin'. If I could read better, there might be other books I'd like. I always liked it when Ma told me stories she remembered from her days in Illinois."

Lena's heart gave a little leap of joy. "Wait right here. I'll be right back."

Moments later she walked back in the room. The boy had plunged himself beneath the covers, his eyelids already drooping. She sat on the side of the narrow bed and lay the book on her lap. "How would you like for me to read to you before you go to sleep?"

"That'd be nice." His words, slurred by sleepiness, were further muffled by the quilt about his head.

Lena ran her fingers across the cover of the book before opening it. Then she read.

"Tom!"

No Answer.

"What's gone with that boy, I wonder? You TOM!"

No answer.

"That's my pa's name." Daniel mumbled.

"Yes, it is. But the boy, Tom, well he's a lot more like you."

"I like this story. Read some more."

And she did until Daniel's soft, little boy snores, filled the empty space of the house with a sweet rhythm

A S the settlement of Galena came into view, Evan breathed easier. The pass behind them, the road down to Ketchum and on into Hailey posed fewer of the threats that the first part of their journey had presented with its steep ascent and narrow twisting trail hugging the face of the mountain. With the worst behind them, he smiled reassuringly at his anxious passengers. "Should make it to Ketchum just after sunset." He shot Naomi an uncertain look. "As long as there aren't any breakdowns."

Naomi's pale, pinched face reflected the tension that had churned in his gut for the last five miles. "That's sweet news. Couldn't take much more of that. I can understand why folks find a piece of land and just hole up. Don't know if I'll ever pull up stakes again."

"At least not in winter, right?"

She laughed dryly. "If I was a cursing kind of lady, I'd emphasize that statement with the strongest one I could think of, and I can think of quite a few."

Evan chuckled and touched the reins to the horses' rumps, urging them to step out. Traveling down the grade at a slightly faster clip cheered the three ladies who must have found the ride less than luxurious. Anxious as they were to be out of the mountains and in the warmer climate, they'd suffer the additional buffeting.

As he'd predicted, they pulled into the outskirts of Hailey an hour after sunset, guided through the streets by oil lamps. Naomi directed Evan to turn up an alley at the far side of town, through what was obviously the livelier part of town. She had him pull up outside a three-story building, one of the oldest on the street. Evan helped Naomi from the wagon, waiting to the side while she knocked on a newly painted green door. In a short time, the door opened a crack, light and laughter pouring out in equal proportions.

"Will you let Helen know Naomi's here?"

The face at the door lifted to take in Evan and the loaded wagon behind. In a less than friendly tone, she instructed Naomi to wait where she was. Naomi looked over her shoulder at Evan, something like an apology written on her features.

For the second time the door opened, this time fully, revealing the buxom figure of a woman who from her warm greeting must be Helen. A round, pink-cheeked face nodded at the travelers shivering in the cold, waving them inside with a sweep of her plump, white arm. "Come on in."

Two hours later, after unloading the girls' belongings, Evan climbed back onto the wagon seat. Naomi stood outside the green door, her arms covered in a thin knit wrap, more appropriate to the surroundings than the man's coat she'd worn down the mountain.

Evan picked up the reins and gazed down at her. "You going to be all right here?"

"Sure. It's only for a little while. I'll get to Boise come spring, thanks to you." She patted the pocket of her skirt. "I'll pay 'ya back, Evan. I'll find a way."

"Don't worry about it. Next time I'm in Boise City, let me pick out one of those fine hats you'll be making."

"I'll make you more than one, but you bring me a lady to wear that hat. I expect you to marry soon. If you don't do it pronto, I might have to marry you myself, since I'll be a respectable lady by then." She waved as he spoke to the horses, urging them into a walk. She called after him, "You're a good and decent man, Evan Hartmann. God'll bless you. I'm for certain of it. If He don't, we'll be havin' us a little chat."

Evan chuckled as he slapped the reins on the horses' rumps.

A few blocks farther and he pulled up the horses under a streetlight, squinting at the paper in his hand. He looked up the street where the business buildings thinned out yielding to scattered residences. Clucking to the team of horses, he drove farther up the road until he came to a white two-story house that matched his scribbled notes.

Evan heard a man's footsteps heavy on the wood floors approach the door from inside. The curtain covering a side window lifted an inch, and a shriveled face peered out at him a moment before the door was opened. "If you're lookin' for a room, I'm sorry, but we're full up. You might try the yellow house up the street, four doors up on the right. Thelma usually has a room for a night." The aging man began to close the door, but Evan gently placed his hand on it.

"I'm looking for a young couple who gave me this address. Do you have a Mr. and Mrs. Long living here?"

The expression altered. The man peered up at Evan with bright curiosity. "You a friend of Jessica and Bart?"

"Evan!" Jessie came bounding down the stairs, Bart a few steps behind. Squeezing past the old man, she flung her arms around Evan's neck. "How wonderful to see you!"

His voice, muffled by locks of blond hair covering his face, came with a laugh. "It hasn't been that long. You only left a couple of weeks ago."

"Oh, but it feels like months! How's Lena? Did she come with you?" Jessie pulled back looking beyond Evan to the team and empty wagon waiting on the street.

Bart clapped his hand on Evan's shoulder. "Come in!" He hurriedly explained to the quizzical landlord that Evan was a close friend, near as a brother.

The old gentleman nodded, his face indicating a more amiable personality than he'd first presented. "Well, any friend of yours is welcome. You make yourselves comfortable in the parlor there. I'll be turnin' in."

Jessie looped her arm through Evan's, steering him to the small parlor at the front of the house. No fire burned in the fireplace, but it was cozy and immaculately clean.

"Tell us everything!" Jessie flopped into the settee next to Bart and reached for his hand.

"Guess, I'd be wanting to know the same of you."

Jessie said, "Oh, we couldn't be happier, unless of course you and Lena were here. That'd make it near perfect, I guess. But I'm working here! It helps with board. And Mr. Simpson may seem a bear at first but he's really quite dear."

"I'm working in the sawmill a mile or so out of town. It beats the mine for pay and hours I have to put in."

"But what about you? And Lena?" Jessie leaned forward, her hands restless in her lap.

Evan slouched against the stiff-backed chair, weariness suddenly overtaking him. "I'm thinking this might not be the best time to explain all that. Need to find a livery or a place to bed-down the horses first and then find a place for me. Right now, I'd be happy to bunk with the horses; I'm that beat."

Jessie leaped to her feet and rushed to Evan's side, her face creased with compassion. "Oh, of course! You must be done in. You traveled all day, just like we did. You poor man." She turned back to Bart. "Can't you take care of Evan's team for him?"

"Sure." Bart obeyed immediately.

Jessie said, "And I'll talk to Mr. Simpson about letting you stay in that empty room at the back."

"But I thought he said he didn't have any rooms."

"Oh, don't mind him. He's just a little suspicious of strangers coming in the night. Don't worry, I'll take care of it."

She left him there in the warmth where the strain of the trail and the lateness of the hour tallied up its due. Jessie had to shake him awake to lead him to his room for the night.

The next morning, feeling rested and eager to get on with his plans, Evan joined Jessie in the sunlit kitchen. She'd prepared a feast of eggs, sausage and donuts. She stood resting with her back against the sink, beaming at him while he dug in to her breakfast.

"These are really good." He shook the donut skewered on his fork in her direction. "Does Lena know how to make these?"

"She should. The recipe is on page twenty-six of *Mrs. Parloa's New Cookbook.*" She waved a hand toward the counter where Evan saw the familiar book.

He gave her a puzzled look. "Did she give that to you?"

"No. I found it at that adorable bookstore she told us about, the one that buys and sells old books."

Evan put his fork down. "Can you show me where it is today?"

"Why of course! I'll bet you want to buy Lena a gift, don't you?" Her freckled cheeks opened into a broad, knowing smile. "I know you're sweet on her, Evan, even if you don't."

He took a long draft of coffee, framing his words carefully. "She's a lovely woman with big dreams. Think I might have just the thing to give her a leg up."

The trembling of the shopkeeper's hands betrayed his excitement. Reverently, the owner turned over the pages. "This is exquisite."

"Does it have any value besides as an old book?" Evan asked, his impatience only barely restrained after the man's inspection of nearly twenty minutes.

Looking up at Evan with an incredulous expression, he said, "You have no idea."

"That's right, I don't." Evan tapped an ill-concealed code of irritation on the countertop with his fingers.

"I mean to say, Mr. Hartmann, that it's difficult to put a price on something as sought after as this. Your copy, Mr. Hartman, with all three volumes in such remarkable condition..." he trailed off, a little dreamily.

Evan drove his hands into his pockets. "Are you willing to buy it or do I have to wait for you to advertise it in a catalog? That's what my friend told me was customary for vintage collectables."

The man nodded slowly. "Your friend is correct."

"Unfortunately, Mr. Cartwright, I have need of the cash now."

"Yes, I understand." He picked up the third volume, stroking the cover. "To be very honest, I would like these for myself, but the prices I'm thinking it would fetch in a broader market, well, it doesn't seem fair to you to offer what I could pay."

"Why don't you make an offer, Mr. Cartwright. You'll never know if you don't ask."

With a wallet in his pocket considerably thicker than it'd been at the beginning of his day, Evan located the brick building where Mr. Baxter's new office was located. He climbed the stairs to find a small, but comfortably furnished room at the end of a narrow hallway.

"Mr. Hartmann, good to see you."

Evan was surprised to be greeted at the door by Baxter himself. Evan doffed his hat and bobbed his head. "Thank you. I was hoping I could talk to you about Miss Sommer and her offer."

Baxter's countenance fell at the mention of Lena's name, and with it, so did Evan's hopes for Lena's dream of owning the lodge.

"She gave this to Mr. Baxter? Oh, she must want that house real bad." Jessie held the brooch in her hand, but looking up at Evan's dour expression she asked, "What's wrong? Oh, I can just tell the rest didn't go well!" She clapped her hands over her ears and did a frustrated little jig. "No don't tell me! I can't bear to hear you say it."

Evan sagged into an old ladder-back chair by the stairs. It creaked mournfully. He held the brooch loosely cradled in his palm. Bart awkwardly patted his shoulder. "She won't sell?"

A sigh expanded his chest. "Can't blame her, really. Sawtooth is dying. With the way things are going, no way Lena could make enough this next year to pay for it in full. Only living things in that town come next winter will be walkin' around on four legs."

Jessie balled her fists. "The old spinster! What's she going to do with the place then? Just let it fall to pieces?"

"Now, now," Bart soothed. "Be fair. Sounds to me like she's looking out for our Miss Sommer as much as herself. Seems she could just as easily take that money without a care for what happened to Lena."

A little puff of dust erupted around Jessie as she dropped heavily into a faded armchair. She gnawed on the corner of her fist. "When you put it that way, I suppose we should be grateful to the woman." There was still an edge of spite on 'the woman'.

Evan doffed his hat and scrubbed at his disheveled hair. "I just don't know how I'm going to break it to her. She had such dreams for that place." He swallowed hard, imagining how her face would fall when he told her. Maybe he could just wait until Baxter sent official word in the spring... After all, she hadn't known of his plans for *Ivanhoe*.

"Well, maybe it won't be so bad."

Evan looked into Jessie's face, a sharp glint in her eye.

Bart spluttered, "Not so bad? She came all this way to marry into a good business, only to arrive and find her man cold in his grave. Now this? Her livelihood pulled out from under her *again*?"

Evan ran his thumb over the scalloped edge of the brooch. "Jessie, I've been running this up, down, over, and around my head for a good long while. If you have some insight into our Miss Sommer, I'd be much obliged."

"It's just that..." She rubbed her hands rapidly up and down her legs. "Well, maybe it's not my place to say, but if neither of you are going to face up to it on your own, then your friends have got to lay it out clear!"

Evan's eye twitched, and he felt his foot threatening to start tapping. "Then by all means," he gritted.

She stood up in a whirl of skirts and curls. "You're thick as a brick, Evan Hartmann. And Lena's as stubborn as a mule. Together you make up half a lousy homestead!" Huffing like a steam engine, she stamped from the room. A fearsome clanking and clattering took up in the kitchen.

Bart's shoulders had migrated towards his ears. Or perhaps his head had tried to retreat into his body. "Sorry about that. Don't know quite what she's so twisted up about."

Evan felt a stinging in his palm and relaxed his grip on the brooch. "I think that might be the point."

With saddle bags packed, Evan prepared to leave the following day. He'd hoped to make his absence from Sawtooth City no more than a week. But when he awoke that morning of his scheduled departure, the day dawned with dark gray clouds, heavy with snow. He walked to a rise at the outskirts of town where the dark fury of a storm in the high elevations north of town made it evident that travel would be imprudent if not a deadly proposition. A knot tightened in his gut.

As much as he wanted to be on the other side of that mountain, to be sitting warm and comfortable by the hearth with Lena, Ely, and the brothers, the prospect of breaking the news to her was a constant knife in his side. He'd hoped for so much more. Far better to have been the one to carry back to her good news, or at least hopeful news.

If only that was his only qualm. An ugly fear was wrapping tight about his bones, digging its way into his marrow as the snows deepened every passing hour. It was about this time last year that Jimmy had gone missing. Evan was not a superstitious man, but love and grief can ravage reason and leave the heart open to all manner of attack.

Four days passed without a glimpse of the sun. In those days, Jessie's coolness toward Evan seemed to wane with the storm. As Evan's mood darkened, Jessie's seemed to soften on the fifth day. She plopped onto the dining chair opposite him that morning. "Evan, you got to stop worrying about what Lena will say or do. If you can't see it, more's the pity. But having you back safe will be enough. I promise."

While very little snow accumulated in the flatter lands around Hailey, no one would argue that feet of it were mounting in those wild upper valleys. When a week had passed, a dusting of snow covered the roof tops and roads, but the sun was shining on the mountain peaks. He wouldn't wait. It had to be now or never. He'd take the risk that the worst of the storms were still weeks out.

Bart and Jessie tried to persuade him to stay a while longer, fearful for him. Jessie insisted on his taking her little mare to get him as far as Galena. From there he'd have to snowshoe or ski. Jessie argued that Becky was sturdy and surefooted. When Evan realized she would not be refused, he agreed, promising to leave her at the Galena wagon station where someone traveling south could bring her home to Jessie.

"I've talked to a number of men who've made this trip in past years," Evan said, while Jessie held onto Bart's arm, her face anxious. "They've made the trip by snowshoe over the pass. They've made it, Jessie. There's even a mail carrier who's been doing it for a couple of years now, once every few months in the winter."

"Oh, Bart, can't you talk him out of this?" Jessie was nearly to the point of tears.

"Jessie, I couldn't do that anymore than I could talk you out of some of the crazy things you've wanted to do. You're both a bit alike, you know," Bart nudged her with his elbow.

"I promise to be careful. I'll talk to the folks in Galena and wait there if I have to until conditions improve higher up." He reached out to her, gathering her into his arms. "Don't worry."

"Of course, I'll worry. Don't tell me a thing like that. It's just plain foolish." She broke from him and turned back to Bart, clutching his arm even tighter.

"I'll send word as soon as the passes clear." He swung into the saddle, looking somewhat out of place, his long legs hanging well below the little mare's stomach. He'd taken her, knowing she was exactly the kind of trail horse that wouldn't shy of a little snow.

"God speed, Evan. Give our love to Lena," Jessie let her tears fall as they waved Evan on his way.

A wagon had passed along the road on its way down from Galena since the last snowfall, making the trail easier to navigate. The mare picked her way through the beaten tracks with precision. With the clear sky above them, the sun made a welcome companion for the lonely trek up to the pass, but it did little to ease the knot ever tightening in his gut. Between him and Lena's door lay ghosts and a shifting sea of snow.

CHAPTER 29

"IT'S been a week, Ely." Lena stood by the window staring out at a field of sparkling snow, wondrous and pure.

"*Ja*, Lena. Would you want him traveling in such a snow?"

She stood like a statue, her arms wrapped tight against her body, answering simply. "No."

"He is a savvy man. I'm sure he's waiting somewhere warm and dry until the snow stops falling."

"You're probably right. Of course, you're right. Jessie and Bart and Evan are settled before a warm fire tonight." She took comfort in the belief.

"But so are we." Ely called her attention to Daniel sitting on the rug before a crackling fire. *Tom Sawyer* lay in his lap, his mouth working out the words, face pinched with the effort.

She looked back at the window where moonlight made shadow play on the fresh piles of snow. "How can something so enchanting be so deadly?"

"You make the mountain sound as though it could reason," Ely said with a hint of bemusement. "It does not think. It only does what the Creator gave it a nature to do."

"Perhaps." Lena frowned, unwilling to consider God as an agent of destruction.

A thunderous crack broke the silence of the muffled night. Lena grabbed Ely's arm, her hand viselike. "What was that?" A thunderous roar rolled from the mountain, echoing and rebounding off the cliff faces.

Heedless of the frigid night, she tore open the door and plunged into the unblemished snow. The Sawtooths rose sharp and fearsome in the moonlight. What started as a small white puff, rising like smoke on a distant mountain slope, grew, swelling, expanding as it billowed, plummeting into the valley below. Gathering not only size, but momentum, the phenomena became more terrifying to Lena in its foreignness. The world of her past held no such terrors. Frozen in place to the ground beneath her feet, she whispered. "What is it?"

In a hushed, thin voice, Daniel answered, "Avalanche."

Lena experienced the sudden chill of frozen night air enter her lungs as she took in a sharp breath. All of Evan's warnings came back in an avalanche of memories. A wordless prayer to a power greater than the mountains rose from her soul. As naturally as the snow falling on the mountain, her heart cried out for two things—mercy for Evan and grace for herself.

The mountain, standing immovable as it had for thousands of years, did not care one way or the other if the lone traveler passed unharmed along its rocky face. Carved by winters, springs, summers, and autumns, each season marked by an artist with a design of his own. Each chipped away at the face as any other master sculptor chips at stone. Summer often ruined the efforts of Winter by filling in those landslides with bits of grass and decomposing granite. And Spring responded to Summer's interference with cascading waterfalls that washed away to the valley floor, her months' long efforts to restore what Winter had destroyed. Like a sculptor of clay, Summer added to the mountain's face, while Winter took away.

Without the cover of clouds, the sun shone brilliant, blinding Evan to a degree where at times the hazy path appeared even less distinct. Unfortunately, the sun did little to warm the biting air. Without the clouds, the temperature plummeted. Every hair of Evan's beard and mustache froze. Icicles dripped onto his lips.

The Galena station owner confirmed the need to leave the pony stabled there. Snow was already too deep, but the snowshoes he'd purchased kept him stable upon the crust. The skis strapped to his back would be used later on the downward slope. As the atmosphere thinned, his pace slowed and his breath became more labored, each step an undertaking. His face burned with the cold while his back dripped with sweat. Wisdom gleaned from more experienced mountain trekkers cautioned him to stop to drink water from his canteen. Blowing on the metal lip to keep from losing skin on the frozen opening, he sipped slowly.

The forest thinned as he climbed higher, opening a vista to the snaking river in the valley far below. Under different circumstances, he might have stopped to appreciate the beauty, but the sun's journey across the sky became a relentless reminder of the urgency to mount the summit and begin the descent before noon. He raced the sun, and his memories. Spring had brought Evan to this pass not to witness the waking of the forest floor, but to uncover the remains of his brother. He thanked God that the obscuring drifts of snow and newly felled trees rendered the exact spot indistinguishable. But he still felt its nearness in his bones.

He pressed on, locking away all fear and unnecessary thought. One misstep could send him plunging down the precipitous cliff to his death. One shrug of the mountain could shift the invisible balance of powder and ice and send everything sliding toward the valley in one thunderous moment. One avalanche would carry not only snow but rocks and building-sized boulders tumbling at mind-numbing speeds, sweeping with it all life in its path. Heedless of ancient trees or innocent beasts, it would take everything in one blinding white explosion of energy. The only warning he might have would be a crack. If he was lucky, he'd hear it seconds before it happened.

The summit came as a surprise. Shielding his eyes with his gloved hand, he looked out over a frozen world of white upon white, rolling and stretching farther than a man could see. Even as he stared out at the vast wilderness stripped of color, reaching miles beyond the river, his thoughts snaked back to Lena. Would she return to Chicago, walking out of his life forever? He needed to know if Jessie's words were true.

Separated from her, for even these few days, had peeled away all the ambiguity from his ambitions. Ranches and rocks were a dull prospect compared with his desire to simply be near her forever. Only in her presence could dreams take on real substance. He wanted to know her. Every detail, every quirk, every heartache and desire, so he could soothe them and fulfill them. As he considered the few miles of trail snaking away to the valley below, he believed he would make it. He also promised himself that no mountains must ever again separate them. These new thoughts pushed back his fear of the mountain, the snow, the threatening winter storms. All that remained was his determination to return to Lena.

After resting there for just moments, he felt the wind shift, the air taking on an even sharper bite. Seeming to lift from the valley floor, he watched as a billowing cloud of snow blew up the mountain. Winds drove the powder of the last snowfall in a rush, up and south to meet him. In the moment it took him to comprehend what was occurring, the wind fell upon him, as if determined to keep him at the summit and out of the valley. Pulling his collar tight to his neck and lowering his head to the onslaught of driven snow, he plunged forward, ready for a battle of the wills, one agonizing step at a time.

Obscuring the trail, snow swirled like angry bees about his head. Evan lifted his hand once to bat at the biting pellets of snow as if he could swat them away as he would a pesky insect, but the swarm was all encompassing. No longer able to track the sun, Evan lost track of time. All that remained was his determination to descend the mountain and return to Lena. The trail disappeared, the sky vanished, all he had to guide him was his hand, flat to the cliff wall. Inch-by-inch, his fingers guided him.

Deprived of senses, he cried out, railing against the roar of wind and ice, "God, if you've got use for this poor pilgrim, I'd appreciate a little help."

Stumbling over some hidden obstacle, he fell to his knees, striking his shin painfully against a rock. The snowshoe slipped from his foot. He groped for it in the powdered snow. His fingers felt the wood a few feet away. Pulling it to him, he squinted, trying to focus his stinging eyes on the laces. He could feel them, but why couldn't he see them? Lifting his hand before his eyes and seeing nothing, he realized in one terrifying instant that his blindness was more than just the storm of white.

As the stinging in his eyes increased, he took stock of his predicament. Survival instincts took hold, reason and logic became his guide, panic damped to a cold lump in his gut. Consciously, slowing his racing heart, he pulled up memories of experiences he'd heard from those who'd found themselves in dire circumstances in these mountains. Snow blindness was just one and what he recalled gave him hope. The condition was temporary, passing in hours, days at the most. Although he could probably not survive days in this climate, he might reasonably be able to wait out hours until some vision was restored.

So, he hunkered down against the rock face, using the tip of the snowshoe to dig out a snow cave to protect himself from the wind. Sweating by the time he'd carved a space large enough to pull himself out of the elements, he closed his eyes, resting his head against the hard rock wall of the mountain. Exhaustion pulled him into a fitful sleep. A nightmare of being buried alive by a mountain of snow brought him almost to the point of wakefulness before slipping back into yet another dream where his brother was calling out to him from beneath a field of ice, only his face showing, twisted into a frozen scream.

By the time he came fully awake, the sun had passed from the sky, revealing to anyone with sight, a velvet sky sprinkled with diamonds. If he had thought it cold before, it was nothing compared to night. If he hadn't been frozen with knees tight to his chest, he feared he might simply shatter into icy shards with the violence of his shivering. An hour passed and yet another. Evan's head nodded, his body struggling to conserve energy. When he at last came fully awake, mouth dry, he pulled the canteen from his satchel. Throwing back his head, he tipped the canteen to his lips. Nothing. He stupidly shook the canteen. Frozen, of course.

With his head tipped back, he perceived a pinpoint of light through the curtain of black surrounding him. He blinked back the tears flooding his burning eyes, straining to see that phantom pin of light. Frustrated, he squeezed his eyes shut again, slouching against the back wall of his cave. It wasn't permanent, they'd said. He'd just have to wait and hope.

Lena sat upright in bed as though drawn by some invisible string. She shivered. Pulling the quilt around her shoulders, she dropped her bare feet to the floor and made her way across the cold wood to the window on the mountain. Silver clouds drifted across the moon, giving it the appearance of some incorporeal being and not the familiar celestial form. Dread gripped her heart. Evan was in trouble. She knew it. The reality of his need was as real and as solid as the wood of the window sill beneath her cold fingers.

Squeezing her eyes shut, she whispered a second prayer. "Oh Lord, help him find his way." Standing there, the cold creeping up her legs and spine, she sensed the light behind her eyelids. Opening her eyes again, she looked out upon the frozen landscape where the familiar peaks were now bathed in brilliant moonlight. Every crag stood out in sharp detail under the silver light of the full moon. Moon shadows stretched out from every cedar, alder, and pine, as though an enormous lantern had been lit in the heavens.

Lena's hands fluttered to her breast, the quilt falling to the floor. She stood transfixed by the beauty, confident that somehow her prayer had been answered. With no thought to the hour, she dressed and hurried downstairs.

Waking suddenly from yet another nightmare, Evan opened his eyes instinctively, then closed them immediately. Afraid he was still dreaming, he pinched his cheek hard and when he felt it, slowly opened his eyes again. This time there was no mistaking the shades of gray that gave the snow dimensions. Looking heavenward, a shimmering orb shone upon the rock face, illuminating the trail. He rose stiffly to his feet, trying out his cold limbs, stamping his feet to restore circulation. His body worked. His mind was alert. More important, his sight was returning.

His cold fingers fumbled with the leather ties on his skis. Next, he strapped the snow shoes to his back. At last, he straightened, cautiously moving forward in the powdery snow disguising the trail. All that stood between him and Lena was a slow ski down the mountain guided now by the full moon.

It was that strange hour before dawn when the world seems to hold its breath. With a lantern in her hand, Lena stepped onto the porch. She hung the lamp on a nail she'd pounded into the sturdy beam by the top step a week ago. Its flame cast warm yellow, fingers of light across the snow. Wrapping her shawl tight to her shoulders, she stared out at the darkened windows of empty buildings in the town below. Just weeks ago, those windows would have been lit by the early risers, the cooks, the men with early shifts. Now they were black and as lifeless as the town. As she had done for the last five days, she spoke into the darkness. "Come home, Evan. You promised. Come home."

Somewhere a wolf bayed to its pack. The answering call came from across the valley. She remained, listening, mesmerized by the lonely voices, knowing they would find each other in the night. She turned aside, desiring the warmth of the fire within the house. But a shadow moved on the road, a wolf perhaps. She waited, watching.

The shape resolved itself to be, not a wolf, but human. A man on snow shoes, trudging up the road, bent, struggling against the drifts. Her breath caught as she grabbed for the railing, straining to see into the darkness. With a cry, she grabbed for the lantern, running in the direction of the figure. Her feet, slowed by drifts of snow, caused her to stumble. Falling on one knee, she scrambled back to her feet, and started again toward the figure. The man so fully wrapped in coat and hat and ragged beard could not be known. But she knew. She knew and she stumbled through the snow until her fingers wrapped around his arm.

Evan inclined his head to her, his eyes squinting and oddly unfocused. With the efforts of a man moving in slow motion, he brought up his gloved hand to reach for her cheek. The frost on his glove nipped at her skin. "Lena, this is you," he rasped. His tone seemed to indicate uncertainty as if he needed her to affirm that she was not a part of a dream.

"Yes, Evan." She took his hand in hers, coaxing off the stiff glove and placing his palm to her cheek. His eyes kept roving, searching, never quite meeting hers. She heard the bang of the front door slamming open against the wall, Ely's voice calling out for her.

"We're here, Ely!"

Ely staggered through the deep snow, puffing great white clouds, still dressed in his nightclothes.

"What's wrong with his eyes, Ely?"

Ely stood beside him, supporting him as the Evan's strength began to crumble. "Snow blindness, I suspect. Is that it, Evan?"

Too exhausted to speak, Evan simply nodded, allowing them to remove his snow shoes. Then they were guiding him into the house. Evan reached for a chair as Lena slipped from under his arm.

"Daniel get some towels. Ely get that wet jacket off him.

Evan looked up at Daniel, standing bleary-eyed in the hall. "Daniel, you here?"

"Hey, Mr. Hartmann. Glad you come back." Daniel gave him a lopsided grin and scurried down the hall to obey Lena.

"Why?" Evan said in a raspy slur.

Ely, tugging on the snow encrusted arm of Evan's jacket, answered, "The boy and his pa have moved into Donal and Carrick's old room. Lena took them in. She's been caring for the boy's father, Tom."

Evan half fell, half sat in the chair, not protesting the ministrations of Ely as he pulled his outer clothing off his stiff body. Evan's body began to react to the shock, trembling uncontrollably.

Lena returned with a quilt to wrap around Evan's exposed chest. Kneeling beside him, she tucked the edges snugly about him. She remained there, kneeling before him, her face pinched with concern while Ely inspected Evan's feet and fingers for frostbite. She followed Ely's instructions and began vigorously rubbing Evan's feet and hands, coaxing blood back into them.

"You're mighty lucky fellow, ja? I do not think you will lose any of these." He straightened, looking at Evan with a broad smile pushing his wrinkles deeper into familiar grooves. "Perhaps Someone was looking out for you, *ja*?"

Teeth still chattering, Evan mumbled softly, "*Ja.*"

Laying his hand on Evan's shoulder, his voice serious once more, Ely added, "It is good you have come home."

Ely stayed with them until Evan's shivering had subsided and he'd seen the man consume a full mug of coffee. Putting his hands to the small of his back and stretching with a groan, Ely said, "This is too much excitement for an old man. Now that I am certain you will live, I crawl back into my warm bed." Then he quietly slipped from the room leaving Lena to care for Evan there in the warmth and familiarity of the great room before the roaring fire.

As Lena adjusted the blanket around Evan's shoulders, he reached for her hands wrapping his stiff fingers around her supple ones. "Lena, I came back for you, only you." His voice still sounded unnatural.

Although Evan still shivered before the blaze, Lena felt a rising warmth in her cheeks, not fueled by the fire behind her. His words stunned her. *For you, only you.*

Still unable to meet his gaze, she remained frozen in place before him. Time slowed, the crackling fire the only sound apart from the pounding of her heart.

Ely had asked that of her. *What do you want, Lena?* She could answer now as she had not then.

Evan leaned forward and touched her face. "Will you get something from my pocket? In the jacket."

She rose reluctantly to her feet and pulled from the pocket a small package wrapped in a familiar handkerchief, her own. Without unwrapping it, she could feel the shape of the brooch inside. She met Evan's solemn gaze with a startled expression.

"It's your brooch," Evan whispered.

Hands trembling, she unwrapping the linen to reveal the silver pin. "But why?"

"He couldn't keep it. He wouldn't keep it in light of the news..."

"You spoke to Mr. Baxter?"

"I'm so sorry, Lena. He heard from Miss Nash." His hands twitched ever so slightly, his face clouded as he gathered strength to continue. Evan reached out to her with one trembling hand. "Come closer, Lena."

She dropped to her knees beside him, her hands resting on his arm.

"She's given him instructions to sell it for scrap." He took in ragged breath. "I'm so sorry." The last words came as a gravelly whisper. "I tried... I offered him more money as a down-payment, but she'd already decided. Your dream..."

Reaching up with one hand, she touched his lips with two fingers and gave him a wan smile. Neither spoke for some time. She could feel his pulse hammering beneath her fingers. "You gave most of what you had to Vicki and I suspect to Naomi as well. What..." She looked to the bookshelf beside the fireplace where the volumes of *Ivanhoe* had been placed weeks ago. "You sold the books," she said softly, shaking her head.

He gave a half-hearted shrug. Lena lifted her hand to his shoulder, hesitating as her fingers touched his skin.

"You dear man. Has there ever been created such a heart as yours? You've given away everything that you could have used to buy your ranch." She shook her head as a tear pooled in the corner of her eye.

"But this place...You made it a home for us, for Ely, Carrick, Donal, Jessie, Bart and I. We became different people, better people, after you came," Evan whispered.

Gripping his arm again with both her hands, she rested her cheek against his shoulder. "I was a fool to stay here. I should have gone with you. My foolishness nearly cost you your life, Evan." Her throat constricted. "I'm so sorry."

What do you want, Lena? "This house isn't what I want." She stopped, suddenly aware of every moment that had cemented this new longing, every smile and kindness that Evan had shown not just to her but to everyone he knew. How could she possibly express her heart's deepest desire?

Fingers still clumsy from the cold, he reached out to her with one hand to cup her cheek. "What do you want, Lena?"

For once, she found all the words she needed to express her heart. She leaned her face against his palm and whispered a single, precious word, "You."

"You lovely, wonderful, incorrigible woman, can that be true? It's all that kept my feet moving forward down the mountain, the thought that you might be able to love me.

But I know you, maybe better than you know yourself. You need more than me to love. I'd be selfish to keep it for myself alone."

She laughed lightly at that, the thought of Evan describing himself as selfish.

"It's true. You have so much love to share with others."

"I think your snow blindness has affected more than your green eyes, Evan Hartmann. I've been cool and afraid to reveal my affections for anyone, for so many years."

"That's not how I see it. In so many ways, not just words, you poured out love on all of us—learning what to cook to please each of us, mending clothes when you saw the need, making us feel like we were part of a family here. You took in Daniel and cared for his father. You have a tender, beautiful heart."

There were arguments that settled into her mind, but this picture he painted of her was new. She remained motionless before him as he stroked her hair with rough hands.

"I want to help you make a new start. Maybe it isn't here. But caring for people is what you were designed to do. You'll bring in new people to pour out your love on, people like Daniel and his father. You can't help it. We could start with a small ranch, run cattle and invite folks to stay like Nash had planned. Add on rooms as we can. Maybe it'd be in Ketchum, where the winters aren't so fearsome, a place where the trains can bring folks from the East for touring."

Enthusiasm lit his face, strengthening his voice. And the dream that he unfolded for her seemed as natural for him as snow falling on the mountain. But it would be a dream they could make together. He had woven himself into the dream, and she with him. Once more, she would have a hearth, and those she would come to love to share it. There would be late night conversations and laughter. And there would be always be love expressed in all the ways her heart could devise.

Worn out from his dream weaving, he held her face in his hands, "Sometimes the road we start down takes a turn we didn't see coming. I know that's true for me. You're my bend in the road. The view I see ahead is better because of you." Breathless, he whispered, "I love you, Lena."

As he held her eyes with his, she saw there that this love, his love, was for her and her alone. She saw there the truth, a clear picture that gave her the full portrait of herself, undistorted by her doubts.

"Can you love me?" Fine lines creased his brow, his eyes searching hers for the answer.

With the snow mounding in deep drifts against the doors and chilling winds moaning through the pines outside the windows, winter had come, its power beating in full force against the sturdy log house. The warmth within stood firmly against it. Spring would come in its time, bringing rays of the first brilliant sunrise to melt the mountain snow fields, forcing winter to release its grip upon the land.

There would be no waiting for Lena. Her heart's winter was over and spring had come.

She answered his question with quiet assurance, pressing her palm to his heart. "I do love you, you wonderful man."

He lowered his face to hers and sealed her declaration with a kiss.

THE BEGINNING

Fair Reader,

Thank you for joining me on Lena and Evan's journey. I hope you enjoyed reading it as much as I enjoyed writing it. If you would like to follow their legacy, visit www.samanthastclaire.net to receive notifications of upcoming publications. Drop me a note. I love hearing from readers.

The best way to thank an author for a good read is to leave a review. Please consider leaving a review on Amazon or Goodreads.

Happily Everafters,

Samantha St.Claire